A Snowy
Christmas

Books by Fern Michaels

Spirit of the Season
Deep Harbor
Fate & Fortune
Sweet Vengeance
Holly and Ivy
Fancy Dancer
No Safe Secret
Wishes for Christmas
About Face
Perfect Match
A Family Affair
Forget Me Not
The Blossom Sisters
Balancing Act
Tuesday's Child
Betrayal
Southern Comfort
To Taste the Wine
Sins of the Flesh
Sins of Omission
Return to Sender
Mr. and Miss Anonymous
Up Close and Personal
Fool Me Once
Picture Perfect
The Future Scrolls
Kentucky Sunrise
Kentucky Heat
Kentucky Rich
Plain Jane
Charming Lily
What You Wish For
The Guest List
Listen to Your Heart
Celebration
Yesterday
Finders Keepers
Annie's Rainbow
Sara's Song
Vegas Sunrise
Vegas Heat
Vegas Rich
Whitefire
Wish List
Dear Emily
Christmas at Timberwoods

The Sisterhood Novels

Cut and Run
Safe and Sound
Need to Know
Crash and Burn
Point Blank
In Plain Sight
Eyes Only
Kiss and Tell
Blindsided
Gotcha!
Home Free
Déjà Vu
Cross Roads
Game Over
Deadly Deals
Vanishing Act
Razor Sharp
Under the Radar
Final Justice
Collateral Damage
Fast Track
Hokus Pokus
Hide and Seek
Free Fall
Lethal Justice
Sweet Revenge
The Jury
Vendetta
Payback
Weekend Warriors

The Men of the Sisterhood Novels

Hot Shot
Truth or Dare
High Stakes
Fast and Loose
Double Down

The Godmothers Series

Far and Away
Classified
Breaking News
Deadline
Late Edition
Exclusive
The Scoop

Published by Kensington Publishing Corporation

A Snowy Little Christmas

FERN MICHAELS

TARA SHEETS
KATE CLAYBORN

ZEBRA BOOKS
KENSINGTON PUBLISHING CORP.

www.kensingtonbooks.com

ZEBRA BOOKS are published by

Kensington Publishing Corp.
119 West 40th Street
New York, NY 10018

All Kensington titles, imprints, and distributed lines are available at
special quantity discounts for bulk purchases for sales promotion,
premiums, fund-raising, educational, or institutional use.

Special book excerpts or customized printings can also be created to fit
specific needs. For details, write or phone the office of the Kensington
Sales Manager: Attn.: Sales Department. Kensington Publishing Corp.,
119 West 40th Street, New York, NY 10018. Phone: 1-800-221-2647.

Zebra and the Z logo Reg. U.S. Pat. & TM Off.

First Printing: November 2019
ISBN-13: 978-1-4201-4608-0
ISBN-10: 1-4201-4608-4

ISBN-13: 978-1-4201-4611-0 (eBook)
ISBN-10: 1-4201-4611-4 (eBook)

10 9 8 7 6 5 4 3 2 1

Printed in the United States of America

Contents

Starry Night

FERN MICHAELS

Chapter One

Jessie Richmond was staring at the calendar. It was October. Her thirty-fifth birthday was in two months, with Christmas coming two weeks later. The fall weather had started to settle in, bringing with it a stunning array of autumn leaves in their colors of red and gold. Mother Nature was decorating the landscape with the accessories of the season.

Jessie loved this time of year, a season when the sky was cerulean blue and big puffs of cumulous clouds served as the background for the foliage palette, telling the world that Christmas would be arriving shortly. Time moved swiftly yet often seemed to stand still.

It had been three years since Jessie had spent the holidays with a significant other, which wasn't such a bad thing considering the alternative. Had she stayed with Dennis, the season would be rife with arguments, and there would be no explanation for his late nights out. And should she dare to ask where he had been and what he had been doing, his expletive-laden response would inform her that it was none of her business. Then would follow the quarrels about with whose family they would spend Christmas Eve and

Christmas. And then there was the always stressful New Year's Eve with Judy and Ernie Stevenson. Nope. It was much better to be spending her time clearing out the bookstore, which had been left to her by her uncle Hugo.

Jessie was his only niece, and she loved books. It would be nice to be away in a place where she had fond memories and not have to deal with her day job at the advertising agency and her nights of comforting and advising the lovelorn.

Jessie was a striking-looking woman, with almond-shaped eyes and olive skin she'd inherited from her Italian maternal grandmother, along with the green eyes, high cheekbones, and straight blond hair from her father's Dutch side of the family.

Blessed with a lean five-foot-ten-inch frame, she was a natural athlete. After earning second-team all-American honors her last two years at Penn State, she had earned a place on the Olympic volleyball team, but the practices were long and grueling. During one practice, a photographer took special interest in her and encouraged her to pursue a modeling career. While she didn't mind the fierce competition among the women, volleyball could get rough, and she decided that a fresh French manicure was much more attractive than the swollen knuckles everyone had from digging balls off the floor.

Even though she was only twenty-two at the time, she knew it was rather late to begin a career in modeling, but the photographer's charm won out. She quit the team and moved to Philadelphia, where he convinced her he could land her a lot of jobs. She was forced to admit that she had been a bit naïve, especially after almost a year with very few paying gigs. She lived month to month, with two, sometimes three roommates, one of whom was her photographer-boyfriend. But Jessie had a strong resolve. She would figure it out—whatever "it" was.

While at an interview for a modeling job, Marjorie Leland, who owned an ad agency, hired her for some print and cable work for a local car dealership. Marjorie knew full well that getting modeling jobs was not easy for most women, however good-looking they might be. But Jessie was attractive, bright, and had a quick wit, and Marjorie took a liking to her. Marjorie saw her potential and offered her a position as her assistant, encouraging her to do some modeling on the side. Over time, however, Jessie became less interested in the runway and much more fascinated by life on the other side of the camera. She began to coordinate photo shoots for clients of the agency. Being a quick study, by the time she was thirty she had worked her way up to account executive.

Jessie had a charisma that attracted the attention of almost anyone who entered the doors of Leland and Burrows. Her alluring smile and the sparkle in her eyes made her instantly likable. She was warm and open to all those with whom she came into contact. It didn't matter who they were or where they came from. As far as she was concerned, everyone deserved respect—until they screwed up.

The ad agency shared the floor with a local radio station, and after spending eleven years in the building, she had become friends with some of the staff. One evening last year, just as she was about to push the elevator button, Brian, the sound engineer, came running out of the studio, grabbed her by the arm, and tossed a headset at her. "Quick. Come with me! I need you to sit in for Megan." Apparently, the regular host of the advice for the lovelorn segment, *Megan Masters, Love Doctor*, had thrown another one of her hissy fits and stormed out over some perceived slight.

"Wait! What?" Jessie had no idea what Brian was talking about as he gently dragged her into the studio.

"Megan split. Had another meltdown. Apparently, the coffee wasn't French-roasted enough. It will only be two hours. Fake it. Whatever. They're mostly a bunch of lonely people who want someone to talk to." He pointed her to the sound booth, gave her a shove, and christened her "Dr. Richie, Romance Professor." God, how she hated that name! After a week's absence, it became abundantly clear that Megan Masters had no intention of returning, and Jessie, aka Dr. Richie, seemed to be holding her own.

Within a very short time, listeners were blogging, posting, and tweeting about the new "Love Professor" and how much better she was: more compassionate, a good listener, asked good questions, gave good, sound advice, and was often very funny. Dr. Richie, Romance Professor was becoming the new "it girl" of the wounded and heartbroken.

By the end of the third week, the station manager offered her the segment on a full-time basis. The pay was adequate and the hours easy. She could keep her day job at the ad agency and work her two-hour radio shift five nights a week.

Although she didn't have a degree in psychology, having majored in English literature, or any other formal training for what she was doing, she certainly had enough experience in the romance department. She knew, from sometimes bitter experience, all of the "what not to do's."

Under the circumstances, Jessie decided that the

best thing she could do was to maintain a low profile. Though she was by no means a shrinking violet, fame for its own sake had no appeal, and she wasn't doing the program to satisfy her ego. She sincerely wanted to help people, and she already had a full-time job. Accordingly, extracurricular activities to promote the show were of no interest, and she made sure that was part of the deal when she agreed to take on the spot. The station could blog, post, and tweet, but personal appearances were not going to happen. She didn't want to find herself defending her position as an advice giver. She knew how mean-spirited people could be, especially on social media. With pure sincerity and without a lot of hype, she became a very popular mentor to the relationship-weary.

After a year of balancing both jobs, she had little time to look for a partner of her own. Listening to all of her callers' tales of woe, she often thought she was being saved from another romantic disaster. She comforted herself with the company of her cat, Mozart, and her dog, Picasso. "Mozart" because he loved to run across the piano Jessie had kept since her childhood, and "Picasso" because, when she rescued him, his paws were covered in paint. Admittedly, she hadn't played the piano for years, and it took up a lot of room, but she had a sentimental attachment to it, and her straight-faced answer to anyone who asked her why she kept the baby grand in her small apartment was "It would mean Mozart would have to give up his piano lessons!"

Sure, she was happy, but she also secretly hoped she would find someone. Someone with integrity, who had a real job, was self-aware, mature, reliable, loyal, kind, generous, and available. Fat chance. Lately, her friends were warning her that she was "too picky," but after a couple of failed romances, she preferred the word "cautious." Thankfully, she wasn't one of the walking wounded or desperate—at least not yet—so she had a different perspective than many of her listeners.

Jessie encouraged her callers to find their own passion, to be their own person, and she was keen on pumping up people's esteem. Broken relationships often create broken people, she would point out. She wanted to help people mend, but she stressed that doing so required self-reflection. "Are you being true to yourself? Do you feel that you have a purpose and are you fulfilling it?"

When callers would complain that they and their partner had "drifted apart," she would ask, "Who were you then and who are you now? Remember, life is a constant work in progress. We evolve . . . or devolve, depending on our choices. We are not the same person we were when we were twelve—although some people still seem to behave that way!"

She would emphasize the importance of communicating honestly and moving toward happiness—whatever that meant to an individual. More of her counsel included statements like: "Challenges are inevitable, misery is optional." Another one of her favorite lines was: "If you were in a foxhole, who would you want there with you?" Quite often, that question was met with a very long pause. Mostly, the calls were about boyfriends who behaved badly and how the women loved them nonetheless. Some people called it "The Bad Boy Syndrome." What caused it was the real question. Why were so many women drawn to that kind of man? Jessie thought that a lot of men were very capable of behaving badly and that, unfortunately, many women let them get away with it. But why? Perhaps it was fear. Fear of confrontation? Fear of being alone?

Yes, fear either propelled you or held you. But what was the point if you weren't happy and someone made you feel bad about yourself? No, Jessie's agenda was to help restore people's sense of self-worth.

But today she was planning ahead for her two weeks off during the holidays. She would finish clearing out Riverwood Books, the bookstore her uncle owned in New York State, in Croton-on-Hudson, a quaint community on the banks of the Hudson River, just forty miles north of New York City.

Over the past few years, Uncle Hugo would constantly complain about how the Internet was killing his business and his customers were all moving south. Then one day, out of the blue, she got a call from him. "I'm following my friends to Florida. The bookstore is yours, honey. Do whatever you want with it. It's paid for, so take the money and buy yourself that house you've always talked about. I'm closing up shop. You know where to find the key."

Jessie was speechless as she stared at the phone. A bookstore? Sure, she had spent most of her childhood there, reading every new book appropriate for her age, but running one? Uncle Hugo was right. Sell it.

The radio station had planned to pipe Christmas music every evening during the holidays, giving the staff a much-needed break and the opportunity to spend time with their families. The only people scheduled to work were Brian, who was filling in for the traffic guy, and Ziggy, the weatherman. Jessie was concerned about her love-starved/love-crazed audience—the holidays could be rough for a lot of folks—but Brian was going to hold down the fort, running previously recorded shows. There was plenty of entertainment and advice in the digital files he kept. He also promised he would get in touch, but only if it was an emergency.

Jessie's parents were celebrating their fortieth wedding anniversary this coming holiday season and were going to Italy and the Netherlands. Her mom had always wanted to attend Christmas Mass at the Vatican, and her dad wanted to see his grandfather's house, which had served as part of the underground during the Nazi occupation.

Jessie was thrilled that they had planned this adventure for themselves. They had worked hard to put Jessie and her brother, Josh, through college. It was time for them to have some fun and excitement.

Even before the news about the bookstore, Jessie had been planning to spend the holidays with her life-long friend in Croton, Lisa. They had been besties since kindergarten. Lisa was married and had two kids, eight and ten years old. They were at that age when they were beginning to question the existence of Santa, but Christmas in Croton would be a very festive atmosphere nonetheless.

Before she could plan her time off, she needed to take a look at what she was getting into regarding the bookstore, so she planned a short trip to Croton early in November. She could assess things, make lists, call a real-estate agent, and contact a local contractor to do the necessary work. If all went according to plan, the bookstore would be in decent enough shape to put on the market by February.

Chapter Two

The weekend after Halloween, Jessie made the drive from her apartment in Philadelphia to New York. It took just under three hours. She was able to beat the commuter traffic and enjoy the Palisades Interstate Parkway as, high among the cliffs, it weaved its way along the Hudson River. New Jersey had some beautiful spots, including the beaches in the east, Kittatinny Mountain in the north, and Buttermilk Falls and Crater Lake Loop Trail in the west. The state always got a bad rap, and that idiotic show *Jersey Shore* had set the Garden State back a few decades. Make that centuries. Jessie shook her head, thinking about how much the entertainment industry was becoming a cultural calamity. It was the equivalent of junk food. No wonder so many people were depressed.

As she began her descent from the Palisades cliffs, she was awestruck by the new Tappan Zee Bridge. It resembled the bridges recently built in Charleston and Oakland—massive sails made of steel beams perched on the asphalt span.

After crossing the river into New York, she saw the familiar signs for Tarrytown, home of "The Legend of Sleepy Hollow." When she was a kid, her uncle would

have Halloween parties at the shop and read the story
to children as they pulled a blanket or sweater over
their heads and shivered in fear. She smiled to herself,
remembering what an exciting world she had lived in
among all those stories and books.

In more recent times—after the spooky story was
read—the kids would head to Van Cortlandt Manor,
an historic landmark originally built as a hunting
lodge in the 1600s and converted into a lavish man-
sion in 1749, to see the Great Jack O'Lantern Blaze,
which featured over seven thousand individually hand-
carved and illuminated pumpkins. Jessie was sorry
that she had missed the Halloween extravaganza, but
she would be there in time for Lightscapes, the holiday
walk-through, land-art experience. Visitors entered
through a pulsating-light Bubble Tunnel and emerged
into a world of wonder spread throughout the historic
landscape.

As she pulled her Audi SUV into the circular pebble
driveway of the bookstore, a rush of mixed emotions
washed over her. The wonderful memories were etched
in her heart, and here she was, about to say good-bye.
It was bittersweet.

The building was a two-story colonial. There was a
porch with a white railing running along the front.
Four large pillars graced the façade. It had been built
in the early 1950s as a bed-and-breakfast, after which
came incarnations as a gift shop and an antique store,
but no one ever seemed to be able to make a go of it
until Hugo bought it in the early 1970s and turned
it into a bookstore catering to the summer tourists. He
and Jessie's dad had pretty much gutted the space,
knocked down some walls, installed columns, and
added a few bay windows that overlooked the grounds
in the back. The exterior remained traditional, but

the interior had a lot of open space, making the shop light and airy.

When you entered the foyer, the room on the right was the fiction section, with the children's area in the back. The room on the left was nonfiction, magazines, and newspapers. Both had a view of the grounds, with French doors that led to the patio area.

The only thing that showed any evidence of its age was the large oak staircase leading to the second floor. On the right side of the second floor was a mezzanine balcony that served as a reading area and overlooked the fiction section on the first floor. There were several lounge chairs, a sofa, and a large coffee table. At one end of the room, a small counter held a Nespresso coffee machine, with a small refrigerator underneath for self-serve. Coffee was a dollar a cup and everyone was on the honor system. Occasionally, the hospital volunteers, called the Blue Belles, would drop off baked goods and leave a jar for donations. Uncle Hugo didn't have the space or inclination to have a full-service café, and most people were content with just a good cup of coffee. It was a favorite place for parents to relax when their kids were below during the children's reading hour.

The skylights gave the space a very open feel, with sunlight filtering down to the first level. On the other side of the staircase, there was an apartment where authors, friends, and relatives would stay. The apartment also had an entrance from the deck in the back, which provided easy access without having to traipse through the store, providing privacy for some of the more famous authors who would occasionally show up.

Uncle Hugo and his wife, Lydia, had their own cottage a few blocks away. It was far enough to be able to leave work behind but close enough to walk. Now they were on their way to palm trees and golf courses.

Croton-on-Hudson was a popular destination during the summer season, and the apartment was host to a variety of people. Jessie hoped it was in decent shape so she could spend her time there instead of at Granger's Inn.

She fished the key from its hiding place, took a deep breath, and slowly climbed the steps leading to the large veranda. As soon as the double locks clicked, she swung the double Tiffany glass doors open. The smell of books took her back so quickly, she almost tripped at the threshold. Uncle Hugo had literally walked away and left everything on the shelves, including several children's picture books spread out on one of the big bay window seats. Entering the bookstore was like being thrown back in time.

She must have been standing in a dreamlike state for a while because she almost jumped out of her skin when Rosemary, the real-estate agent she had spoken to, walked up behind her.

"Excuse me. Are you Jessie Richmond?" an equally startled Rosemary inquired.

"Oh yes! Sorry. I was reminiscing and lost in thought!" She extended her hand and gave the woman a warm smile. "It's been a while since I've been here. Brought back a lot of memories."

"I can imagine! I'm Rosemary Bidgood from the real-estate agency. Didn't mean to scare you!"

"Nice to meet you, Rosemary. I just got here, so I have no idea what to expect." Jessie guessed that Rosemary was around her own age, maybe a few years older.

"No worries. We'll figure it out. Did you grow up in Croton?"

"Yes. Spent almost every Saturday here when I was a kid. Uncle Hugo would unpack the children's books and ask me to pick one or two for the Saturday children's reading hour. It made me feel so important! He called me his Young Reader Assistant." Jessie was overcome with nostalgia.

"Children's books?"

"Yes, some of it, but he carried the usual literary, mystery, and romance genres as well."

"I was never much into books. I confess, I don't think I've ever been in here. When I was growing up, it was all about makeup, hair, and teen magazines. Couldn't wait until I could dye my hair blond, or red, or purple! I must have driven my mother crazy."

"I think that's part of our job as daughters!" Jessie gave another slight chuckle, remembering all the teenage arguments she would have with her mother.

"I think you're right." Rosemary nodded in agreement.

Rosemary was a petite brunette with shoulder-length wavy hair. She wore a simple suit with high-top sneakers. She noticed Jessie looking at her feet. "Oh, I usually wear normal shoes, but I busted a heel at the last house, and these were in my trunk."

"I hate when that happens. Actually, I think it's kind of a cool look. Savvy yet casual."

"Ha. Don't tell my boss. She is a stickler for conservative fashion." Rosemary rolled her eyes, displaying more of her playful personality.

"I know what you mean. I'm not much for business suits, but working in an office, it's like wearing a uniform. I can't wait until I get home and put on some comfy clothes and roll on the floor with Mozart and Picasso."

"Mozart? Picasso?"

"My cat and dog. They're my kids!" Jessie laughed. She felt very comfortable with this woman—she was down-to-earth.

"I don't want to hold you up, so let's take a look at what we have going on here." Jessie gestured for Rosemary to take a tour of the shop. "There's also an apartment upstairs to check out. There's an entrance up the stairs as well as a deck with stairs in the back."

Rosemary pulled out her retractable tape measure and took copious notes, checking the floorboards for squeaks and the windows for drafts. She inspected the two private bathrooms, the storage area, the kitchenette, and the outdoor patio that had hosted many author events. To one side of the patio, a wooden staircase led to the balcony deck that served as a separate entrance to the apartment. Rosemary appreciated that feature.

When they entered the apartment, aside from a few dust bunnies and some stagnant air, Jessie decided it was good enough for her stay over the holidays. Rosemary recommended a cleaning service to get the place spick-and-span.

The two women leaned on the railing of the balcony and enjoyed one of the last few days of crisp autumn weather. The building sat on an acre and a half that was landscaped with a high stockade fence and a variety of evergreen trees. Jessie pointed out certain shrubs where she would hide Easter eggs for the hunt. "Some of the kids would try to bribe me to tell them where they were, or try to come up here to get a bird's-eye view. But I was implacable." Jessie gave Rosemary a wink.

"This is a lovely place. Sure you want to sell it?" Rosemary could hear the nostalgia in Jessie's voice.

"I have a good job, an apartment, and a life in Philadelphia. I couldn't even begin to think about running a bookstore. Sure, I spent what seems to be half my life here, but you have to have a feel for bookselling. I'm just a reader."

"Too bad. I mean, it's a shame you can't keep it in the family."

"Uncle Hugo told me to sell it and buy a house with the money. Honestly, I don't know where I would buy a house. I've been living in an apartment since I was twenty-one! And I don't want to be exiled to suburbia and have to commute. I kind of like my life, actually." *Or do I?* she mused. She had been so caught up with her day job, and now the radio gig, that she realized she hadn't given her actual life much thought. How does one get from one place to another without thinking about it? Maybe that was much of most people's problems. They just do. They don't think. *Note to self: Make a checklist for your life. Pay attention.*

Rosemary instinctively glanced at Jessie's left hand. No ring, but she was curious. "Married?" Again, Jessie was pulled from her daydreaming.

"Me? No. I did have a live-in boyfriend for a few years, but that ended three years ago. I've had a few stalled relationships since, but there's no diving into the dating pool—it's too shallow!"

Both women broke into laughter. "And you?" Jessie tossed back.

"Divorced. We were too young. I'm pretty sure neither of us knew who we were or what we were doing. Let me rephrase that. I know for sure *he* didn't know who he was because, shortly after we got married, he decided he wanted to become a priest."

"Are you serious?" Jessie had heard this story more than once on the phone lines.

"As a heart attack." Rosemary gave her a look of resignation.

"How did you handle it?" Jessie was genuinely curious, but also doing some research for her audience.

Rosemary shrugged. "I was always a little suspicious. The romance left right after the honeymoon, which was not all that exciting to begin with, for one thing. And he was always talking about religion and different saints. We got divorced after a year. He went away to seminary, then came back to the area as a priest in a nearby diocese. We're still friends, though, and I see him every once in a while. I think the endorphins or dopamine or whatever the heck happens to your brain when you have sex masks reality. I was twenty-two at the time. Now, fourteen years later, I'm still single."

"Good point about the endorphins," Jessie replied. She realized that so many women their age were single. "Seems like a national epidemic."

"What?" Rosemary looked confused. "Endorphins?"

"Single women!" Jessie laughed out loud. "I hear it all the time!" She stopped short of revealing her other job. "I mean, I meet so many of them!"

"Yeah, it seems like there are a lot of single people, but none of them are making a love connection!" Rosemary sighed. "Dating kind of stinks, ya know?"

"I do indeed." Jessie was replaying dozens of phone calls in her head.

"Well, let's finish up here, and I'll give you the names of two of the best contractors around. Have you decided what to do with the inventory?"

Jessie remembered that most books were returnable, but that would be a beastly job, dividing them by publisher, boxing them up, and shipping them back.

Plus she would have to find the invoices. Nope. She would donate them to the local library, school, and hospital.

Once they reached the ground level, Jessie showed Rosemary the way to the door that led to the basement. The building was on a slope, so there was access from the side as well as from the interior. With some trepidation, Jessie pushed the door open. It was a little musty, with boxes of file folders lined up against the walls. There was a carpet remnant on the floor that hosted an old walnut partner's desk and a rickety banker's chair. Otherwise, it was relatively neat.

"I guess I could call someone to clear this out. I know I'm not going to have any time to go through all of it." Jessie had another pang of nostalgia. "Although all the holiday decorations should be somewhere around here." She scanned the large room and noticed some garland peeking out of a box in a far corner. She heaved a big sigh.

Rosemary walked up and put her hand on her shoulder. "This must be kind of hard for you. With all the memories?"

"Yeah." Another big sigh. "Maybe I'll have one last holiday party here. Hey! Here's a thought. I'll have a holiday book giveaway party."

"That's a great idea!" Rosemary was delighted. "I can help you organize it."

"Wow—that would really take a lot of pressure off me to pack everything up." Jessie was starting to feel as if some of the weight had been lifted from her shoulders. "And it would be a fun 'going-away sendoff.'"

"I like it." Rosemary took a few more notes. "I'll order cartons so people can pick and pack."

"Thank you, Rosemary. I cannot tell you how grateful I am." Jessie's eyes were welling up.

"My pleasure. It will give me something to look forward to during the holidays!"

After the walk-through and several pages of notes, Rosemary wrote down the names of the contractors and handed the paper to Jessie. "I'll get back to you with what I think should be the asking price. It could use a little TLC and a new toilet, but the building itself seems sound. And then we can talk about the holiday party. I'll be in touch." Rosemary turned and headed toward the door as Jessie stared wistfully at the bookshelves. For the moment, she felt less depressed about abandoning the bookstore. Now she needed some expert advice as to how to put a little sparkle and shine on the place, so she pulled out her cell phone and dialed the phone number of Evan Becker, the first of the contractors on the list.

"Becker Contracting, this is Evan," a strong-sounding voice answered.

"Hello, Evan. My name is Jessie Richmond. Rosemary Bidgood suggested I get in touch with you. I am at my uncle's shop, Riverwood Books, and need an estimate to get it ready to put on the market."

"Nice to meet you, Jessie. What day and time did you have in mind?"

"I'm only going to be here through tomorrow. Is it possible to stop by this afternoon to do a walk-through?"

"I could be there within the hour."

"Terrific. You know the place?"

"Sure do! See you in a bit."

As Jessie hit END, a feeling of apprehension crawled up her neck. "You're doing the right thing," she told herself.

* * *

When Evan Becker arrived, his six-foot-three-inch frame filled the doorway. Strong facial features revealed a charming smile that curved toward his dark, smoky-brown eyes.

Handsome is an understatement, Jessie thought, as she once again looked for a wedding band. *You have to stop doing that,* she told herself. No ring. But that didn't mean anything. A lot of men didn't wear one, especially if they were in the trades. But there was an animal attraction she hadn't felt in a very long time. *Too long—stop it . . .* she admonished herself again, also being very aware that her hands were trembling when he extended his.

"Sorry, I was outside, and my hands are a little cold." *That's so lame.*

"No worries." He responded with a handshake. "Mine are a little rough."

And that smile. She thought she was going to faint.

"Okeydokey, then. Shall we get started?" Jessie was hoping her knees wouldn't buckle under her.

"I remember coming here a few times when I was a kid." Evan glanced around the big room. "I would visit my grandparents in the summer, and truth be told, I dreaded coming here." He said this with a sheepish grin. "I was only interested in sports; anything requiring a bat, stick, or ball. I only agreed because we would go out for ice cream afterward."

Jessie was trying to size up his age. His salt-and-pepper hair made him appear to be in his early to mid forties, but she didn't think he was that old. Obviously, people change, but she was sure that she would have remembered those eyes and that smile. She shrugged.

"Funny, I was here every summer. I don't remember

rowdy boys in the reading group!" She was starting to relax with a bit of teasing.

"Oh, I wasn't rowdy. In fact, I was a bit shy. Intimidated, to be honest. I wasn't much into books, so I felt a little stupid, especially when that girl would start reading to us. She was a little younger than I, and had mastered the art of storytelling!"

Jessie's face began to turn red. "Uh, I believe that would be me you're talking about."

"Seriously? You?" Evan was dubious.

"Yep. I was Miss Bossy Pants, instructing everyone to sit still and be quiet."

Evan let out a guffaw. "Well, I was impressed. You actually held my interest . . . at least for a few minutes!"

"That is just crazy." She had once intimidated *him*! The irony was not lost on her. "Well, Evan Becker, it's nice to meet you again!"

They took their time inspecting the walls, floors, and trim. "Looks like they put up those columns where there was a load-bearing wall."

Jessie gave him a perplexed look. Evan continued when he saw her questioning brow. "You need to support the beams for the roof or second floor. That's what walls are for, besides designating space." *That smile again.* "Nowadays they put up steel beams if you want an open expanse like this. Doing it now would be very costly, which is why you have these columns. Nice that they kept them natural." Evan scanned the room again.

"My dad and Uncle Hugo renovated it sometime back in the early seventies. Not exactly professionals." She hoped they hadn't committed any kind of construction faux pas that a real professional would find.

"They did a pretty good job, actually. This is going to be a large space once you move out the sofas and bookcases." He continued with his assessment. "I would suggest replacing the molding around the floor and doors. I know some people think keeping old wood is important—antique or some such nonsense—but this stuff is just old pine. The storage and bathroom doors are in pretty good shape. We can refinish them and clean up the knobs. The problem may be the floor. When you take out the bookcases, it's going to need to be stripped, sanded, and refinished."

Jessie's head was reeling. "Darn. I hadn't thought about that part. I was more focused on getting rid of the books." Her mood shifted.

"You sure you want to sell this place?" Evan sensed her reluctance.

"I do have mixed feelings about it. I have no idea how to run a bookstore, and I have a life in Philadelphia."

"Philly?"

"Yes, that's where I live and work now."

"What kind of work? If you don't mind my asking." Evan sounded genuinely interested.

"Advertising. I did some volunteer work for a suicide hotline, but that got a little heavy after three years. Now I . . ." She immediately stopped that train of thought. "I just seem to work all the time." She was proud of how she managed to save her secret, but that was twice in one day that she almost spilled the beans. She had to be more careful—but being back at the bookstore, her façade had disappeared.

"All work and no play . . . I'm sure you've heard that before," he chimed in. "I'm afraid that I'm guilty of the same thing."

"Must be rough on your wife and family." Jessie was horrified that she had gone there so quickly, but then again, she only had one day to find out.

"Wife? That was the problem. I worked too much, and she got 'distracted.'" He used air quotes to illustrate the word. "Been divorced for several years. But my son and I have a great relationship. He's going to be ten in February. I see him almost every day, and I get him every other weekend. I coach his Little League team."

"Ah. Now I see why you were anxious to get out of the bookstore with your bat and ball." Jessie chuckled. *He's not married! Girlfriend? Too much to push at the moment.*

"Yes. I was actually drafted by the Astros when I graduated from college, but I broke my arm in my second game and lost my swing." He sounded disappointed but not bitter. "They say God does things *for* you, not *to* you."

Handsome, not married, and philosophical. Jessie was beginning to think there was hope for the opposite sex.

"Does your arm affect your construction work?" she asked, curious.

"Most of what I do is the designing and estimating." His face lit up once more with that smile. "I have a partner and a few guys on a crew that do all the heavy lifting. I do the planning and some of the finish work. The thinking part can be stressful, so the finish work helps me to relax."

Jessie finally took notice of what he was wearing. His handsome face had been a huge distraction when he first walked in. He was in what looked like a new pair of jeans with a tailored, button-down shirt, and what appeared to be a Hugo Boss belt. *Hmmmm . . . good taste.* And his work boots were shined. *Slow down, girl.* The fact that a member of the opposite sex was grabbing her interest was heartening. She was beginning to think she would never find another man attractive, especially hearing all the horror stories from her show.

She wasn't a man-hater by any means, but more of a hesitant party. She reminded herself that *cautious* was the key word.

"I would suggest replacing the toilets and the sinks in the bathrooms, and the floors could use some help, too." Evan was talking, but Jessie was lost in thought.

"Huh? Oh, sorry. I was getting ahead of myself." *If he only knew.*

"Nothing to worry about. Renovating a place can be overwhelming, and given that you want to sell the place, that adds another layer of stress. I was saying that the floors in the bathroom could use some help. Right now they're wood and have been abused, if you get my drift. I would suggest tile. You don't want to start negotiating a sale when there are obvious issues."

"I agree. I want this to look inviting." She smiled at him, noticing the early signs of crow's-feet around his eyes. It gave him a look of experience more than age.

"Okay, so I'll include the removal of the book-shelves, refurbishing the floors, bathroom fixtures, ceramic tile, refinishing the doors, paint, and new molding. What do you want to do about the ceiling fixtures? The ceiling fans look like they're about to retire."

"Might as well replace them." Jessie started to add up the costs in her head but realized she was clueless. She had only lived in apartments, so she had never had to deal with any homeowner issues. She cringed at the next sentence. "We still have to check the apartment upstairs. Follow me."

Because the interior entrance to the apartment was rarely used, they went outside and climbed the steps to the second level. "The deck appears to be in very good condition. And the yard just needs a little cleanup. If you need some assistance with landscaping, I have a guy who is good and reasonable." Jessie opened the apartment door and gestured for Evan to walk in.

The main living area was adjacent to the deck overlooking the large yard. The full-sized kitchen was equipped with stainless-steel appliances, including a dishwasher and a peninsular counter with stools. There was a dining alcove that accommodated a long, rectangular table, all opening into the large living room, which had a small corner fireplace.

"Nice space." Evan took a sweeping look. "I like the open floor plan and the skylights. With a northern exposure, it really brightens up the room."

"My uncle and dad were nuts about natural light—hence all the skylights in the place. Our house was chock-full of them. You'd have thought they hijacked a truck!" Jessie let out a small snicker. "We had one in almost every room—including my bedroom. I loved lying in my bed and looking up at the stars, especially in the winter, when you would get those glorious starry, starry nights. I would watch for shooting stars and, of course, Santa!" Jessie was enjoying her reminiscences. "But we couldn't go to sleep on Christmas Eve until we made snow angels outside. That was how we knew Santa would find us." She stopped short. "I must be boring you to tears."

"Not at all." Evan gave her a warm smile.

Jessie regained her poise. "Anyway . . . Uncle Hugo would let authors stay here when they would do a book signing. During the summer months, we always had friends or family popping in when there wasn't an event. There was always a lot of activity, that's for sure."

Jessie made her way through the apartment. "The bedrooms are average size, but the living area is quite comfortable. I think he was hoping I'd move in and take over the store."

"No interest?" Evan queried.

"Oh, nooo. I had to go to Philadelphia to be with my then new photographer slash boyfriend. That lasted a few months. But I have a good job, friends, and I love the city. But . . ." Her voice trailed off, as she thought she was sharing too much information.

"I get it. I moved here because I had met Alicia one summer when I was visiting my grandparents. After my baseball career ended, including my time as a coaching assistant at Oklahoma, where I went to school, I thought about moving my family back to Albany, where I grew up. But my cousin was starting his construction company and needed a partner. So here I am." Evan once again spoke with clarity, not regret.

"So what do you think?" Jessie implored, hoping there would be no additional costs to getting the place in shape.

"Let me take a look at the loo."

Jessie pointed in the direction of the bathroom. There was only one, but it was a split bath. The tub and toilet were separated from the long double-bowl sink by an interior door, allowing for more privacy. There was also room for a tall linen cabinet on one side.

After a little scrutiny, Evan said, "You might want to think about replacing the light fixtures, but a couple of coats of paint should be fine for up here."

Jessie was relieved that this part wasn't going to cost much. "What about the deck?"

"A good power wash should do the trick."

"We still have to check the basement. Uncle Hugo kept a lot of records down there."

"Lead the way." Evan appeared to be easygoing, with a healthy dose of self-confidence.

A quick inspection revealed that the foundation was solid: no leaks, no mold. "Maybe have Servpro come in and give it a good cleaning. But otherwise, there's nothing I need to do down here."

As they returned to the main level, Jessie was feeling some anxiety. She wasn't sure if it was being around him or the impending cost. "Any idea what this is going to run?"

"Everyone asks the same question before I pull out the calculator." He grinned. "This isn't too complicated. You have approximately twenty-three hundred square feet on the first level. Should take me a day or so to write it up. You said you were leaving tomorrow?"

"Yes, but I'll be back the week before Christmas and staying through New Year's. The office closes for a few days during the holidays, and I have some extra vacation days I have to use up."

"I have my son for the week, so I wouldn't be able to do any work until after the first of the year." Evan was hoping that wouldn't be a deal breaker.

"Oh, no problem. My original plan was to pack everything up, but Rosemary and I concocted an idea to have a holiday book giveaway party, where people can come and take whatever they want." She was feeling more lighthearted again. "My goal is to get it on the market by end of February."

"That should be plenty of time, unless we find some hidden disasters." Seeing the shocked look on Jessie's face, he continued, "But I don't expect to. These buildings were built to last."

"Whew. I was thinking about that *Property Brothers* show, where they have to tell the owners they need a new retaining wall for twenty grand!"

"Yeah, that kind of news is never fun to deliver, especially if you're a reputable contractor—you don't want to profit on someone else's misfortune." Evan let another side of his personality show—decency.

"Will you be around during the holidays or are you planning on taking your son to someplace fun and warm?" She was trying not to sound like she was giving him the third degree.

"This year, we're staying local. My parents are coming up from Myrtle Beach to visit my sister in Troy, just outside of Albany. She and I decided to split their travel expenses to make it easier for us, actually. She has three kids, and I have Connor. Lots of moving parts. It's just over two hours by car, and they'll stop by to see some of their friends who haven't become snowbirds." *Again—that alluring smile.*

"I hope you and your son can come to the party. Maybe he can snag some books for his school library. You're welcome to bring a date." She tried to hide her mortification. To be sure, since she had started the radio gig, she had learned to cut to the chase, but this was bordering on ridiculous.

"Date?" Evan raised an eyebrow. "Most women my age are either married or divorced with kids and don't want any more, including only part-time."

"It's funny. People don't want to be alone, but they make up so many rules that it's almost impossible to find someone to even *think* about having a relationship."

"Sounds like you have some experience in that arena." He stopped writing and glanced up at her.

Jessie was on high alert. She could not take the conversation any further for fear of revealing her radio persona. She'd rather keep that undercover.

"Yeah. I seem to be an expert in 'what not to do' in that arena." She giggled at her self-deprecating remark, then flashed him her most winning smile. A long pause hung in the air.

"Well alrighty then! I'll get this written up and send

it to you. What's your e-mail address?" He held out his massive hand with the pad and pen.

"Thanks, Evan. You and Rosemary have been very helpful." She jotted down all her contact information and handed the pad back to him.

As she watched Evan stroll back to his truck, she realized that she had a great big smile on her face. She quickly turned back into the store, not wanting him to see her "teenage-like" moment. *Huh. Who knew you could have a crush on someone at this age?*

Jessie pulled out her cell phone and dialed Lisa. "Hey! Got a lot accomplished. Ready to grab some dinner?"

Lisa sounded excited. "You bet. Kenny and the kids are going bowling. Give me fifteen minutes to get them out the door! Meet you at the Pour House?"

"Sounds good! I could use some comfort food and ale right now!"

Chapter Three

As Evan pulled out of the driveway, he was a little uneasy. But not in a bad way. The fact that she was very attractive had caught him off guard. He really didn't know what to expect. Niece to a bookstore owner? She could have had that long-skirt-granny-glasses look to her, but she didn't. Slim jeans, sweater—which skimmed her toned body—and knee-high riding boots. No. This was no shrinking violet of a bookworm. She was a very attractive woman of purpose, charm, style, and magnetism. It had been a long time since he had been in the presence of a woman who was confident and in charge of herself, a woman not afraid to acknowledge her limitations and comfortable enlisting the assistance of others. No. She was different. She was special.

Evan tapped his head with the pencil that often sat behind his ear. He didn't want to allow his thoughts to wander any further. *She lives almost three hours away, you don't know her situation, and she is selling her property and getting the heck out of here. It's a job. Business. Period. But still . . .*

With the prospect of finding a significant other

seemingly out of reach, Evan had resigned himself to a life of being single, raising his son, and working. He liked to kayak, hike, and fish, activities that helped him relax and forget the loneliness that would set in from time to time. *Yes, men get lonely, too.* He remembered reading a short article in *Men's Health* magazine. Dr. Somebody or Other. She was giving advice to the newly divorced and single. He had taken his son, Connor, to the dentist when he noticed the sidebar story as he sat in the waiting room. Evidently, there were a lot of people bemoaning the fact that life hadn't turned out the way they had planned. He guessed it was the same thing that has plagued men for centuries: midlife crisis. This professor person was advising people to "try to find something to be passionate about—not necessarily through another person. A hobby? Sports? Cooking? Even gardening. Or challenge yourself to do that one thing you always wanted to do. At least you would have tried. Reclaim yourself. Once you do that, other people will be drawn to you. Loneliness can lead to depression, and that helps to create a vicious circle. Get out there! Do something!" Evan thought the article had some very sound advice. He recalled that when he had first gotten back to Croton, he was deflated and in a bit of a funk.

After the divorce, he decided that if he couldn't actually do the thing he felt passionate about, he could at least continue to coach. Once word got out that Evan Becker wanted to coach softball and baseball, he had offers from Little League to the local community college. With Connor in grammar school, he picked the teams that would fit into his schedule. Working for yourself had its advantages. He could arrange his time so that he and Connor had something to share.

He thought back to his relationship with Alicia.

They had met during the summer between his junior and senior year at the University of Oklahoma. She was from Schenectady, a year younger than he was but also a rising senior at Oklahoma. Strangely enough, they had not known each other at Oklahoma but had met at a party in Utica after a college league summer baseball game, and romance followed. During their senior year, they were inseparable. Alicia, the social-butterfly cheerleader type and Evan, the star center fielder who batted .450 his senior year with eighteen home runs and fifty-three RBIs while leading his team to the NCAA Division I national championship. They married right after graduation, and he reported to the Houston Astros' Pacific Coast League team in Round Rock, Texas.

During his second game, he broke his arm in a freak accident when he, the second baseman, and the shortstop all went after a pop fly behind second base and collided. The injury not only put an end to his fledgling baseball career but also, he now realized, to his romance.

When Evan was benched and told by the doctors and specialists that he could no longer swing a bat in a manner consistent with being a professional baseball player, the excitement that had marked their young lives collapsed. Granted, people lose much more than a job or a career, but the loss of his proved to be the deal breaker in their romance though the marriage continued for a number of years.

After he was cut loose by the Astros, the University of Oklahoma offered him a graduate assistantship to continue his design studies and be an assistant coach for its championship baseball team. They spent the next three years in Oklahoma, where Alicia gave birth to their son. When his studies were over, and while contemplating what to do next, Evan received a phone call from his cousin Reed in Croton. Reed had been working construction and decided to open his own contracting business, and asked Evan if he would consider going into partnership with him. Evan decided to accept Reed's offer and move his three-month-old son and wife back to New York State.

That's when things really began to sour. During their time back in Oklahoma, Alicia had been spending his $300,000 signing bonus as if that level of income were going to continue, and by the time he had finished his studies, their credit cards were maxed out. He tried to reason with her, but she persisted in demanding the lifestyle she had become accustomed to on the basis of the bonus. The arguments increased in volume and intensity over the course of the next few years after they had returned to New York. She couldn't understand why he couldn't get a job in baseball "like one of those guys on TV who talk about the games and the players and give play-by-play descriptions of what's happening."

Evan tried to explain that those jobs went to people who had experience, not guys who get cut from a team after their second game in the minors. Besides, he had no interest in becoming a sports commentator. Alicia's blistering language still echoed in his head. "If you really loved me, you'd try harder!"

One night, when Evan was sitting on his son's bed, Connor asked him why Mommy and Daddy didn't like each other. Evan was struck by the innocent but cutting words from his little boy. He saw the dismay on Connor's face and knew something had to change. So he asked Alicia for a separation. She had a fit and blamed him for everything, which only confirmed that getting a divorce would be the healthiest course of action for all of them.

When the divorce became final, they had no assets, and he would be paying off credit card bills for years. It was almost comical, therefore, when Alicia told the judge that she was entitled to alimony because Evan could be making more money but wasn't trying hard enough. The judge was stunned by her bizarre demand. She had a college degree, was almost the same age as Evan, able-bodied, and perfectly capable of finding gainful employment. The judge had no sympathy. "Get a job, young lady," he told her. "Use your brains to support yourself. Your ex-husband is only responsible for child support. Period." It was a victory for Evan. All of it.

He finally relaxed his shoulders and headed to his usual stop for a quick bite to eat. Then he'd go home and start working on the estimate for "Miss Bossy Pants." He smiled to himself, recalling her voice and self-deprecation. He had to admit, she was cute. More than cute, actually. And she was coming back for the holidays. That's when the wheels began to turn.

Chapter Four

There was a squeal of glee as Lisa and Jessie hugged and kissed each other on each cheek. "So good to see you!" Jessie was beginning to feel less isolated and overwhelmed. Lisa had been her best bud through elementary and high school, and they still kept in touch with weekly phone calls. When Jessie had left for Penn State on a volleyball scholarship, Lisa enrolled in the local community college to study nursing. During her last year, when she was thinking about completing her studies at a four-year college, she met Kenny, a sophomore at SUNY Albany who had grown up in Montrose, and fell head over heels in love. Luckily, he did also.

So instead of continuing her studies, Lisa moved to Albany, got a job as a home health aide, and moved in with Kenny while he finished studying for his accounting degree. They got married in August after graduation and moved to Croton, where he took a job with a local accountant. Three years later, she gave birth to her first child and Kenny took over from his boss, who had decided to retire to Arizona. The good news was that she and her hubby were still crazy about each other fifteen years after they had first met.

"What a day. My head is spinning." Jessie plopped herself into one of the old red leather barrel-shaped chairs. She loved the Pour House. It was a throwback in time, with old photos of the town, model ships, a dartboard, and a small standing shuffleboard table. "Rosemary, the real estate agent, was terrific. She's going to help me organize a book giveaway over the holidays," she said, with a sigh of relief.

"That's a great idea!" Lisa chimed in. "It should be fun. We can decorate the front porch like we used to."

"Oh, I don't know about that. I'm only going to be here for a little over two weeks, and I imagine I'll be engulfed in packing whatever is left and working out details with the contractor."

"Which contractor did you call?"

"Evan Becker." Jessie took a small pull on her glass of water, not wanting to reveal her almost secret crush.

"Evan Becker? He's quite a scrumptious piece of man cake!" Lisa stated with certainty. Her gaze lifted across the room. "Speaking of Mr. Scrumptious, he's across the room right now." Lisa immediately put her arm up to wave, but Jessie caught it in midair. "What?" Lisa quizzed her.

"Nothing. I just don't want to get too chummy with someone who is going to work for me. You know, keep it professional." Jessie tried to hide her private interest, but the blush on her face gave it away.

"Ooohhhhh . . ." Lisa gave her a sideways glance. "You've already inspected that big hunk o'man." She couldn't help but tease her old pal.

"Shut it," Jessie said with a smile. "Yes, I found him

very attractive, which makes me think I should get a second opinion."

"On what? That he's handsome?"

"No, silly. On the construction work." Jessie motioned for the waitress while she tried to keep Evan from spotting them. "By the way, how do *you* know Evan?"

"He coaches the kids' baseball team."

"Ah. And you never thought of mentioning him to me?" Jessie chided her.

"I thought you were off men for now."

"I feel like that's been a career." Jessie slumped farther down in her chair.

"Time to dust off your perky self and get out there!" Lisa, who had settled into life as a stay-at-home mom and looked more matronly than perky, had always admired Jessie for being in shape and keeping a good attitude no matter what.

"Yeah, yeah . . . one of these days."

"What about Match—" Lisa was just about to recommend online dating when Jessie interrupted her.

"Don't even go there!" Jessie realized she had raised her voice a little louder than normal. "There's no diving into that dating pool!"

Lisa laughed out loud. Jessie continued, "Rosemary and I were discussing this earlier. Considering that the divorce rate is hovering around fifty percent, there still seems to be a drought of eligible men. Have you seen some of these guys?" Jessie sat back and folded her arms across her chest. "Why do men think a photo of themselves in a hot tub is alluring? It's gross!" The two doubled over in laughter.

Lisa sat up straight and scoped the room. "Yep. The only thing worth looking at is looking at us right now."

"Oh no . . . Did he actually see us?" Before she could finish the sentence, Evan stood and started walking toward them.

"Dang it. I didn't even brush my hair!"

In a conspiratorial whisper, Lisa leaned in again. "You look fine." Sitting taller, she continued, "Well hello, Coach Becker!"

"Good evening, Lisa. Jessie. Nice to see you both. May I buy you a drink?" Evan seemed taller with Jessie seated. Almost Paul Bunyan-like.

"Sure. Thanks. Want to join us?" Lisa threw that out immediately, as Jessie kicked her under the table.

"Yes, please do." Jessie made the obligatory remark.

"Thanks, but I have to get back to the office. I have an estimate to write up, but I wouldn't mind a rain check next time you're in town." He nodded toward Jessie.

"I think we can arrange that." Lisa was all over this, returning the kick and almost knocking the table over.

Jessie smiled. "Yes, that would be nice."

"Great. I'll look forward to it. I'll have Nancy put your cocktails on my tab. Have a good evening." He gave them a two-finger salute. "I'll be in touch."

"He can touch me anytime," Lisa said dreamily.

"Aren't you the comedienne?" Jessie finally felt she could exhale.

"Hey, I may be happily married, but I'm not dead!" Lisa chortled, almost knocking over her glass.

Chapter Five

Confident she'd covered her bases with Rosemary and Evan, Jessie packed her weekend bag and began her trip back to Philadelphia. During the drive, she realized she had said "no diving into the dating pool" twice in a single day. Plus she heard that story repeatedly on the air. Maybe she could do something to change that, and the idea of speed dating came to mind. It saved a lot of time instead of fishing for love on the Internet.

She reviewed the process in her head. The number of women and men who attended would determine the number of small tables, with one woman seated at each table. The tables would be numbered, and the women sitting at them would remain seated while the men moved from one table to the next. Each couple would spend ten minutes talking, a bell would ring, and the men would move to the next table. Everyone would have a card, so they could take notes as to whom they might want to see again. At the end of the event, the participants would turn in the card, and the host—who would be Jessie—would send private e-mails to all the participants as to who wants another opportunity to meet. The only snag was when/if someone didn't get any requests. She'd figure out some sort of consolation prize—maybe a free personal half-hour phone session with Dr. Richie. Since her radio show was available to stream on several different sites, she could promote the event to people in the Croton area that way, in addition to putting it up on the local Patch. Lots of lonely people during the holidays, and she wanted to spread some cheer.

As she crossed the Betsy Ross Bridge, she finally had most of the logistics figured out. She could do the book giveaway party, have the bookcases either moved or removed, then host the speed-dating night. She then wondered if she was taking on too much. *Nah. It will keep my mind occupied,* she thought to herself. She would need to rent a few tables and chairs, get some pads and pens, and stands for the table numbers. Easy-peasy . . . she hoped.

When she got to her apartment, she dropped her bag and immediately called Lisa.

"Okay, Miss Smarty Pants, Miss Bossy Pants calling. I have an idea."

Lisa knew the translation—"*And you will help me.*"

"Okay. Shoot."

"Speed dating!" Jessie said gleefully.

"Speed what?" Lisa sounded perplexed, so Jessie began to explain, trying to elicit enthusiasm from her friend.

"Oh, I get it. Musical chairs, kinda." Lisa was trying to be supportive.

"Yeah. Kinda."

Chapter Six

Like every year before, the hallway the ad agency shared with the radio station was chock-full of jingle bells, wreaths, reindeer, elves, ubiquitous garland, and the stealthily hung mistletoe. Jessie would always chuckle, wondering who was trying to kiss whom because no one seemed to know where the mistletoe came from. She suspected that the source was Ziggy the weatherman. He had a secret crush on Valerie the receptionist, who in turn seemed to have some interest in Ziggy. But he never made a move. *Maybe this year.* Jessie was always thinking in the most positive light.

It was two weeks before Christmas, and each night, the phone calls during her talk show became more frequent and desperate. The oddest call was one in which a woman was upset because her boyfriend did not want to go to her family's house for any of the holidays. Jessie, aka Dr. Richie, explained that a lot of people feel stressed during the holidays, and meeting someone's family is stressful in itself. Too often, people put too many "special occasions" on top of the holidays, creating a giant panic attack waiting to happen.

Then, about an hour later, another woman called with the same issue. Jessie gave her the same explanation, but the woman persisted. "We've been dating for four months, and he hasn't wanted to meet my family, not even my twin sister! And *her* boyfriend doesn't want to meet the family either! It's not like we're weird or something!"

Jessie got a little bit of a chill. "So you've both been dating men who have an aversion to meeting the family?"

"Yes. Roger missed the Labor Day barbecue, and now he won't come to Christmas dinner. My sister's boyfriend says it's too soon for him—they only started dating about a month ago. We're both single. She's divorced, and I'm a widow."

Listening to the woman's voice, Jessie guessed the caller to be somewhere in her fifties. "Have you ever seen a photo of your sister's boyfriend?"

"No. Why?"

"Isn't it odd that with everyone having a camera on their phone, your sister hasn't shown you a photograph?"

"Yeah, I suppose." The woman sounded befuddled. "Believe it or not, we don't do a lot of social media . . . we're not very tech-savvy. Kinda old-school. I have to confess, I hardly ever text. But now that you mention it, Roger won't let me take any photos of him."

Jessie was beginning to get a creepy feeling about the situation when the light bulb went on in her head. "I have an idea, but it may make you uncomfortable. This is what I suggest: You and your sister get together and bake some cookies. Then you both bring them to Roger's house as a surprise. This way, he won't have a choice about meeting her." Jessie was regretting the words as they were falling out of her mouth, but confronting the issue was the only way to clear up this situation, which she felt involved a grand deception.

Three days later, during her show, she got a frantic phone call from a man who admitted that he had been dating twins behind each other's back. He insisted it was an honest mistake the first time he met Emily. He was at the grocery store and thought she was Elizabeth. When he realized he had mistaken her for her sister, he failed to mention that he knew her and introduced himself using his nickname, Bucky. They flirted, and he asked her to have dinner. After several dates, he realized he needed to make a choice. Trying to rationalize his behavior, he decided he wanted to set things right with Elizabeth; he had decided she was the one for him. Unfortunately, he was in hot water now.

Evidently, when the sisters got together to bake the cookies, they had discovered they both had a boyfriend living at the same address. Coincidence? That would be a big *no*. Rather than get angry with each other, they decided to teach him a lesson. They thought of switching up and going to see him, but agreed that the switching-identities bit had been overdone. And, they wanted to see the look on his face when he was with both of them at the same time. So instead of cookies, each prepared a fruitcake heavily laden with nuts and baked them until they were hard as a brick—even harder than the usual fruitcake, that is.

When Roger/Bucky/whatever his real name was opened the door, he was surprised by identical women with what seemed like two identical blocks of raisins, dried fruit, nuts, and spices. Each took a turn throttling him with the baked goods and mashing them into his beard.

He continued to whine about his predicament and said it was "an honest mistake. I really love Elizabeth!"

Jessie simply replied with, "I hope they left the nuts in the shells," hit the red, one-inch square DUMP button on the console, and disconnected him.

They called it a "dump button" so the host could dump the caller if they became abusive. It sat just a few inches from her microphone and came in handy when necessary. Luckily, the need to use it rarely arose, but there was a certain sense of gratification when it did. It was like the good old days, when you could slam the phone down on someone. Now with cell phones it wasn't the same just hitting END. No drama in that and not very satisfying.

As she wrapped up the final call, Brian gave her a signal, and she signed off.

"Wow. That was crazy."

"Yeah. I know. I think I may have stepped out of line there, but I didn't know what else to tell that woman. My instincts were correct, unfortunately. I hope I didn't start a family feud." The studio phone line was lighting up again, but it was after the show went down. Both of them glanced at the blinking light.

"Whaddya think? Answer it?" Brian asked.

"Sure. Why not? How bad could it be?" Jessie's eyes widened.

Brian hit the speakerphone button. "WQPK."

"Is Dr. Richie still there?" the voice on the other end queried.

"I believe she may have left for the night. If I can find her, who should I say is calling?"

"Emily and Elizabeth Wilson. The twins. We want to thank her."

Jessie and Brian almost doubled over, and Jessie gave him the thumbs-up.

"Hang on, let me see if she's still in the building."

Pausing a reasonable amount of time, Jessie picked up the phone. "Hello. This is Dr. Richie."

"Dr. Richie, it's the woman who called a few nights ago about my boyfriend who wouldn't come to the house for the holidays. Well, it turned out the jerk was dating both me and my sister, and if it wasn't for you, his little game could have gone on for months! She and I made the discovery when we were baking the cookies. We switched to fruitcakes. When we got to his house, we took turns smacking him over the head with it. Right on his front porch, for all the nosy neighbors to see! It was great! I never felt so vindicated. Now I can get on with my life and not waste any more time with that loser! So thank you, and have a very Merry Christmas!"

Jessie could hear the twin sister echoing her words in the background.

"Glad it worked out for you. Merry Christmas!"

Brian gave her a sideways look. "How did you know?"

"Just a hunch. But I have to say that is probably the best use of a fruitcake ever!" Jessie laughed, winked, said good night, grabbed her coat, and headed toward the door.

"Aren't you forgetting something?" Brian stopped her. "Like your birthday dinner with Mac, Kelly, Ryan, and me?" He almost looked hurt.

"Oh my goodness! I've been so caught up in the plans for the shop and the holiday calls, I wasn't paying attention to the date. The older I get, the less celebrating a birthday appeals."

"Stop it, young lady," he ordered, emphasizing the word "young." "Obviously, you need a little break, and dinner tonight should do the trick."

They were going to Barclay Prime, a sleek-looking

place with hints of a European library. Brian thought the décor was appropriate: books! But it was the steaks that had everyone drooling in anticipation.

"Ahh, yes . . . Hunk O'Meat." Jessie's face went soft, relaxing for the first time in weeks. "Let's get going! What are we waiting for?"

The two headed for the elevator and proceeded to the parking garage. Brian opened the passenger side of his Ford Explorer and, with a great flourish, proclaimed, "Your chariot awaits."

Brian was thirty-three, tall and lanky with a great sense of humor, and kept Jessie on an even keel when the phone lines got hot. It was especially entertaining and challenging when listeners would call in and offer their own advice to a previous caller. And boy, sometimes it got very heated. Jessie and Brian would make crazy faces and hand gestures to each other. His "crazy in the head" was one of his favorites, while Jessie's was pretending her head was exploding. They were good pals.

Jessie often wondered why Brian didn't have a steady girlfriend. He was cute in a nerdy way, wore black jeans, black shirts, thick-rimmed black glasses, and a black leather blazer with a black tie almost every day. Thing was he had several of each so he always had a clean set of his favorite outfit. Said it helped him blend into the engineering room, where the walls were covered in black, soundproof acoustic panels. He referred to it as his "uniform." Plus he never had to think about what to wear. Jessie had once asked, "Is that a geek thing or a nerd thing?" Brian preferred "geek." It was a bit more tech-sounding.

As they pulled away from the building, they discussed what they might have for dinner. Jessie was vacillating among the jumbo shrimp cocktail . . . or maybe the Alaskan king crab, or maybe the oysters . . . but she was most definitely chasing it down with the eighteen-ounce rib eye, medium rare, baked potato, and a side of creamed spinach. Then maybe a soufflé for dessert.

Brian was strictly a meat-and-potatoes guy, so he was going to order the same main dish minus the spinach. When he said, "That's only for Popeye and birthday girls," Jessie smacked him on the arm.

The restaurant was elegantly adorned, with gold-trimmed cranberry-colored velvet ribbon and miniature lights. Simple large crystal bowls held golden glass apples and pears, and sprigs of white birch served as centerpieces on each table, as soft classical holiday favorites played in the background.

When they arrived, their friends were waiting at the bar area with suspicious-looking packages. Birthday gifts. Jessie had been adamant about "no presents!" But her words were ignored by her good friends. After the "Happy Birthdays" and hugs went around, they perused the menu. As the waiters carried food to the other tables, everyone kept changing their mind about what to order. The restaurant was named for its beef, so Jessie, while distracted by the poached lobster, returned to her original plan and decided on the crab cocktail and the rib eye.

The conversation was casual, everyone talking about their holiday plans. Jessie sat back and listened. It was nice to be able to unwind among friends and not think about the two daunting tasks that lay ahead—make that three, counting selling the store. Everything seemed under control, including her stupid crush on that contractor dude. For now she had kept her thoughts at bay. They had been communicating strictly by e-mail. Professional. Succinct. Not a personal "How are you?" The only thing he asked was when she was planning on getting back. She wasn't sure if she was relieved or disappointed, but she knew it was best to keep it at a professional level. She shifted her thoughts to the two events she was hosting before the big FOR SALE sign went up. Jessie did her utmost to have a positive attitude, but she would often fret about details and getting everything right. That was also part of her charm. She was vivacious and sincere, and very detail-oriented.

Relaxing in the large, comfortable dining chair, she took in the restaurant's warm holiday vibe. Steering herself away from thinking about her trip to Croton in a stressful way, she eased into thinking that all of it would be a grand adventure. She made up her mind. It was going to be a good Christmas this year.

Chapter Seven

During the weeks leading up to Christmas, Jessie, Rosemary, and Lisa planned out the book giveaway and the speed-dating event. The book party was the easy part, and they decided to make it a "bring a box, take a box" event. People were asked to bring a toy for the Children's Hospital and some nonperishable items for the food pantry. In return they could take up to ten books: a win-win for a lot of people. It was the speed-dating part that had her traveling into uncharted territory. Jessie kept asking herself, *What was I thinking?* But she was all in now, and there seemed to be some excitement surrounding it.

She had attended two speed-dating events in the past—neither of which produced any romantic prospects for her, but the events themselves didn't appear to be very complicated; and it seemed like the people who attended were willing to spend $35.00 on the chance to meet someone. The proceeds would go toward refreshments and a donation to Animal Care Sanctuary, the largest and oldest no-kill shelter in the country. The money would help pay for a special

Christmas dinner for the dogs and cats who were still looking for a forever home.

Jessie had posted it on her Dr. Richie Facebook page, and there were some ads on the radio station home page and on the local Patch in Croton.

NEED A DATE FOR THE HOLIDAYS?
SPEED YOUR WAY THROUGH THEM!
JOIN OTHER SINGLES FOR AN EVENING OF SPEED DATING.
FINALLY AN OPPORTUNITY TO "INTERVIEW" DATING
POTENTIALS FACE-TO-FACE IN TEN-MINUTE INTERVALS.
NO SURPRISES, NO BAR SCENE.
A PLACE TO MEET NEW PEOPLE—FOR REAL.
DECEMBER 23—6:00 P.M.
$35.00*
Riverwood Books
Croton-on-Hudson, New York
For more info visit:
www.drRichiemeetup.biz
*INCLUDES REFRESHMENTS AND A DONATION
TO ANIMAL CARE SANCTUARY

The notice listed all the information as far as location, time, etc. and an RSVP. It also had a disclaimer that Dr. Richie was only a sponsor for the event. Jessie would simply be "Jessie" throughout.

Jessie and Brian were shocked that over twenty people had signed up. What made it better was that it was an almost equal number of men and women, and the age ranges were within ten years of each other. This might not be the nightmare she feared it could be. Now she was on a mission: someone was going to have a date for New Year's Eve, even if it wasn't her.

She packed two suitcases of clothes because she

wasn't sure about the weather. It had been very inconsistent. Climate change. Whatever.

The doorman would hold her snail mail, and she had her laptop for whatever work-related issues should arise for either job. After reminding the neighbor who watched Mozart and Picasso when she was away, Jessie left a little later than planned, and dusk was already upon her. She knew it would be dark by the time she got to Croton, but she was still familiar with the roads and settled into her seat. When she got to the Tappan Zee Bridge, the hillside was alive with Christmas lights. Some twinkling, some all white, some with bright LED colors. This was the first Christmas in a very long time that she was looking forward to. Yes, there was a lot of work to be done, but also a real change of scenery was beckoning her. Old friends, familiar surroundings. For a moment, the sense of bittersweet wafted over her again, but she smiled, knowing that all those books would be enjoyed by so many, and she was providing what could turn into a love connection for two or more of her guests. "You never know," she said out loud.

As she rounded the turn for the shop, she became disoriented. Slowly tapping on the brake, she blinked several times. White fairy lights adorned the roofline, garland graciously wrapped the columns, wreaths appeared in each window, and an eight-foot tree decorated in twinkling lights was perched on each side of the porch. An elegant life-size Rudolph proudly welcomed visitors at the bottom of the steps.

The illumination and the ornaments were stunning. She gasped in wonder. "What the??? Who??? Wow! Holy Cow! Holy Rudolph!" Almost forgetting to turn off the engine, she jumped out of the car and found herself standing in front of her own winter wonderland. Tears of pure joy streamed down her face. It was exquisite. But who did this? She was sure it was Lisa. Jessie was so shaken by this surprise, she fumbled for her phone and punched Lisa's speed-dial number.

"Oh my goodness! This is spectacular!" Jessie was gushing.

"What are you talking about?" Lisa was puzzled.

Jessie was panting at this point. "The lights! The decorations!"

"What lights? What decorations? Where are you?"

"At the shop! It's beautiful!" Jessie still did not comprehend that Lisa had no idea what she was referring to. "When and how did you do this?"

"Okay, girlfriend. I need to know what the heck you are talking about."

Jessie repeated, "The lights! The decorations!"

"Where? At the shop?" Lisa was totally confused at her friend's enthusiasm.

Jessie finally slowed down. "Yes. The shop. Decorated. Beautiful. Why don't you sound like you know what I'm talking about?"

"Maybe because I don't. Are you saying someone decorated the shop?"

"Yes. How many more times do I need to tell you?"

"None. But honestly, I don't know anything about it. Sit tight. I'm on my way over. I'll be there in a few minutes." Lisa had to see this for herself.

Jessie stared at the phone for a moment. Maybe it was Rosemary? Maybe she wanted to show how glorious the place could look during the holidays? She shrugged, but she couldn't stop staring at the display. Walking around to the back, she saw that the landscaping there was also illuminated and adorned.

As promised, a few minutes later, Lisa's car quickly turned into the driveway, kicking up a few pieces of gravel.

"Wow! This is incredible!" Lisa gasped as she took in the atmosphere of the holiday magic.

"So you didn't do this?" Jessie looked at her suspiciously.

"I swear. No! Maybe it was Rosemary?" Just as Lisa was offering the explanation, Jessie hit the button on her phone for Rosemary's number.

"This is Rosemary Bidgood. Happy Holidays!" a very cheerful voice answered.

"Hey, Rosemary, it's Jessie. The place looks spectacular. Is it you I have to thank?" Jessie was sure she would get a "yes" but instead got another questioning retort.

"I'm sorry. What are you talking about?"

"The shop. It's decorated beautifully. I'm stunned."

"Jessie, I don't know anything about it. I'm a little confused." Rosemary certainly sounded it.

"Now *I'm* confused," Jessie responded, thinking maybe she was actually in the wrong place. No. Lisa was there with her. And it looked like the shop. How strange.

"I'll be over in a few minutes. Don't go anywhere." Rosemary quickly ended the call.

Jessie turned to Lisa, and they both gave a huge wide-armed shrug. "Santa?" Jessie said jokingly. "Do we dare go in?" It had occurred to her she had been standing outside for a half hour.

"You bet. I'm game!" Lisa giggled as they climbed the stairs to the porch. With key in hand—a slightly shaky hand—Jessie unlocked the door.

They both stepped back from the doorway, their mouths agape. In the foyer, a twelve-foot spruce decorated with Victorian ornaments stood proudly.

"What the???" Jessie slowly walked around the glorious spruce, shaking her head in disbelief. She was almost afraid to check the other rooms. *What's next?* As she peeked around the corner she was almost relieved there were no other surprises. She couldn't remember the last time she was so overcome with the joy of such a display. It was breathtaking.

"This is amazing. I don't remember its ever looking this good." Lisa gave Jessie a poke with her elbow.

"No kidding." That was all she could muster in a much-exaggerated exhale.

Several minutes later, Rosemary arrived. "This is quite spectacular." Her eyes were wide with awe.

"So you didn't send your elves?" Jessie was quite perplexed.

"No. No, I didn't."

When Evan told his son, Connor, about the book giveaway, he was so delighted he suggested to his father that they should do something nice for the lady. That was the validation Evan needed to go through with his crazy idea. He wanted to do something special as a send-off for the shop. He, too, had great childhood memories, so he knew how difficult it must be for Jessie. With the book giveaway party, and that other crazy thing she was hosting, he felt it needed to be rightfully festive. *Speed what?* He figured he'd find out, but not before he and his crew gave the place its due.

Jessie had had Rosemary make a spare key for him so he could do some measurements and planning. The cleaning crew had come in the week after Thanksgiving to do the apartment and make the shop presentable. Now all it needed was some embellishment. He had to admit he might have gone a little overboard, but once he got started, it just kept growing, with Connor and his friends finding more places to hang lights. But Evan drew the line when it came to the mistletoe. That could be a little risky, especially with that speed-dating thing. No one needed a free pass at making one, especially with all the sensitivity to sexual harassment and the like.

His only real concern was whether it would freak her out. He was, after all, trespassing.

Lost in thought, he almost jumped out of his seat when his cell phone rang, and he saw it was Jessie calling. He hadn't thought about what he would say to her. He had been caught up in the holiday spirit with the kids. Taking a very deep breath, he answered, "Becker Contracting and Flash Mob Holiday Decorating!" Cringing he waited for a response—the seconds were interminable.

After a short pause, the words finally sank in, and she let out a guffaw. "Am I speaking with Santa?"

"That all depends on the subject. If it's about Riverwood's decorations, I'm afraid he's busy with his elves."

"Oh, what a shame. I was going to thank him. It was such a wonderful surprise!" Jessie could not believe she was flirting with this man. Jessie laughed softly this time. "I cannot tell you how much I appreciate this. It must have taken days!"

Evan's voice was level. "Actually, my son, Connor, and some of his friends were the real instigators and perpetrators. I hope you won't press charges for trespassing!"

"You're joking, I'm sure. But I would like to thank them!"

"You are. It was his idea because of the book giveaway event. He wanted to do something nice for you."

Jessie thought to herself, *And a nice kid to boot!*

"I don't know what to say. That was so very sweet and thoughtful."

"I'll let him know you're pleased." Evan cleared his throat, fishing for the courage to invite her on a date. But he stopped. He didn't want to come on too strong considering he had covered her entire building with holiday decorations without her permission. He also didn't want her to think he was a stalker/weirdo, so he backed off. Besides, if he was going to work for her, it could make things between them awkward and strained.

For a moment, Jessie thought he was going to ask her out, but then he ended the conversation with, "So, I see we're scheduled for a meeting tomorrow morning at ten thirty?"

"Yes. Ten thirty. See you then." She pushed the END button on the phone. She couldn't decide if she was excited or anxious. Why couldn't she shake this? It was so unlike her to feel her emotions out of control. Lifting her head from the phone, she realized that Lisa and Rosemary were beside themselves with curiosity.

"Well? So? Was it him?" Both were chiming in over each other.

"Yes. His son and his friends." Jessie's eyes welled up with tears. "That was probably one of the nicest things anyone has ever done for me."

Lisa wrapped her arm around Jessie's shoulder. "But what about the time I got that bubble gum out of your hair?"

Jessie let out a laugh. "But if I recall correctly, you were the one who put it there in the first place!"

"A total accident. I had no idea that bubble would get so big and burst in your face!"

"Yeah. My bangs were stubs by the time you cut the gum out of them! I had to wear a headband for months!"

"You were always so fashionable." Lisa hugged her friend. Lisa had been more of a tomboy when they were growing up, so it was surprising that she was the one to get married and have kids. In reality, Lisa was a better athlete than Jessie though she was uninterested in going the college route, and once she fell for Kenny, her thoughts turned to a more traditional life.

Jessie grabbed Rosemary by the arm. "Come and look at the tree."

"There's a tree?" Rosemary was still recovering from the overwhelming display of lights.

"Yes. A very big tree." The three women linked arms and marched up the front steps and into the foyer, where the magnificent spruce stood.

"I should start showing this property tomorrow!" Rosemary exclaimed. "The place looks so absolutely festive and inviting!"

"Oh, Rosemary, I can't wrap my head around that right now. Evan is coming by tomorrow to go over the estimate, and we have to move our butts for the last-minute details of the book giveaway. We only have two days. And after that's done, we have to get ready for the speed-dating event."

Rosemary cocked her head. "Yes. About that. I signed up for it, but I need some coaching."

Jessie gave her the same explanation she had given Lisa. She finished by saying, "At the end of the evening, everyone turns in their cards and I get in touch with the people who have other people interested in them. They can choose to pursue or not."

"Sounds a little awkward."

"Any kind of dating is awkward! But this way you're not wasting time in front of a computer screen not knowing what you're really getting."

"Good point. Okay. I'll have to trust you on this!"

"We have eleven women and nine men, so two women will be alone at a table for ten minutes. The two tables will be away from each other, so neither woman will be alone for more than ten minutes. Considering so many of us are alone for days and weeks, that's not too bad! And you know my motto: 'You Never Know!'"

Chapter Eight

Once everyone got over the shock of the magical display, they went out for a quick bite to eat. Jessie had a lot of work to do and was a little road-weary. Traffic had been a beast. She needed—and wanted—to be sharp and look her best for her morning meeting with Evan.

By ten o'clock the next morning, she was pacing the floor. Why was she so nervous? She went down the list: *1. You're packing up your uncle's store and selling it. 2. You are holding two jobs, one of which is being done anonymously. 3. You're hosting not one but two events at the same time you're getting the bookstore in shape for the market. 4. You have a stupid crush on a man you met for fifteen minutes two months ago. Yes, but that man created a winter wonderland. Okay. 5. What is going on in Evan Becker's head?*

She nearly jumped out of her socks from a knock on the door. She steadied herself and proceeded to greet her contractor/holiday decorator. How should she approach him? A hug of gratitude? Nah. Too much body touching. A peck on the cheek? Nah. Too . . . too . . . just too whatever. She got it—a handshake with her right hand, then her left hand on his arm. Like guys do to each other in that "How'ya doin' good to see you "gesture. This way it's informal but not touchy-feely in any way. Boy was she overthinking this.

By the time those thoughts flew through her mind, she was standing with her hand on the doorknob. A quick inhale and voila!

"Oh, Rosemary. Hi."

"Well, don't sound so excited to see me." Rosemary took another long, gaping look at the tree. "Unbelievable."

"Sorry. I just wasn't expecting you." Jessie was an inch away from embarrassment, thinking her excitement to see Evan was obvious.

"I have the cartons for the books. I figured I would drop them off now." Rosemary turned and pointed to a flat of boxes. "There are more in the car. We're going to have to assemble them and tape 'em up. Didn't want to wait until the last minute."

Jessie was impressed with Rosemary's efficiency. "I appreciate that."

"By the way, I put up a notice in the teachers' lounge at the middle school and high school and also in the cafeteria at the hospital."

"I am thoroughly impressed." Jessie helped her unload the remaining flats of cartons. Each carton, when assembled, could hold about twenty books.

"And here's the packing tape." Rosemary pulled two big dispensers from her tote bag and a few large magic markers. "I think we should assemble a dozen and line them up in the entry. We'll have people write their name on the box. If there's only one copy of a book and more than one person wants it, I have a few coins in my purse. Heads or tails. That's how we play it."

"I don't know what I would have done without you."
Once again, Jessie felt a deep sense of gratitude.

"Oh, I'm sure you would have been just fine. And I
am happy to do it. I told you, it was going to keep me
occupied." Rosemary started toward the car. "I'll be
done around three. If you want, I'll come by, and we
can finish setting everything up for tomorrow."

"Sounds like a plan." Jessie waved from the porch
steps.

Just as Rosemary was heading out to the road, another vehicle pulled into the driveway. For a brief
moment, Jessie had forgotten that Evan was coming.

Jessie watched as the long, muscular legs of Evan
Becker appeared from the door of his truck. He truly
looked like the Marlboro Man, with a red-and-black
flannel shirt and jeans. The only thing missing was the
cowboy hat. Working in advertising, Jessie was very
familiar with the evolution of ad campaigns. Too bad
that one was for cigarettes.

"Hey!" Jessie brushed her hair from her face. She
felt a little disheveled from carrying the flats of boxes.
Making a grand gesture toward the shop, she said,
"Nice work!"

Evan took a small bow. "My pleasure, although I can't
take all the credit."

"If your contracting work is as impeccable as your
decorating, I am sure this place will look spectacular."

Evan was carrying a leather portfolio under his
arm. It contained a written estimate and brochures for
doors and light fixtures, and a few small samples of tile
for the bathroom floor. He had found that it was
always easier to discuss everything in person so as
not to cause any confusion. People can rarely visual-
ize what something is going to look like, so it was

better to talk it through, answering any questions and frequently offering advice.

They took a seat on one of the sofas, and Evan placed the papers and tile on a coffee table Jessie had cleared earlier.

Jessie was fidgeting with the tiles when Evan told her she wouldn't need a lot, so he suggested a small Carrara white polished hexagon mosaic. "It's neutral and a very popular style, so it will give it an updated look. I also brought a catalog for you to pick a new toilet and sink. I suggest a pedestal—easier to keep the floor clean. I know you won't be the one cleaning it, but it is a good selling feature."

For a moment, Jessie almost forgot she was selling the place. "Right. Good idea."

"Here are some light fixtures I recommend as well." Evan pulled another catalog from the portfolio. "I'm assuming since you want me to take the bookcases down, you're going to put it on the market as open retail space?"

"Yes. That was the plan. Why?"

"You may have to widen the doorway to the bathroom to accommodate the Americans with Disabilities Act. People need to be able to get a wheelchair in there."

"Right." Another lame response.

"I put an extra line in the estimate if you wanted me to do that now, or wait to see what prospective buyers may want."

"Good idea." She was beginning to feel a bit stressed. The details were intimidating. She could run an ad campaign from beginning to end, but remodeling was completely foreign to her.

"You okay? You seem a little shell-shocked, and I haven't gone over the numbers with you yet!"

Jessie wasn't sure if it was being in his presence or the renovation that was making her light-headed.

"I'm fine. This kind of thing is very new to me. I never had to pick out a tile, or a light fixture in my life. Funny, huh?"

"Not really. Most people only deal with paint, furniture, drapes, and linens. Unless it's a custom house, people buy it and move in. I know it can be confusing, so I try to narrow down the choices for my clients—as long as I know what style or taste they have. In your case, I went on the assumption you wanted to keep things simple, clean, and easy since you are putting it on the market."

"Yes. Yes, you're right." She could not believe she was stuttering. Maybe she had taken on more than she could handle.

Chapter Nine

Things were relatively quiet at WQPK . . . finally. All the promos for holiday gift giving and people calling in for contests and promotions were winding down. Just a few more days of holiday-madness shopping were ahead, and Brian was keeping the airwaves filled with prerecorded content.

Ziggy the weather guy came huffing and puffing into the booth. "Hey, looks like there's a major low in Canada—could turn into an Alberta Clipper, which will probably make its way here in a few days. You know how brutal those storms can be."

"I do indeed." Brian was nonchalant.

"Well, the radar models, which are always contradicting each other, are actually on the same track, and it looks like we could get hit with a few feet of snow by the weekend."

"Goody. A White Christmas." Brian was still blasé.

"Yeah, but isn't Jessie up in Croton?"

"She is. But she's not due back until the second."

"But isn't she hosting some kind of meet and greet up there?"

"The last time I looked it was called speed dating."

"Yeah. Whatever. Just thought you might want to pass the info along to her."

"Will do." Brian finally looked up from the control panel. "Thanks, Zig. I'll let her know."

Brian grimaced, thinking maybe Jessie could use a hand with the event—especially if it was going to be in the middle of a blizzard. He picked up the phone and punched in her cell number.

"Brian! You promised you wouldn't call!" Jessie was half serious. "Everything okay?"

"Hey, Jess. Ziggy just rolled into the booth and told me there may be a storm forming in the upper Midwest, possibly clipping the East Coast. It may hit us in the next few days. I wanted to give you a heads-up because of your event."

"Really? Seriously?" Jessie sounded forlorn.

"Yeah. Could be a doozy according to Ziggy. It's called an Alberta Clipper. Moves really fast, with lots of wind and snow."

"I haven't heard anything."

"Not yet. It's a low-pressure system now, but all the models are showing that it's going to pick up some speed. Could slam into your party."

Jessie was silent for a moment.

"Jess?"

"Yeah, I'm still here. I don't know what I should do."

"Things are pretty quiet here. Why don't I take a couple of days and run up there and give you a hand? Ziggy can hold down the fort, and the intern we have seems to be capable of running the recordings we have lined up. I can always bring some equipment and content to do remote broadcasts if necessary."

"Are you sure? I have some friends who are helping out."

"But if there's a storm, you could be stranded with a bunch of single people!"

Brian tried to sound lighthearted.

"Good point. But I'd think they would stay home, too, no?"

"Desperate people, desperate measures. You oughta know."

"You've got a point. But I don't want to put you out. Don't you have plans?" Jessie did not want to put any pressure on him.

"Not until Christmas Day. If we do get hit, that will give me enough time to dig out and get back to Philly."

"Sounds good to me. If you're okay with it, then come on up. There's a spare bedroom in the apartment. I have the book giveaway tomorrow night and the speed-dating event two nights later."

"I'll try to get up there day after tomorrow. Just text me the address, and I'll let you know my ETA."

"Thanks, Brian. I really appreciate it."

"No prob. Besides, I want to see how this speed-dating thing works. I'll ping you when I leave."

"Sounds like a plan. Be safe." Jessie clicked off the line. Knowing she had help, she also recognized that everyone had lots to do for their own families, and she didn't want to impose any further. Her meeting with Evan had left her rattled and feeling a bit over-whelmed. Brian would be a welcome addition to her crew.

She did a few yoga stretches and breaths, then picked up the dispenser of packing tape and began to tackle the folded cartons Rosemary had dropped off. After assembling thirty of the fifteen-by-ten-by-ten-inch cartons, Jessie decided to take a coffee break and went up to the apartment.

She switched on the TV. She was instantly riveted by

the true crime–type show that was playing: a plump, lonely, sixtysomething widow from Nevada had signed up with a dating site a year ago. Her name was Eleanor. She had connected with a man who was slightly younger, and very handsome—according to his posted photos. His profile said he was an interpreter for a charitable organization and traveled a lot, making it difficult to meet a woman and have a relationship. They began e-mailing and exchanging photos. He told her she was lovely. After several weeks of online inter-action and sharing stories about their lives, he said he would love to meet her when he returned to the States. He began writing poems and pulling quotes from romantic films. He told her he was lonely and tired of traveling. He confessed that what he really wanted in life was a partner—a woman with whom he could share his dreams. Eleanor was beginning to fall in love, in love with a man she had never met.

He told her he was currently working at an orphan-age in Spain and would be away for three months but would plan a trip to Nevada on his way home from Europe. She was thrilled and asked him if they could start talking on the phone somehow, or maybe video chat. She wanted to hear this engaging man's voice.

He said he would have to buy a special phone that cost $500 and he didn't have that kind of cash on him, so she offered to send him the money. She could barely contain her excitement. He gave her the infor-mation, and the next day, she made arrangements to wire the money into an account of a friend of his in Florida. That friend would get the money to him. Eleanor was more than happy to oblige.

Several days later, she received that highly antici-pated phone call. She was all atwitter. His silky voice was captivating—captivating with a slight accent that she could not quite place. When she asked him about it, he said it was because he spoke many languages and traveled so much. That seemed to satisfy her curiosity. They spent some time with idle chatter, and he said that he didn't want to incur more charges on the phone but made a plan to speak with her again in a few days.

For the first time in two years, Eleanor felt happy. Happy, wanted, and needed.

Jessie knew this woman's story. Women like her had called in to Dr. Richie's show. Eleanor had become suspicious but did not want to believe she had been scammed—and up until that point she was only on the hook for a few thousand dollars.

Over the course of several months, Eleanor's suitor had concocted several scenarios where he needed money. One was that his passport and wallet had been stolen and he needed $1,000 to get to the embassy and file his papers. Then he needed hotel and travel money. Within three months, Eleanor had sent him $30,000 and had still not met Prince Charming. Eleanor finally shared her situation with a friend, who was horrified. She knew Eleanor had fallen victim to "catfishing," or a "love bomb." Eleanor didn't want to believe it, but in her heart, she knew that something was wrong. Her friend encouraged her to do a search as well, and when she did, she found nothing on anyone named David Shoemeyer. Nada. Zip. Zilch.

Eleanor's reaction was surprising. She wasn't shattered. She wasn't devastated. She was furious. The expression "hell hath no fury like a woman scorned" became her battle cry. The creep preyed on her vulnerability, but after all the pain she experienced after the loss of her husband, she wasn't going to crumble over money. No, she was going to find that jerk. Maybe she wouldn't get her money back, but she would get satisfaction.

Completely engrossed in the television show, Jessie followed the trail of lies—e-mails and phone calls to a small group operating out of a warehouse in Texas. They had scammed over forty women to the tune of $5 million. As the segment ended, it showed the FBI arresting several men. Eleanor became a spokesperson for stronger laws against Internet fraud, and met her new husband during one of her speaking events.

Jessie felt both relieved and dismayed. Dating could be a dangerous undertaking. She felt sorry that the woman had lost so much money but happy she finally tracked him down, got her revenge, and actually met a decent man.

She wondered if it was merely a serendipitous coincidence that she happened to turn on the TV at the time she did. Even so, it was satisfying. Maybe it was a sign that things would work out for the best.

Chapter Ten

The afternoon and evening before the giveaway, Rosemary, Lisa, and Jessie assembled a few more boxes and stacked them in the large foyer. There was a small table for people to sign the guest book—a fond farewell to Riverwood Books—and several magic markers to use for putting their names on their boxes.

Rosemary had found a small wooden cart about the size of a picnic table on one of the properties she was listing. The owners were going to junk it, but Rosemary decided that a few cans of spray paint and some garland could turn it into a sleigh for the children's gifts. She was able to get Evan to bring it over in his truck, and he and a few of his men lugged it up the porch steps.

"Hey, easy, guys. Do not disturb the decorations! A lot of hard work went into this," Evan said, half joking.

The men carefully placed the makeshift sleigh next to one of the Christmas trees. Jessie stepped outside to see what the ruckus was about. She didn't think she could be any more surprised than the night she'd arrived to see the array of garland, lights, trees, and wreaths. But she was. And it wasn't just the sleigh. It was the effort everyone was making. She was feeling a true sense of community among these people whom she had just recently met. She felt somewhat lighter. *De-light,* she thought to herself. *Interesting. The light.*

"Wow. This is incredible." Jessie took a few steps around the sleigh. "The only thing we're missing is Santa." Her smile was so big she thought her lips would pop off her face. "Rosemary, you are a woman of many talents."

Rosemary was deep in thought. "Huh? Oh thanks. I'm wondering what we should do for the other side of the porch. For the food pantry items." She snapped her fingers. "Oh duh. Shelves. We have lots of 'em. We just need to clear one off and bring it out here." She looked straight at Evan.

He held up both hands as if to say, "I surrender." He followed with a "Lead the way," and swept his hand across the threshold to allow Jessie and Rosemary to enter the shop.

"So which books and where do we put them?" Jessie's eyes scanned the space.

"Let's pull the science and nature books and put them in a box. I know Connor's school will want them," Evan offered.

"Good idea. I'll go assemble a few more boxes." Rosemary went into the large closet that held the rest of the unassembled cartons.

Once they cleared the shelves, Evan's two crew members moved the bookcase out to the other side of the porch. "Hey, easy, guys. Do not disturb the decorations!" There were grumblings of "Yeah, yeah . . . A lot of hard work went into this" mixed with laughter from the crowd.

Jessie thought her knees were going to buckle under

her. The kindness of everyone was awe-inspiring. This was truly the Christmas spirit. Strange. Even though she had friends and was very social in Philadelphia, there was nothing like this sense of community. Maybe it's because it was a big city. Sure, you knew your neighbors and frequented local restaurants; you'd attend fund-raisers and special events, but there wasn't the same type of connection. The people she was standing with were rooted in this hamlet. They might not all socialize with one another on a daily basis, but they pulled together for the good of the local townspeople and showed great pride in their village on the Hudson.

Jessie ran up the stairs to the apartment and pulled out a box of rice, cereal, and pasta, and a few cans of soup, corn, and beans. When she returned everyone gave her an odd stare. "What?" she queried.

"We were wondering what you were doing. What ARE you doing?" Rosemary asked.

"Setting up the display. This way, when people arrive, instead of just piling stuff, we can pre-organize. Makes it easier for the pantry."

"Brilliant!" Lisa chimed in. She had been on the other side of the shop, where they had set up a table with eggnog, cider, and cookies baked by the Blue Belle volunteers from the hospital. "Jess, do you have a bowl?"

"What kind of bowl?"

"Something for donations."

"What donations?"

"The Blue Belles. The hospital volunteer group. They're donating cookies, so I figured if we put a little bowl out, they can collect money for the family-care group. You know, the little fund they have to help out families with expenses," Lisa explained.

"Oh. That's lovely. I had no idea."

"Yeah. They do a fund-raiser every summer. Old-fashioned barbecue. Chicken, ribs, corn on the cob. Yum. Lots of fun."

"Corn on the cob. I can't remember the last time I had any." Jessie thought carefully. "Seriously."

"Seriously?" Lisa sounded leery.

"Yes. Seriously."

"Oh, girl, you need to get your butt back here in the summer."

Jessie glanced over in Evan's direction. Looking back at Lisa, she said, "I sure do."

Chapter Eleven

Surveying the foyer, then the interior of the building, Jessie was feeling confident that everything was well organized and ready for the giveaway. She had about an hour to freshen up. She thought about her dog and cat. They were being looked after by a neighbor, who she quickly called to check on them. Jessie realized that most people would think she was a little kooky for missing them so much, but they were her little family. She also knew that dragging them up to Croton for two weeks would be traumatic and chaotic. After the brief phone call, knowing Mozart and Picasso were lounging in their favorite spot in the living room, she shifted her thoughts to the evening ahead. She hoped she had packed something a little dressy yet practical. It was the first time in a while that she even cared about attracting a man's attention. She got a little shiver up the back of her neck. *Easy girl. Focus on the task at hand.*

She took the interior stairs to the apartment and rummaged through her clothes. After trying on several outfits, she finally settled on a pair of black slacks that were slim enough to show off her trim legs and a forest-green cashmere sweater that emphasized her eyes. She finished the look by doing her hair up in a ponytail and putting on her grandmother's emerald-stud earrings. A pair of high-cut boots rounded out the look: perky, cute, and a little alluring. After looking at herself in the mirror on the inside of the closet door, she thought, *Who said that I just turned thirty-five?*

She applied a modest amount of makeup, lipstick, mascara, and a touch of her favorite Hermès perfume. Voila! Yes, she was feeling and looking a little sassy.

As she made her way down to the main level, her phone chimed a text from Lisa. **On my way.** A second came from Brian. **Be there tomorrow around noon.**

The first person to arrive was Paula, the local librarian. Jessie was surprised that the woman was about her own age, mid-thirties. She really didn't know what to expect. Paula was cute in a nerdy way. She had semi-spiked short white hair with pink streaks, a pair of black Clark Kent–type glasses, a plaid skirt, and knee socks.

"Hi, I'm Paula. I run the public library."

Jessie was taken aback but broke out in a warm smile. "You sure don't look like the librarian who used to work in town when I was a kid!"

"Ha. I get that a lot." Paula made her way over to the sign-in table. "I think what you're doing is wonderful, I mean about the books and all." She let out a big sigh. "I am going to miss this store, though. Hugo would let us use the back patio and grounds for special events."

Jessie got a pang of guilt. "He always looked like he was going to snarl at you, but he was really such a teddy bear."

"Yeah. I remember the first time I met him. I was a little anxious. But when he offered us the use of the grounds anytime we wanted it, I knew he was a good egg."

"Yes, he's a character all right. He dropped this surprise on me." Jessie swept her arm around like a game-show hostess, indicating the store.

"So you don't think another buyer will take over?" Paula was searching for some comfort.

"Uncle Hugo was able to keep the place afloat, but it got harder each year. It was only his robust investment portfolio that allowed him to continue to run the bookstore at break even or maybe a bit of a loss. And I have no portfolio, robust or otherwise, and know absolutely nothing about running a bookstore, let alone how to make money doing it. And I don't know if the area can continue to support one. Publishing is a crazy business, and so is retail—especially with all of the online options, like Amazon."

"It's a gosh-darn shame. But what can you do? Gotta move on." Paula pulled out one of the markers and wrote the word "library" on her box. "Do you mind if I get a jump on everyone? I have some specific types of books I could use for the library."

"By all means. Here, I'll mark a few more cartons for you." Jessie was feeling a sense of betrayal to the community.

"Oh, that's so nice. Thank you."

"It's the least I can do." Jessie almost got a little misty-eyed. She hoped that it wouldn't happen again this evening. This was no time to be emotional. Besides, it would smear her mascara. She laughed quietly, pulled her shoulders back, and stood tall. She reminded herself, *It's a good thing I'm doing.*

"Let me know if you need any help," Jessie said, as Paula began to survey the shelves.

Shortly thereafter, dozens of people started pouring

into the large front entry. Lisa and Rosemary had the process well organized. Once people dropped off their toy in the sleigh or placed pantry items on a shelf, they would come through the door, hang up their coat, sign the guest book, pick up a carton, write their name on it, and leave it in the foyer. This way they didn't have to carry the box around the shop. They could browse and select at leisure. That was until Mickey Clark and his brother Danny began a tug-of-war over a dinosaur book and the screaming and kicking started.

Before Jessie could blink, Evan had soared across the room and separated the boys. He squatted and spoke to them in a very low voice. Mickey handed the book to his younger brother, and tranquility returned. Their parents were startled at how easily Coach Becker had untangled them. Mrs. Clark looked at him with amazement. "How did you do that?"

"Trade secret." Evan winked at the couple.

Jessie watched the incident from the other room. It lasted less than a couple of minutes. *Very impressive. No wonder he's a coach.* She walked toward the peacemaker. "Thank you. That could have gotten ugly, and people would have been uncomfortable."

"You're quite welcome. Have you met my son yet?"

Jessie was surprised that question made her a little nervous. "I would love to meet him and thank him for all his hard work."

Evan walked over to a small group of boys looking through some of the graphic novels. "Connor, come meet Jessie, the lady who did this. You too, guys." He gestured for the group to follow him.

Jessie was talking to one of the Blue Belles when Evan returned with his son and a group of his friends. As she turned, she saw a young version of Evan, who was almost as tall as she. "You must be Connor."

"Yes, ma'am. Thank you for donating the books."

"Well, I think I owe you—all of you—a huge thank-you, too! What a wonderful surprise! The place looks like a winter wonderland."

The boys beamed with pride, one pointing out his personal contribution of wrapping the garland around the banister. "Great job, guys!" Jessie had an urge to hug each and every one of them but thought that might be a bit much. Instead, she shouted, "Group hug!" A few were a little standoffish, and some snickered, but Connor gave her the biggest hug in return. It was interesting to see the difference between an eight-year-old, a ten-year-old, and a twelve-year-old. Some still thought girls gave you cooties, while others were thinking about ladies' boobies. She cracked a smile at that off-color thought.

After an awkward moment, Jessie gave a directive. "Okay, guys, go get your books!" Who she really wanted to hug was Evan. He had been so thoughtful. She put her hand on his arm, feeling his muscle beneath his shirt. "Your son is quite impressive, and you've been so kind."

"You haven't seen the estimate yet!" Evan teased her.

"You're a comedian, too? I'm surrounded by them." At that moment she thought she could wrap her arms around his neck and kiss him. She felt her face become flushed and pretended Lisa was motioning to her from across the room. She squeezed his arm one more time. "I think Lisa needs me. Excuse me for a sec."

She made her way over to Lisa, eyeing the room as people picked their favorite authors' books. Lisa turned. "Looks like you and the coach are hitting it off."

"Don't start. He makes me nervous." Jessie was almost trying to hide behind her friend.

"But why? Because he's handsome, built, charming, and single?"

"You forgot thoughtful. And yes, all of the above. I feel like I'm back in high school." Jessie was fanning herself. "Is it warm in here or is it me?"

Lisa cracked up laughing. "All of the above! Let's go out on the porch and check the toys and pantry stuff."

As they made their way toward the door, people stopped Jessie to thank her and tell her how much they were going to miss the patio events in the summer. She smiled, then muttered to Lisa, "Sure, make me feel guilty."

"Well, they're not wrong. The summer reading circles were always fun and enlightening." Lisa took her own jab.

"Thanks a load for laying on more guilt."

"What are friends for?" Lisa wrapped her arm around Jessie's shoulders. "I know it's a big tug-of-war for you, but you're right. You have a life in Philadelphia."

"Do I?" Jessie was wary thinking about it.

Rosemary sidled up to both of them. "Jessie, do you mind if we have a little shop talk? No pun intended."

"Of course. Let's go up to the mezzanine."

Rosemary followed Jessie up the stairs, where she started toward the counter. "Can I interest you in a cup of coffee, espresso?"

"Why yes. Thank you."

"Large, or 'grande' as they call it, or demitasse?" Jessie asked.

"Grande for me! I love the taste of dark, rich coffee. I can't stand the swill they serve in the office."

"I'm a bit of a coffee snob myself. I'd rather have none than a weak cup. You know the kind that stays an ugly shade of brown no matter how much cream you pour?"

"Yep. That's my office rotgut." Rosemary sat back on one of the lounge chairs as Jessie fixed their drinks.

She handed Rosemary her cup and sat across from her, each enjoying their java. "So, what's up?" Jessie asked.

"I think I can get about $650,000 for this place. We'll ask for $700,000, which will give us lots of negotiating room."

"Seriously?" Jessie was stunned. She had no idea what property was worth here.

"Because it was zoned as commercial with residential clauses, we can pitch it either way. It could become a two-family house or a commercial building with rental income. Lots of ways to go." Rosemary was very animated, more so than usual.

"Wow. I had no idea." Jessie was contemplative. What would she do with that money? Pay taxes on it, for sure, but could she find a suitable home for herself in Philadelphia?

"Yep. And when they clear out the lower level, it will be amazing."

Jessie felt a surge of sadness and relief at the same time. She had been on an emotional roller coaster for several days. "Well, okay. At least I know there'll be enough money to cover any construction work."

"For sure! Do you know when Evan is going to get started?"

"Sometime in early January. He hasn't given me the total estimate yet because he didn't know how much damage there would be moving the shelves. Ballpark is fifteen grand, which includes remodeling the bathrooms with new toilets, sinks, tile floors, and fixtures." Jessie felt like she was in a dreamlike state, the words slowly coming out of her mouth. It was really happening—selling the bookstore.

As she peered over the railing, she saw that most of the books had been spoken for and that Evan and another guy were helping people carry the boxes to their cars. Lisa had started packing the pantry items.

"Who is that guy with Evan?" Rosemary asked.

"That's Gerry. He works for Becker Contracting."

"New in town?"

"I have no idea. Why?" Jessie realized that Rosemary was curious about the nice-looking, quiet man who had helped with the sleigh and pantry shelves.

"He's a man, and he's breathing." Rosemary nodded. "Let's go see what everyone is up to."

Jessie burst out laughing, then asked the obvious question. "Did you check for a ring?"

"Yes, and no, he's not wearing one."

In unison they said, "But that doesn't mean anything!" They laughed their way down the stairs to the few stragglers who couldn't decide on Agatha Christie or Minette Walters. Jessie said, "Take them all!" She wanted as much gone as possible to save herself from packing what was left over. Surprisingly, there wasn't much, which was a relief.

The Blue Belles had collected almost $100, the pantry shelves were bursting with nonperishable items, and the sleigh was packed with dozens of toys. It would have put Macy's to shame.

Jessie stood in the foyer with her arms folded across her chest, still reeling from the dollar amount Rosemary had quoted her. Thinking of that much money was overwhelming.

Within a short time, the crowd had thinned out, leaving Evan, Gerry, Rosemary, Lisa, and Jessie. Connor was spending the night at a friend's house. The Blue Belles had cleaned up the refreshment table, and there was little else to do at that point. Tomorrow, they would finish packing, and Evan's crew would make room for the speed-dating event.

Everyone was commenting on how successful the evening had turned out and the generosity people had shown. Jessie felt a huge surge of relief and had to remind herself that she had done a very good deed for the town. With a little luck, the dating event would be successful as well.

"The tables and chairs will be delivered late tomorrow afternoon. Will that be enough time to clear out some space?" Jessie hoped that moving to the next event wouldn't be problematic.

"Sure. You said ten small tables and twenty chairs? Should fit in here easily enough and have plenty of room between each one for privacy." Evan was back to business.

"Excellent. Thank you. I hope you're adding all this extra work to your estimate, right?" Jessie didn't want Evan to think she was taking advantage of him in any way, shape, or form.

"Don't be ridiculous. We'll be in and out of here in less than an hour. There's a storage cottage behind the library. Paula made sure there was room to store the shelves until the spring, when they can refinish them. She is going to use them for the new annex."

"Yes, she was over the moon when I told her she could take them."

"I know it's sad that the bookstore isn't going to reopen, but your incredible generosity is much appreciated." Evan put his hand on Jessie's shoulder.

She felt the warmth of his smile, his words, and his touch. Once again, her knees turned a little rubbery.

"And all of you have gone above and beyond for me. I could never have done any of this without you." Jessie found herself getting teary once more.

"We're not done yet, girly-girl." Lisa poked Jessie with her elbow. "You can thank us after the Date-O-Rama is over."

"Speed dating," Jessie corrected her.

"Tell me again how that works?" Evan asked. "I signed up for it."

Jessie's heart sank. It occurred to her that she hadn't read the e-mail Brian had sent of the final list of names. She could barely speak. "Oh, it's simple." She explained the process yet again. She was fighting not to say, *"But I will throw any cards you get into the trash and pretend no one was attracted to you."* As if that were remotely possible.

"Should be interesting." Evan was cool about it.

"Yes, that would be one outcome—interesting." Lisa chimed in, knowing Jessie was a little unglued by Evan's willingness to participate. "It's getting late, folks. Time for me to get back to my brood." After she slipped on her coat, she gave Jessie a hug and whispered, "Don't freak out. It's going to be okay."

Rosemary took the opportunity to turn to Gerry. "Did you sign up for this speed-dating thing?"

"I hadn't thought about it, but it could be 'interesting,'" he replied, using air quotes and mimicking Evan. "Is it too late?"

"What? No, of course not. The more the merrier," Jessie said blankly.

Rosemary quickly put his name on the yellow pad that was sitting on the foyer table.

A few more hugs with the women, and handshakes with the men, and Jessie waved them off and shut the big doors behind her as tears ran down her cheeks.

As she was opening the apartment door, her cell phone beeped. It was Lisa, sending her a text. **R U okay?**

Jessie replied with **Not sure.**

Lisa pinged her back with **Want to talk?**

Nah. I'll be fine. Time to get some z's. Sleep tight. And she turned off her phone. She didn't want to know if anyone was trying to reach her, or worse NOT trying to reach her. She would sleep on it. All of it.

Chapter Twelve

The day after the book giveaway started slowly for Jessie. She didn't realize how exhausted she was—she guessed she had been working on a combination of adrenaline and emotions over the past few days. She tried to shake off the nagging disappointment that Evan was signed up for speed dating. *I thought he wasn't interested in dating. Although I can't blame him for trying, especially if someone puts an opportunity right in front of him. Yeah, Jessie. Great idea.* She stretched and began a slow crawl out of the bed, wrapped herself in a warm robe, went to the kitchen, and made a cup of coffee. She padded across the landing to the mezzanine and sat on the large sofa overlooking the main floor. A fleeting thought of her sitting at one of the dating tables went through her mind. *Too desperate.* She shrugged off her silly idea and decided she was going to deal with it as business as usual and stick to her original mission.

Her phone buzzed her out of her daydream. It was Brian sending a text. ETA noon. Need anything?

Nope. Good. Drive safe Jessie tapped back, then pulled herself off the comfy sofa and headed into the apartment. A nice, long, hot shower should help her get in the mood to be a hostess again.

"Never mix business with pleasure," Jessie muttered to herself. "And don't even THINK about mixing them. Change that channel in your head! What will be will be." She then started singing the chorus of "Que Sera Sera"—something her mother would sing to her whenever she faced a disappointment. Thinking she was alone, she started belting out the words at the top of her lungs. That actually made her feel better until she heard a voice from the lower level.

"Is that Doris Day up there?" Evan's voice boomed up at her.

Jessie was mortified. *What is he doing here?* "Ah! You caught me!" was all she could say, feeling her face turn beet red. She regained her composure and came bounding down the steps, hiding any sense of embarrassment.

"You've got quite a set of lungs on you," Evan teased.

"I was checking the acoustics," she said wryly, as they both broke into a comfortable chuckle. *Comfortable.* That was the word Jessie was searching for regarding Evan. Even though she had a silly crush, he made her feel safe and comfortable in the place. The place she was about to sell.

"I wasn't expecting you so early."

"I wanted to be sure there was enough room for the tables and chairs. Sorry if I encroached on your space. I knocked, but no one answered."

"I must have been in the shower. But no problem. You just startled me a bit. Go do what you need to do. I have to run some errands." She checked her watch. She would be back before Brian got there. Grabbing her jacket, she headed toward the door.

"Okay. See you tomorrow night. The speed thing." Evan made a gesture as if tipping his hat.

"Yep." She scooted out before any emotion showed on her face. As she hopped down the steps, she got a sense of snow. Even though the sky was clear, a deep color of blue, she could smell it. She jumped in her SUV, and headed toward one of the warehouse clubs to confirm her food order and pick up the beverages and paper items. She ordered several platters of sandwiches, a case of water, cookies, iced tea, and coffee. She realized that she probably ordered enough for an entire football team, but that was Jessie's way. She was an impeccable hostess, and food and drink were always in abundance.

An hour later, she returned just before noon as Brian's SUV pulled in.

"Right on time to help with this stuff. I figured I'd get the nonperishables today and pick up the food tomorrow."

Brian paused abruptly as he approached the porch. "Wow. Who did all of this decorating?"

Jessie tried to stifle a blush. "The contractor and a group of his son's friends. It was a thank-you for donating the books."

"Impressive." Brian didn't know what to look at first.

"Wait until you see it at night. It's quite the spectacle!"

"And with the snow, it will certainly look like a winter wonderland, I imagine." Brian reminded her of the impending storm.

"Oh. Right. The snow. Do you think we'll get slammed?" Worry crossed her face.

"I'll text Ziggy in a bit and see if he has any updates."

"I haven't heard anything on the radio or TV, although I have to admit I haven't been paying much attention. There's so much going on." She grabbed a big bag filled with snacks.

"This is a pretty cool place." Brian scanned the interior. "Those skylights are a nice touch. I always think of bookstores as being dark."

"That's exactly why Uncle Hugo and my dad installed them. Uncle Hugo wanted the place to be open and bright. In fact, we had several in my house when I was growing up, and there are a couple of them upstairs in the apartment. I think they must have raided a Home Depot!" Jessie let out a laugh.

Within a couple of hours, a truck arrived with the tables and chairs. Evan and Gerry created ample space for the layout, allowing enough room for private conversations at each table.

"Looks like you're going to have a cocktail party . . . and candles, too!" Brian stepped back to review the scene. "Very nice touch."

"I wanted to make it as comfortable as possible." There was that word again: "comfortable."

"It should be a very interesting night."

"Yeah. That seems to be the theme—interesting," Jessie mused.

Brian felt his phone vibrate on his belt. "It's Ziggy." He read the text out loud. "Get out the snow shovels and flashlights."

Brian texted back, What's the ETA?

"Late tomorrow night," Brian said, once again reading the message out loud.

"Oh shoot." Jessie sat on the staircase with a thump. "What should we do? Cancel?"

"Nah. Let's see if people cancel. What's the worst that can happen?" Brian was making an effort to be supportive.

"We eat a dozen caprese sandwiches?" Jessie was still

making a gallant effort to be positive, knowing the prosciutto, mozzarella, tomato, and basil on a ciabatta roll was one of Brian's favorites.

"Yeah? But what are *you* going to eat?" Brian was trying to keep the mood light.

"The roasted vegetable paninis, I suppose. I only got six of those." She sighed. "And a half dozen roast beef with cheddar, turkey with a cranberry spread, ham and brie, smoked salmon and cream cheese, a cheese platter, and crudités."

Brian was counting his fingers. "That's over forty sandwiches! We only had twenty responses."

"Yes, but . . ." Jessie attempted an explanation.

"But, it's you, Jess! The quintessential hostess. I'm sure none will go to waste."

"Indeed! One more sweep of the place, and we'll go to the Pour House for a real meal since we'll probably be living off sandwiches for the next couple of days!" Jessie finally sounded like her optimistic self again.

When they reached the pub Jessie was welcomed by a number of patrons—most had heard about the giveaway or were the recipients of some of the books.

Several rounds of drinks were offered to Jessie and Brian, and many toasts were made. In spite of her generous donation, Jessie's conflict resurfaced and she felt disloyal to this lovely community.

Brian looked at her quizzically. "What's up?"

"Oh nothing really. Well, really yes, there's something. I feel like a traitor."

"What do you mean?"

"Closing the bookstore. People really seemed to depend on it . . . not just for books, but a place to gather."

"Your uncle would have stayed if he felt there was a need. From what I heard, they have an incredible library here."

"Yes, but they don't have the space for events." She still felt a pang of guilt.

"I'm sure someone will figure it out. Hey, you didn't bring this on, and you did a good thing." He adjusted his glasses and took another pull on his beer.

"I know you're right. I'm just beat and a little stressed. I'll be fine."

They had to beg off many more offers for drinks—Jessie knew her limit and wasn't about to cloud her brain any further. When they made their way out, bystanders raised their glasses to her. As she gave everyone a big wave, she choked back a tear.

Chapter Thirteen

The morning of the speed-dating event drew a number of phone calls and texts asking about the weather and possible cancellation. The cheerful response was "We'll be here!"

Jessie and Brian headed out to pick up the rest of the food. When Brian saw the number of trays, he broke into laughter. "I guess you're right! We'll be elbow-deep in snow and sandwiches!"

"Please don't mention the snow. I'm this close to a panic attack." She made a gesture with her fingers, indicating about an inch of space, thinking about Evan's impending attendance.

"When we get back, we can put all of this outside on the patio. It's cold enough to keep everything fresh, but not enough to freeze the cheese." Brian led the way through the building and out the French doors, carrying two trays at a time.

After several trips, they both stared at the bounty. "And yes, enough to feed an entire football team!"

The afternoon passed quickly with nine people canceling. Each had an hour drive and was concerned about the weather. The rest were local and used to the snow. Jessie's next challenge was what to wear.

She chose a white-cashmere cowl-neck tunic sweater, leggings, and her riding boots—although she figured she would be changing into her Sorel Snow Angel boots at some point in the evening.

She smiled as she pulled them out of the closet. She bought them because of the name of the style: Snow Angel.

The first to arrive was Rosemary, wearing a red blazer and black trousers. "I brought dessert!" she said proudly as she presented a stack of boxes filled with Italian pastries.

Brian let out a huge laugh. "Wait until you see what's on the patio!" He took the packages from her and put them with the rest of the food.

"The place looks very cozy!" Rosemary wandered through the downstairs, taking in the setup. "Now I can envision how this works. Even though you explained it, it still wasn't clear in my mind."

"I don't know what was going on in mine when I thought of it." Jessie rolled her eyes.

"It will be fun!" Rosemary was her usual animated self.

"I hope so. With the weather, I'm not sure how many people will actually show. Nine have already canceled."

"Oh, who cares?" Rosemary said. "I mean, it's not that you haven't put a lot into this, but there's nothing we can do except have a good time!" She put her arm around Jessie and gave her a hug.

"You are absolutely correct. I hope you like sandwiches."

The second to arrive was Paula the librarian, wearing pink leggings with an abstract duster that resembled Joseph's Amazing Technicolor Dreamcoat. She looked like a giant Christmas ornament, but in a very cute way. Brian was immediately drawn to this kooky character. "Hey, we have the same glasses!" Brian put out his hand to welcome her. "I'm Brian, a friend of Jessie's."

"Cool beans! I like your tie," Paula replied, noticing that Brian had opted for a candy-cane tie instead of his usual black leather. He fidgeted with it for a moment.

"Thanks. I'm usually much more monochromatic."

Paula let out a loud "Ha! And I'm usually . . . um . . . as colorful! I'm Paula, the librarian."

"Not the usual librarian garb, eh?"

"Nah. That's so old-school . . . and I mean as in an old school! Ha!"

Brian adjusted his glasses again—a nervous tic when he would get a little uneasy. He thought Paula was a little quirky, something that was very appealing to him. Most single women his age were uptight and anxious about settling down and having a baby. The biological clock syndrome. Paula seemed to be a free spirit.

Within a few minutes Lisa arrived to inspect the premises. "It looks like a nightclub. Just need some cool jazz."

"It does look quite chic, if I say so myself." Jessie gave her friend a big hug. "Thanks for coming. I know you have your hands full at home."

"What? And miss this? Besides, I needed a break from all the hyperactivities. Kenny can take over for a few hours."

The next to arrive were two women in their early fifties and a tall, well-dressed man Jessie put in his early sixties. The odds weren't looking good as far as a male-to-female ratio. She was relieved to greet another man in his mid to late fifties wearing a blazer, flannel shirt, and khakis. Not a fashion icon, but he was clean-shaven and had all his teeth—a joke that she and Rosemary had made to each other on more than one occasion when discussing the event.

By six fifteen, it seemed obvious that no one else would be attending; and the snow was beginning to fall.

Jessie realized that in order for this to work, she and Brian would have to sit in at the tables. Yikes. "Awkward" was the word that came to mind.

Jessie explained how the event would proceed and invited everyone to have something to eat, hoping to ease some of the self-conscious tension her guests seemed to be experiencing.

A half hour later, she seated the women at different tables—five including herself. It became clear that this was not going to turn out the way she had expected, but at least it was a social gathering if nothing else.

Jessie sorted the men so they would start with someone close to their age, which meant she would be seated with Evan or Gerry. She picked Gerry because she already knew Rosemary was interested in him and would send him to her during the next round.

She and Gerry made small talk about the town and how long he had lived there. He was very articulate and had a little twinkle in his eye. Jessie thought he would be a good match to Rosemary's joie de vivre. After Lisa rang the bell, everyone got up and moved to the next table. Sort of like musical chairs, but all the chairs stayed in place.

Jessie got a little bit of a shiver when Evan took his seat across from her. He leaned in so close she could almost feel the heat from his body. Or was that her having an early hot flash? She hoped it didn't show on her face.

Evan wasted no time in saying, "So how did you get involved in this? Are you friends with Dr. Richie?"

Jessie's palms began to sweat. Stammering a little,

she replied, "I . . . uh . . . work on the same floor as the radio station. Brian and I are pals, and I got roped into it." There. That should cover her bases.

"Seems like a big undertaking considering all the other things you have going on." Evan was just shy of sounding like he was interrogating her.

"Yes, I know, but they were in a bind. Why do you ask?" *Let him answer a question or two*, she thought to herself.

"During one of our conversations when we were talking about relationships, you said a few things that rang a bell. A while back I read an article in a magazine; and then, when you were picking out tile, you said something else that sounded familiar. I'm pretty sure the article was by this Dr. Richie, and now this." Smiling the entire time, he made a gesture with his thumb, pointing to the group.

Jessie's mind was racing when she was literally saved by the bell. She must have been holding her breath for a full minute.

"We're not finished with this, young lady." Evan smiled, showing his dimples.

Funny, she hadn't noticed them before.

Not long after the wind started to kick up, the lights flashed on and off, and then went off entirely. Really off. Fortunately, Jessie had tea-light candles on the tables, so it wasn't a complete blackout. Everyone waited a few beats, hoping the power would be restored, but after several minutes and a lot of grumbling, Evan dialed his friend at the Department of Public Works. "Hey, Rick, any idea what's happening?"

"Downed power line." Evan had it on speakerphone so everyone could hear.

"Not too bad. Should be no more than two hours. I'll let you know if it's going to take longer."

"Thanks, pal. Be careful out there." Evan hit END.

Jessie, Lisa, and Rosemary gathered together and decided to rearrange the tables and bring in the rest of the food. No one had eaten much earlier. Most likely from jitters about the evening ahead.

Brian pulled his portable speakers from his back-pack and hooked them to his phone. He found a good retro playlist, and the bop of 1960s Motown Christmas songs filled the room.

Gerry politely bowed to Rosemary. "May I have this dance?"

Giggling as she stood, Rosemary proved to have another talent. The two of them began to do the twist when Brian shrugged at Paula and joined in the dance. It took no longer than a minute for Richard, Lorraine, Harold, and Mabel to kick up their heels as well. Jessie stood in wonder at how proficient Brian was on his feet but even more amazed at how this evening had gone from an awkward date-if-you-dare gathering to a holiday dance party. Jessie, Evan, and Lisa were totally entertained and clapped after each song, encouraging more.

As promised, the power went back on in less than two hours, which seemed to disappoint everyone in an ironic sort of way.

A couple of inches of snow had fallen at that point, which spurred people into leaving. As they gathered their coats, hats, and gloves, Jessie prepared bags of goodies stuffed with sandwiches, cookies, and pastries for everyone. She thought to herself, *If not potential dates, perhaps people made new friends.* Jessie could not have asked for a better outcome until she stepped out onto the porch and was stunned by the twinkling of the lights filtering through the snow. Truly a winter wonderland. *Awesome* was an understatement.

Everyone stopped for a moment to marvel at this special display, while the oohs and aahs floated through the air in a way that can only be heard while snow is falling.

Brian offered to drive Paula home since her MINI Cooper wasn't the best for driving on slippery roads and already had a few inches of snow covering it. The two other gentlemen, Richard and Harold, offered to drive Mabel and Lorraine home as well. Evan had to pick up Connor, but before he sauntered down the front porch, he took Jessie's hand and said, "To be continued."

She stood in silence for fear of breaking what felt like a magical moment. As he was getting into his truck, he paused and gave her a smile that melted her heart. She gave him a soft wave as he pulled out of the driveway.

Rosemary and Gerry helped lug the remaining food up to the apartment, and Rosemary asked if Jessie would be okay.

"I'll be fine. I'm going to light a fire and shove a few of these capreses into my mouth!" With that, Gerry and Rosemary headed out, grabbing a goodies bag for each of them.

"Call if you need anything!" Rosemary said over her shoulder.

"Will do!" Jessie stepped out far enough to feel immersed in the glow of the twinkling lights. Turning toward the front door, she stopped for a few moments and took in all that had occurred over the past ten days. It was surely a remarkable community, with wonderful people. A big lump formed in her throat.

Several hours had passed when it finally dawned on her that Brian hadn't returned. She pinged him, **You OK?**

He quickly replied, Yes. Sorry. Paula's power is still out, so I think I'm going to crash here. You okay with that?

I am so okay with that. And she was. The feeling of camaraderie she had been experiencing was seeping into her bones as she realized she had been smiling most of the night.

Chapter Fourteen

The snow continued to fall until the wee hours of the morning of Christmas Eve, leaving over two feet on the ground. Jessie wondered if the roads were clear enough for travel since she was supposed to help Lisa with the presents for the kids. It was still early enough in the day, but by noon she hadn't heard any plows out on the roads and gave Lisa a call. "Hey, any word on the condition of the roads?"

"It's slow going. Kenny checked. Lots of people on vacation. They're hoping to have the main roads cleared by tomorrow morning, so people can attend church, visit relatives, etc."

"So I might be snowed in?" Jessie was bordering on being concerned.

"Maybe for today. But like I said, should be okay for tomorrow."

"But I promised I'd help you."

"Don't be silly. Kenny and I can handle it. You just relax today. You've done enough this week." Lisa was making sense, and Jessie appreciated it.

"Thanks, pal. I'll give you a buzz later. Love you!" Jessie signed off.

She quickly sent off a text to Brian, wondering how his evening had gone.

Hey! All good? Roads are still covered. May take a while. Hope you're having fun!

A minute later, Brian responded, All good here! Paula is a gaming junkie. Has cyberpower pcgaming supreme! She throttled me in Minecraft. You okay?

Jessie responded, I'm fine. Enjoying doing nothing. Have fun!

Brian texted, I am! Will try to get there ASAP to dig you out!

Jessie wrote back, No worries. I'm really okay! Lots of sandwiches! See you prob tomorrow.

Brian ended with, Roger that.

Jessie spent the day doing exactly what Lisa had suggested. She made a few phone calls, took a shower, put on a fresh pair of lounging pajamas, and lit a fire. After finishing her annual reread of Charles Dickens's *A Christmas Carol,* she watched a movie and chomped on a few more sandwiches.

It was around eleven o'clock when she decided it was time to turn in. Even though she had dozed a few times reading her book and watching movies, she was ready for a good night's sleep.

As she flung herself on the bed she looked up and noticed the clear starry night through the skylights. She bounced back up and said, "What in the???" She looked up again. Sure enough, she could see the sky. She pulled on her boots and wrapped a blanket around her as she made her way out onto the deck. She stopped in her tracks when she saw a large snow angel on the ground. Peering at it closely, she noticed writing in the snow: *Hi Santa!* Jessie was dumbfounded. Looking around, she saw what appeared to be footprints. But they were messy, as if someone had tried to cover them up. She rubbed her eyes and pinched herself in the arm. Was this for real? She knew right then that there was only one person who could have done this. But when? She shook her head. It didn't matter when. It only mattered that it was.

When she awoke on Christmas morning, she had a new sense of purpose and exhilaration. She couldn't wait to tell Lisa about the skylights and the snow angel.

Around ten in the morning, Brian pulled onto the snow-covered drive. Jessie was relieved that she wouldn't have to dig herself out by herself. As they were clearing off her car, she teased him about Paula.

"She's a pretty cool chick," Brian offered. "She's going to come to Philly for Martin Luther King weekend." Jessie wasn't sure if he was blushing or if it was the cold air.

With a big smile, she tossed a handful of snow at him. "Well, whaddya know. Speed dating wasn't such a bad idea after all!"

Brian made a loose snowball and threw it at her. Once they were satisfied the driveway and car were clear, Brian gathered his things and headed out.

"Brian. Thanks so much for everything. I really appreciate your coming up here and helping out."

"I should be thanking you, Jessie. You and your crazy idea!" He pecked her on the cheek. "See you next week. Merry Christmas!"

"Merry Christmas indeed!" Jessie was overjoyed. She packed up all the gifts for Lisa, Kenny, and the boys and searched for any remaining pastries. She thought she could never look at another cannoli again.

Lisa and Kenny's house was abuzz with kids laughing and running around, and the wonderful aroma of food being prepared wafted through the air. Jessie was relieved to be off the sandwich and pastry diet. She had to admit, she really overdid it with the platters of food. Thinking about the past few days she smiled to herself and decided that this had truly been the best Christmas she had experienced in a very long time.

Lisa was about to burst from the joy she felt as Jessie told her about the skylights and snow angels. "So? What do you think?"

"About what?" Jessie was trying to be demure.

"Funny girl. About Mr. Man Cake?"

"Please stop calling him that," Jessie pleaded. "I don't know what to think. I'm trying *not* to think, actually. You know me . . . overthinking gets me into trouble. I'm going to try to enjoy these next few days. I mean, I'm sure I am going to see him, but maybe he's just trying to be nice."

"Are you serious?" Lisa was incredulous. "That guy decorated the entire building and the grounds, helped with everything *plus* cleaned your skylights and made a snow angel? And you think he's just trying to be nice? He likes you, girlfriend!"

"I must confess, I kinda like him, too. As in *really . . . really like.*" Jessie was recalling the words they used to use when they were in high school describing how they felt about their latest boy crush.

Lisa gave her a poke in the arm. "Go for it!"

Jessie thought she just might.

After several hours of gift giving and stuffing themselves with Lisa's glorious dinner, the kids and their dog, Boogie, were all tuckered out. Jessie, too, was feeling a bit drowsy and decided to call it a day. Lots of hugs and thank-yous were in abundance as Jessie headed out, reminding Lisa she would be going into the city to meet Marjorie on the twenty-seventh.

She had wondered how Evan was enjoying his time with his son and family. For a moment, she didn't feel like a silly schoolgirl—but the moment didn't last long when her phone pinged and she saw it was Evan. **Got a minute?**

She sent back a **Yes.**

With that her phone rang . . . *butterflies again.*

She took a deep breath. "Merry Christmas!"

"And a very Merry Christmas to you!" Evan's strong, smooth voice replied. "Hope you didn't get snowed in."

"No, Brian dug me out this morning." There was a long pause, then she continued, "Speaking of digging out, someone cleaned off my skylights and left a message for Santa." Yep, she was going for it.

"Imagine that," Evan said softly.

"Yes. Imagine that," Jessie spoke in the same tone.

Evan cleared his throat. "Listen, I want to apologize if I was being too pushy about Dr. Richie. You seemed a little taken aback. I didn't mean to pry. Just a bit of curiosity."

"Oh, no. It's fine. I can explain when I see you. That is, assuming you still want an explanation."

"I do indeed. So how about that dinner meeting we were discussing?"

"Yes, the dinner *meeting.*" Jessie emphasized the word "meeting."

"I have Connor until New Year's Eve morning." He hesitated. "But I am free New Year's Eve." Before he gave her a chance to answer he quickly added, "I know New Year's Eve is a big deal for most people, but I haven't taken it seriously for years."

"What a coincidence. Neither have I." She could not wipe the smile off her face.

"Excellent. I'll pick you up around seven that night.

As I said New Year's Eve isn't a big deal. Casual. Wear something warm and comfortable."

Jessie pulled the phone away from her ear and gave it a strange look. "Something warm?"

"Yes. Boots, scarf, gloves. The usual winter garb."

"Okay." She was a bit puzzled, but she was up for whatever he had in mind. "See you then!"

Two days later, Jessie took the train into Manhattan and met Marjorie at the Blue Box Café at Tiffany's. The sidewalks were packed with crowds of tourists getting a glimpse of the beautifully decorated windows. Of course, her favorite spot—and everyone else's—was Rockefeller Center. From Fifth Avenue you could see the giant angels flanking the promenade leading to the magnificent and famous tree. It was breathtaking. Before leaving, she stopped at St. Patrick's Cathedral, beautifully adorned with hundreds of poinsettias and thousands of candles. She walked over to the Altar of Saint Jude and lit a few candles of her own and said a few prayers. Even though he was known as the patron saint of those who are in despair, she still felt a kinship to the revered and beloved disciple, remembering all the times she had prayed for his help. This time she was thanking him.

Chapter Fifteen

After four days of packing up what remained in the store, Jessie was looking forward to her "Un-New Year's Eve date." *Is it a date?* She remembered Lisa's words: "The guy did a LOT to make your Christmas special." So, yes, she was considering it a date. End of matter.

After changing her outfit three or four times, she decided on a Norma Kamali soft V-neck jumpsuit and a cashmere scarf. He had said "casual and comfortable." She was thrilled she had an excuse to wear her Sorel Snow Angel boots. There certainly seemed to be a snow angel watching over her in addition to welcoming Santa.

At seven o'clock, she heard the sound of a vehicle enter the driveway. She thought it a bit odd that he would arrive in his pickup truck instead of his SUV, but tonight she was going to let him take the lead, knowing full well they had a lot to discuss. After a brief hug, he opened the passenger door for her. "You look great. And appropriate!"

"Ha. Funny, I was thinking the same thing." She chuckled, thinking about her "appropriate" boots but she was going to keep that her little secret. At least for now.

As they were driving, she noticed they were heading away from the town and going to higher ground.

"Where are we going?"

"Just a little side trip." He glanced over at her with his charming smile. Jessie thought she was going to burst with excitement.

They arrived at an open field. For a split second, Jessie didn't know if she should panic. This was a very strange place for him to park.

Without saying a word, Evan opened her door and escorted her to the back of the truck. He jumped into the flatbed and held his hand out to help her up. She was quite confused at this point until he opened two anti-gravity chairs. He then began unpacking a cooler that contained a bottle of champagne, cheese, bread, and a variety of charcuterie; a large satchel held two soft blankets.

Sensing her confusion, he looked at her and said, "Ten minutes." He offered her a glass of the bubbly wine, then cut some of the cheese and bread and gave them to her.

Jessie kept staring at him as she took the plate. Yes, he even had melamine dishes.

Sitting back in his chair, he motioned for her to do the same. Checking his watch, he pointed north. "Look."

Jessie's jaw dropped as she witnessed first one and then dozens of shooting stars. The sky was alive with what looked like thousands of fireflies. She was astounded by its beauty. "I've never seen anything quite like this," she whispered softly, as if her voice would shoo them away.

"It's the Quadrantid meteor shower," Evan explained.

"I remember how you said you used to look up at the stars when you were staying at your uncle's."

They sat quietly for quite a while and then, as if on cue, they both began to speak.

"Please, you go first," Evan offered.

"Evan, there is something I have to tell you," Jessie started.

Evan thought he heard concern in her voice. "Is this about Dr. Richie?"

"Oh no. Well, not exactly. Kind of, but . . ." Trying to find the right words—the words she had practiced for two days—she began, "When Uncle Hugo told me to sell the store and buy a house, I was stunned and excited. I had thought about buying a place, but everything is very expensive in Philadelphia, and I didn't want to be flung out to the suburbs, especially since I don't know a soul outside of downtown Philly. After being here these past two weeks, I've come to realize what a wonderful community this is, and the people, well, they are incredible." She took a sip of her champagne and continued, "I'm afraid I'm not going to have you renovate the bookstore."

"Are you saying you're keeping the store? Or are you firing me?" Evan had a look of surprise and confusion on his face.

"Not exactly. I met with Marjorie, my boss, a few days ago. She told me that she was going into partnership with an ad agency in New York. She needs someone to take meetings twice a week and asked me to be her liaison person." Jessie took in another deep breath. "I can work from home the other days."

Evan was still unclear. "So you'll commute to New York from Philadelphia?"

"No, not from Philadelphia." Close to losing her

nerve, she went on, "I want you to remodel the store so it can be my home."

"Does this mean that you're staying here?" Evan's voice was a bit shaky.

"Yes. Yes, I am." There. She'd said it. "I spoke with Paula and told her that I want to renovate and make the area that is now—was—the nonfiction section into a solarium to host author signings, weekly book readings, recitals, and other fund-raising events. And it will finally give me some space for my grand piano. Mozart will be thrilled."

She was almost giddy. "We'll—I mean you—if you still want the job—can put in French doors, so I can close it off for privacy and it will still lead out to the patio." Jessie became even more animated as Evan hung on every word. "I'll use the mezzanine as my bedroom and remodel the basement to be my home office, and keep the apartment for friends and family. Obviously, I'll need a real kitchen, too." Jessie's head was reeling, contemplating the next phase of her life.

"That will be quite a renovation," Evan said evenly, as he processed this new, happy turn of events.

"I know, but the property is worth quite a bit of money, and I can get a home equity line of credit. I felt bad about telling Rosemary she wasn't going to get a commission, but she was totally fine. She's happy to have made a new friend." Jessie paused for a moment. "Actually, two new friends. She and Gerry are going to Van Courtland Manor to see the Lightscapes." She sat back in her chair and placed her hand on his arm. "I do hope you'll help me with this."

He brushed a strand of hair from her face. "Of course I will. Anything you want."

"Oh my gosh. I can't believe I'm doing this." She sat back in the chair, letting the reality of it sink in.

"And I am so very glad you are." Evan gave her hand a comforting squeeze. "So, now tell me about Dr. Richie."

"Ugh! That subject again?"

"Yes. Let's just get it out of the way."

Jessie explained about her evening job counseling the lovelorn and how she wanted to keep a low profile. As she recounted some of her funnier stories, Evan became more impressed with this remarkable woman.

"So what will happen to Dr. Richie when she moves to Croton?"

Speaking in the third person, Jessie went on, "It will be a couple of months before I can move here permanently, so Dr. Richie will continue for a while until they can find a replacement. She is a little burned out from doing both jobs and wants to spend more time working with the people in her new community."

"That sounds like a very reasonable plan. She sounds like a very bright woman."

She rested her head on his shoulder and sighed. "Perhaps. But nowhere near as bright as this starry, starry night."

Mistletoe and Mimosas

TARA SHEETS

Chapter One

It's not that Layla Gentry hated snow; it's that she just wasn't prepared. For starters, her outfit was all wrong, and that was enough to throw her off her game. As a top real estate agent on Pine Cove Island, she prided herself on looking her best at all times, and stepping through icy sludge in her favorite stilettos was not part of the plan this morning. Why didn't she check the weather forecast before leaving her house? It wasn't unheard of to get mid-December snow in the Pacific Northwest, but it had happened so fast. When she pulled out of her driveway, the sky had been a crisp, clear blue. But by the time she drove into the Daisy Meadows Pet Rescue parking lot, the snow flurry was in full swing.

A thin layer of frost blanketed the pavement, and the brisk wind caught at Layla's dark hair, pulling strands free from her carefully crafted bun to tumble around her face. Unfortunately, her thin pencil skirt did nothing to block the chilly breeze, and her fitted silk blouse was already scattered with dark water droplets from melted snowflakes. Layla sighed. So much for looking pulled together for the weekly office meeting. Maybe today wasn't the best day to surprise her friend Kat with holiday cupcakes on the way to work, but it was too late now.

Balancing the Fairy Cakes bakery box with one hand, Layla shut her car door and tiptoed gingerly through the slushy parking lot. The front entrance of the newly remodeled animal shelter was decorated with a Christmas wreath, jingle bells, and a bright red welcome mat.

Layla pushed through the front door and paused to admire the view. If it weren't for the surprising distraction in front of her, she might've taken a moment to appreciate the soft holiday music or the fresh scent of evergreens from the little tree in the front window. But the tall, dark stranger standing at the reception desk stole all Layla's attention.

She didn't have a clear view of his face since he stood with his back to the door, but it was a *nice* back, so she wasn't complaining. He was wearing jeans and a blue flannel shirt, and he had broad, muscular shoulders, a trim, athletic build, and glossy dark hair. Even his voice was appealing—low and whisky-smooth. There was something vaguely familiar about it that made Layla's skin prickle with physical awareness, which was unusual. Her reaction surprised her even more than the sudden snow outside.

Layla's friend Kat sat behind the reception desk, her red hair frizzing around her head like a fiery halo. When she caught sight of Layla standing inside the front door, her face lit up in a mischievous smile. "If you linger beneath what hangs above, you'll soon be falling deep in love."

The man tilted his head. "Pardon?"

"Not you," Kat said with a laugh. "My friend over there." She pointed toward Layla. "She's standing under my cousin's magic Holloway mistletoe. It's charmed to help people find true love."

Layla glanced up at the fresh sprig of mistletoe tied with a red satin ribbon hanging above her head. Fall in love? Not a snowball's chance. She wasn't interested in falling, thank you very much. Occasional dating was fine, but that whole dream of "always and forever" just wasn't for her. If there was one thing she'd learned growing up with a single mom, it was that relationships were messy, tricky things, and tumbling head over high heels for someone wasn't worth the trouble.

Layla grinned at her friend as she approached the desk. "You should know by now, I have no intentions of falling, tripping, or stumbling into anything."

The tall stranger turned to face her.

Layla glanced up and stutter-stepped, her smile fading fast.

No. It couldn't be!

Her fingers clutched the bakery box to her chest in surprised shock. Of all the good-looking backsides, why'd it have to be attached to *him*?

Sebastian Harrington, her high school nemesis, stood smiling down at her as if they were old friends and he'd never left Pine Cove Island all those years ago. What was he doing back?

Kat introduced them, oblivious to Layla's inner turmoil. "Dr. Harrington is taking over the new veterinary clinic down the road," she chirped happily. "He just stopped by to check on one of our rescue dogs."

Sebastian's gaze settled on Layla, and his mouth curved into a slow smile—the same smile that used to grace the halls at Pine Cove High. Cocky and confident. Teasing. Bothersome. "Hi, Layla." His voice was warm and deep, coming from some far-off place in her past she'd rather forget.

Oh, no. He didn't get to say "hi" like it was nothing. Like they were just passing in the grocery aisle. Like he wasn't the one who'd traumatized her with his rich kid cronies and defined the meaning of the word "humiliation."

She lifted her chin and tried to look unmoved. It wasn't easy, because Sebastian was one of those people who glowed. He always had been, even back in high school. It was totally unfair, in Layla's opinion, for someone so annoying to be blessed with both a rich family and the kind of sinful good looks that could melt polar ice caps. Now, after so many years, he looked even better. He'd filled out in all the right places, and there were faint laugh lines at the corners of his dark blue eyes. Luckily, all she had to do was remember his personality, and it kept her grounded. He'd been self-centered and condescending back then, and she doubted much had changed over the years.

"How are you?" he asked. There was a flash of warmth in his eyes that, if she didn't know better, seemed almost genuine.

"Good." Layla cleared her throat. "Just great." She gave him a tight smile, the kind she reserved for difficult clients or the grouchy cashier at the Gas 'n' Go. Forcing herself to turn back to Kat, she set the box of cupcakes on the desk. "I brought you some holiday cheer."

"Hallelujah! I knew you were more than just a pretty face." Kat flipped open the lid and eyed the delicately frosted cupcakes with glee.

The heavenly scents of French vanilla and rich caramel wafted up from the bakery box, teasing Layla's senses and making her mouth water, which really just seemed wrong. The delightful cupcakes were marred by the presence of the man standing next to her who, in Layla's opinion, was the furthest thing from delightful.

"Dr. Harrington, you have to try one," Kat said. "They're so good, they'll change your life."

"No, thank you." Sebastian held up a hand. "I don't have much of a sweet tooth."

Kat gasped. "No sweet tooth?" She lifted out a fluffy white cupcake with caramel drizzled over the top. "That's a tragedy right there. I'm so sorry for your loss."

Sebastian chuckled, and the sound of it did warm, tingly things to Layla's insides, which she promptly ignored.

"Layla will have one," Kat said, pushing the box toward her. "She's a sucker for anything sweet."

"Not today," Layla blurted. "Sorry. I'm in a huge rush, so I can't stay and chat, but we'll catch up soon." She backed away from the desk.

"Wait!" Kat said. "You're coming to the holiday party at the community center on Saturday, right? Don't you dare say you're too busy. There's more to life than just work, Layla Gentry, and you need to let loose once in a while."

"Okay, okay. Fine." She hadn't given the holiday party much thought, but if she said no, Kat would demand reasons, and Layla didn't have time to make anything up. All she knew was that she really didn't want to chitchat with Sebastian standing there watching her. It was unsettling to realize that she still felt like the poor girl from the wrong side of the tracks in front of him. Even after all this time. *Get a grip!*

"One more thing," Kat called out as Layla pushed open the front door. "You're up next on our pet volunteer list. I've got a kitten coming in who needs a temporary home, and you're it."

Layla groaned. "So soon?" Two weeks ago, over

drinks at O'Malley's Pub after work, Kat had convinced Layla to become a pet shelter volunteer. Layla had no idea why she'd said yes. She lived alone and was always at work. She often worked on weekends and had no time in her life to even take care of a plant, let alone a pet. But Kat could be as sparkly and charming as a Tiffany bracelet, and somehow Layla had agreed. She suspected it had something to do with Kat ordering the next round of top-shelf margaritas on the rocks with extra salt. She was brilliant like that.

"Yup, you're foster mom of the week," Kat sang out with a huge grin. "I'll bring the kitten by tomorrow after work."

Layla grumbled something she hoped sounded positive and dashed toward her car. She had the oddest feeling that Sebastian was still watching her, but she refused to turn back and check. Why waste even another moment on him? Sure, he'd hurt her feelings back when she was young and poor and vulnerable, but she wasn't that person anymore. She'd grown up, and now she was a successful businesswoman with stability and enough money saved aside for even the rainiest of days. Running into him felt like a trip down memory lane in a rusted jalopy with bald tires, so she forced herself to take a mental U-turn. No more thinking about those days. The past was in the past, where it belonged.

Getting into her shiny Lexus, she smoothed her hair, checked her lipstick, and dusted some errant snowflakes off the shoulders of her blouse. Life was good. She had everything she needed, and she was perfectly content. Everything was just fine. She lifted her chin and pulled out of the parking lot.

Movement in the rearview mirror caught her attention, and she saw Sebastian's tall form leaving the animal shelter, sauntering toward his truck. Why'd he have to saunter? Did he even know he was doing it? It's like every step he took bragged, "Here I am! Look at me."

No, thanks. She tore her gaze away and pulled out onto the highway, her eyes automatically flicking to the rearview mirror one last time. Now he was leaning against his truck with his arms crossed. It looked like he was watching her drive away, and there was a crooked half smile on his face. She flipped her rearview mirror up and kept driving.

Chapter Two

The next afternoon, Layla stood in the kitchen at Pine Cove Real Estate staring glumly at the prepackaged snack foods. This is what happened when she didn't take her mother's advice to take the time for real lunch breaks. Doomed to another day eating at Chez Vending Machine. She sighed and opted for the peanut M&Ms.

"Nice choice," her coworker Jay said as he breezed into the kitchen and made a beeline for the coffee machine. "You can feel good about eating the protein when really it's all about the chocolate."

"Exactly." Layla reached into the machine and pulled out the yellow bag of candy.

Jay Sheridan was the newest addition to their office. He was several years younger than Layla and still "wet behind the ears," as their boss, Albert, liked to say, but Jay's easygoing nature made him a great asset to the team. He was funny and charismatic, and people automatically felt comfortable around him. Layla had no doubt he'd do well in the real estate business.

She glanced over at him and gaped. "What happened to you?"

Jay's normally smooth, boyish face sported a stunner of a black eye and a split lip. On him, it looked bizarre. He was always so perfectly groomed and put together. Even now, with a face that looked like he'd just gone a few rounds in an MMA fight, his light brown hair was neatly combed and his clothes were impeccably tailored.

"Bar brawl at Goalies." Jay stirred his coffee, careful not to splash any on his silk tie. When it came to his clothes, Jay was like Layla. He did not mess around.

"You were in a fight?" Layla asked in disbelief. "At a *sports bar*?" That made no sense. Jay was more of a wine and crossword puzzle type guy. She'd never even seen him at the local pubs.

"I wasn't there by choice," he said glumly. "Some clients wanted to meet there, and after they left, I decided to stay and have another drink. But then some game came on TV, and people got all hot and bothered about the score. Shouting happened. Fists began to fly. Somebody threw a chair, and well . . . I caught it with my face."

Layla slapped her hand over her mouth. "That's terrible. Does it hurt?"

"Nah, I'm over it. Besides, it's getting me all kinds of sympathy, so I'm milking it for all it's worth."

"What game were they arguing about?" Layla teased. Jay had as much interest in sports as she did, which was about zero to none. Their friendship was based on a mutual love of fashion, music, and real estate trends.

"Who knows?" Jay joined her at the small kitchen table. "I think there was a ball in it."

"Sounds fascinating." Layla popped an M&M into

her mouth, savoring the sweet, sugary goodness. "Were we winning?"

"Yes, I believe our local sports franchise was performing admirably." He raised his coffee mug and took a sip. "We sportsed a lot of points."

"Well, at least we can be thankful for that. Here." She shook the bag of candy at him.

He made a face. "If you come at me with one more sugary treat, I will explode. I already ate three doughnuts this morning."

"Just have some," Layla pressed. "Chocolate cures all."

"Amen to that," a woman sang out as she bustled into the kitchen. Mindy Martin was one of Layla's favorite people at the office. They'd both started in real estate around the same time, and they kept each other grounded whenever things got too hectic. Mindy was adorably curvy with black ringlets and a face like a cherub. She had a penchant for wearing trendy accessories, such as the big jingle bell earrings she had on today. "Hey, are we still going to hot yoga on Sunday morning?"

"Yes," Layla said firmly. "We made a pact, remember? Do or die, so don't try to get out of it this time."

Mindy sighed heavily and slapped her lunch bag on the table. She shoved her frizzing curls out of her face and fake-scowled. "I wish you weren't so goal oriented, Layla. It really puts a damper on my plans to procrastinate."

"That's what makes her good at her job," Jay said, toasting Layla with his coffee mug. "She's driven. We should all try to emulate her."

"Oh really?" Mindy smiled sweetly. "Then why don't you come to hot yoga with us, Jay? It's the eight o'clock class at the Waterfront Gym. We'll save you a spot up front."

"Hard pass," Jay said, dusting a piece of lint off his sleeve. "I've got plans to be deeply asleep at that time, but I'll be cheering you both on in my dreams."

"Speaking of dreams," Mindy said excitedly. "Did you guys see my new dreamboat of a client? He's gorgeous, and charming, and he's in the market for something fabulous on the waterfront, so there'll be a big commission there. And there's no ring on his finger, which makes him even hotter."

Layla shook her head, smiling. Mindy was always on the lookout for a future ex-boyfriend. She reveled in the chase and was constantly falling in and out of love at the drop of a hat. It seemed like she dated a different guy every week. Sometimes Layla thought Mindy wasn't really looking for Mr. Right. She seemed more interested in just finding a Mr. Right Now.

"Does this dreamboat have a name?" Jay asked.

"Sebastian Harrington." Mindy sighed softly. "Even his name sounds delicious, doesn't it?"

Layla's chocolate candy high took an instant nosedive. She opened her mouth to tell Mindy exactly what she thought of the man, then decided to stay out of it. It was better not to interfere with Mindy's first impression. If Mindy was lucky, she'd never discover what Sebastian was really like, she'd make a quick sale, and that would be that.

"I'm going to show him that property next to your place, Layla. You know, that gorgeous house with the huge backyard overlooking the ocean? It's got bay windows and an infinity pool. Can you imagine if he went for it? Cha-ching!" Mindy squealed.

Layla choked on an M&M, and Jay thumped her

hard on the back. "No," Layla said, coughing. "That property needs work. It's a bad investment. I don't think you should waste your time showing it."

Mindy shrugged, then launched into a story about her latest Christmas shopping drama.

Layla only half listened to Mindy, too busy contemplating the terrible notion of Sebastian Harrington moving into the house near hers. *Not going to happen.* She'd worked too long and hard to find her place on the waterfront. It was a peaceful, two-bedroom home with a modest yard and lovely floor-to-ceiling windows facing the ocean. All her life, Layla had dreamed of living in a beautiful house, a real house, instead of the trailer she'd grown up in with her mother. Now that she finally had it, her life felt complete. Layla tossed the rest of her candy into the garbage, no longer hungry. Her home was a haven, and no swaggering hotshot was going to mess with that. She'd make sure of it.

Later that evening, Layla gently arranged her newest picture frame on the console table in her living room. The small frame was embellished with green and blue Swarovski crystals, and it held a black-and-white stock image of a couple and their dog on the beach. She took the image out, then stood back to admire her collection. Several crystal-studded frames of varying sizes sat on the table like sparkling gems in a jewelry box. One of these days, Layla was going to actually get around to putting photographs in them, but for now it made her happy just to see the bright, colorful arrangement.

"Mom, I'm fine," she said into her phone as she padded barefoot into the kitchen. "I did eat lunch, and

I have dinner in the oven right now." Well, technically it was a frozen Hot Pocket in the microwave, but her mom didn't need to know that.

"You know I worry about you in that house by yourself." Her mother's voice sounded stern through the phone, and Layla could just imagine her mom shaking her head, gray wisps of hair floating around her heart-shaped face. "A beautiful young woman your age, it's not right for you to be so alone. I saw a documentary the other day about a serial killer who breaks into houses and hides under bed skirts, waiting for victims to fall asleep. Did you know they're more common than you think?"

"Bed skirts?" Layla poured herself a glass of merlot.

"No, serial killers," her mother said in exasperation. "I just want you to be safe. Think about getting a dog at the pet store, maybe. Or better yet—get a nice strong man."

"Last I checked, they don't sell nice strong men at Pet Palace."

Her mom let out a huff, then continued to fuss in her sweet, endearing, completely nosy way. She'd always been a worrier, but Layla never faulted her for it. Her mom had struggled all her life to make ends meet for them. Now she insisted on living in a small apartment on the other side of the island. It wasn't great, but it was near the diner where she worked, so Layla gladly helped pay the rent. It had been one of Layla's greatest joys to be able to provide a place for her mother and get them out of the trailer park. The two of them had come a long way, and even though life hadn't been easy for them, they'd always remained close.

"I have a state-of-the art security system in place here," Layla assured her. "I also took that self-defense class, remember? I don't need a dog or a man, Mom. I'm totally fine."

After promising to consider the benefits of owning a pit bull or a German shepherd, Layla finally said good-bye, just as the doorbell rang.

She opened the door to find Kat standing on the welcome mat with a pet carrier in one hand and a big bag of cat supplies in the other. "Greetings, foster mama!"

"Oh, that's right." Layla blinked down at the fluffy gray face staring out at her through the bars of the pet carrier. The kitten was a few months old, and it looked part alien, with its huge headlamp eyes and its narrow chin. What was she thinking, agreeing to this? She knew nothing about cats. "Well, come in."

"Try to contain your excitement." Kat pushed through the door. "It's just for a couple of weeks until we find him a permanent home. Is that the hall bathroom? You two get acquainted while I set up the litter box. Food dishes go in the kitchen, okay?"

Layla nodded as Kat chatted away, zipping through the house. Within just a few minutes, all the kitten supplies were put away, and the gray tabby was now sniffing around the living room. He crouched low, glancing around for a few moments, then crawled behind the curtains.

"This is Toonces. He's a little shy," Kat said. "But once he gets used to the place, he'll be a total love bug. He's definitely a lap cat, so you're in luck."

Layla scrunched up her face. "What kind of a name is Toonces?"

"Smitty named him." Kat's tone of voice implied the reason should be sufficient, and maybe it was. Layla had only met Smitty at the Daisy Meadows Pet Rescue a few times. She was the office manager. An older woman with a sour expression and teased and sprayed hair out to there. She smoked like a chimney and still wore acid-wash jeans—not because they were retro-cool now, but because she'd been the front-runner in fashion back in her heyday, and she'd never changed.

"She's a die-hard vintage *Saturday Night Live* fan," Kat added. "I think she named him after one of the old skits. Something about a cat who drove cars? I didn't ask too many questions."

"Are you sure he'll be okay here all day while I'm at work?" Layla asked.

"Totally fine. Just give him some extra snuggles when you get home."

Kat set a basket of small toys on the living room floor, coaxing the kitten from behind the curtains with a feather on a stick.

He took a few tentative steps toward it, then pounced. After a few moments, Kat grinned and stood, slapping her hands together. "He feels comfortable enough to play now, so my work here is done."

"Stay and have a glass of wine," Layla offered.

"Can't. I promised Emma and Juliette I'd meet them for movie night. Hey, you want to come?" Kat usually met up with her cousins once a week, and even though Layla had only met the Holloway women a few times, she liked them a lot. They were just like Kat— open and easygoing and a little on the quirky side. "We're going to watch *Elf* to get in the mood for Christmas."

"I wish I could, but I'm wiped. It's been a long day."

"Next time." Kat made her way toward the front door. "I'll see you on Saturday night for the holiday party. It's cocktail attire, so be sure to dress sexy." She wiggled her eyebrows. "I think Dr. Harrington's going to be there."

"Not my type," Layla said firmly, taking a gulp of wine.

Kat tipped her head back and laughed. No, she *guffawed*. Like, on purpose. Layla could see all her molars.

"Honey, I know you aren't interested in getting tangled up in anything, but that man is anyone's type." Kat waved her hand in front of Layla's face.

Layla frowned and jerked her chin back. "What are you doing?"

"Just checking to see if you've gone blind. I mean, did you *see* him? He's gorgeous. He's charming. And he genuinely loves helping animals. It's like his superpower. What's not to like?"

Layla pressed her lips into a hard line. "Let's just say I knew him back in high school. I wasn't impressed with him then, and I'm not impressed now."

"You used to know him?" Kat's leaf-green eyes sparkled with interest. "Spill, girlfriend!"

Layla shook her head. "It was a long time ago. I'll tell you some other time over drinks. Lots and lots of drinks."

"Huh." Kat narrowed her eyes. "Gotta run, but I'm going to hold you to that. See you Saturday!" With a final wave, she was out the door and gone.

Layla wandered back into the living room and sat cross-legged near the kitten, who was now stalking a cloth ball with a bell inside it. He really was adorable.

"Toonces, huh?" Layla jingled the cloth ball and rolled it on the carpet. "Sorry about the name."

Toonces swiveled his ear, as if he couldn't care less. Then he pounced on the ball.

She snapped a quick picture and texted it to her mom. *Behold, the fierce attack cat. He'll be staying with me for two weeks, so you can rest easy now. I'm safe.*

A few moments later her mother responded. *What a cutie! Not as fierce as a rottweiler or a big strong man, though.*

Layla sighed. *Good night, Mom.*

Night, hun. Don't forget to check under the bed skirt before you go to sleep.

Chapter Three

Sebastian entered the community center on Saturday night with a sharp sense of nostalgia. The big gym had been decked out for the holiday with sparkling Christmas trees and giant snowflakes hanging from the ceiling. Onstage there was a local band singing holiday tunes, and crowds of people were grouped in lively conversation or milling near food tables and a bar along the far wall. The air was rich with the scents of fresh baked gingerbread and sweet rum punch, which made him smile. The locals in this town always did know how to party.

Ever since he'd moved back to Pine Cove Island last month, he'd been surrounded by the familiar people and places from his childhood. It was both heartwarming and bittersweet. The island was a glowing reminder of the easy, carefree days of his youth, filled with backyard barbecues and baseball games and fishing trips on his parents' boat. But it was also a reminder of the harder times that came later, when everything began to fall apart. Still, he didn't regret moving back to open his veterinary practice here. He still loved the town and all its quirky people, and the longer he stayed, the more convinced he was that he'd made the right decision—even if it had meant giving up a piece of his soul to do it.

He adjusted the sleeve on his designer suit, shoving away the painful memories he left back in San Francisco. What's done was done, and he was here now. Nothing to do but embrace his new life and find joy in what he loved most.

"Seb!" a booming voice called through the crowd. "Is it really you?"

Sebastian turned to see one of his old high school buddies barreling toward him with a glass of whiskey. Keith Miller had been a linebacker for the Pine Cove High football team, and they used to call him The Hammer because he was always ready and willing to beat someone down. Now, with his thinning blond hair, florid complexion, and beer belly, he looked less like an imposing linebacker and more like a middle-aged armchair quarterback.

"Keith." Sebastian reached out to shake his hand. "It's been a long time."

"No kidding, man!" Keith grabbed Sebastian's hand and yanked him closer, thumping him hard on the back. Sebastian winced. Keith might be older and pudgy, but he still had the hammer fists.

"I heard you moved back here," Keith said. "Veterinarian, huh? What about your family's wine business?"

Sebastian kept his expression carefully neutral. "I chose a different path."

"But, dude. All that *wine*." Keith stared dreamily off into the distance, as if he were imagining a swim through a Willy Wonka factory–sized river of booze. He finally snapped out of it and held up his glass in salute. "Veterinarian. That's good, I guess. Dammit, man, time is your friend. You look great. What'd you do, make a deal with the devil?" Keith snickered and took a swig of his drink.

Sebastian gave him a wry smile. "Something like that." Sometimes, those long hours he spent running or working out at the gym did feel like hell, but he did it anyway. Years ago, he'd discovered that hard exercise helped clear his head and stay focused. It had been the one thing he could control when the rest of his life careened out of control, and the habit had stuck.

"Who'd have thought," Keith said. "Seb Harrington. Back in Pine Cove. We should get together with the boys and talk about the glory days."

Sebastian gave a noncommittal reply, because as far as he could remember, those days weren't all that glorious. There was nothing he cared to recall about that time in his life . . . well, almost nothing. Only one person had remained in his thoughts over the years, and even though the memory came with heartache, it still glowed like a bright star on a moonless night.

Keith lifted his drink, downed it, then glared into his empty glass.

Sebastian could tell from Keith's bleary eyes that The Hammer was well and truly hammered.

"I'm going to go for a refill," Keith said with a hiccup. "My wife's gonna be pissed because I'm designated driver tonight, but what the hell, ammirite?" He cracked himself up. "Catch you later, man."

Sebastian watched him weave through the crowd, pretty sure they wouldn't be catching up later. Most of his old high school buddies had been big partiers, and Sebastian ran with that crowd because it was the easiest form of escapism. He'd done and said stupid things, all in the name of fun, when really he'd been miserable inside. It wasn't until he'd moved away that he realized how much time he'd wasted pretending to be the carefree party boy everyone thought he was.

For the next hour, he wandered through the crowd, stopping once in a while to engage with old acquaintances and meet new people. It came as no surprise that he was actually enjoying himself, even the ramblings of old Mrs. Mooney, who'd latched onto his arm to discuss the many ailments of her dog, Bonbon. Sebastian was reminded again of why he'd chosen to move back. There was a deep-rooted familiarity with the people, and the small-town atmosphere stirred his spirit and soothed his soul.

When he stepped outside for some fresh air a few minutes later, he spotted a person in the garden gazebo. Suddenly, his soul stirred in a different way. Sebastian's mouth kicked into a smile and he started toward her, unable to help himself.

Layla Gentry sat on the steps of the gazebo sipping a drink. Hundreds of white twinkle lights were woven through the slats along the roof, lending an almost ethereal glow to the place. She was wearing a knockout black dress that showcased her lethally gorgeous legs, made even hotter by the strappy stilettos and her dainty, red-painted toenails. *Damn*. Sebastian swallowed hard. She had definitely grown up. The Layla he remembered had been a skinny girl in scuffed-up tennis shoes and hand-me-down clothes that always seemed too big for her. But as she tipped her face up to the sky and closed her eyes, he came to an abrupt stop.

There she was. With the same innocent, radiant glow on her face that made her look like an angel. God, she was beautiful, but that came as no surprise. Layla had always been stunning, radiating an inner peace that used to make Sebastian crazy. In her circumstances growing up, she should've been bitter and jaded, but she wasn't. He never could understand how she always managed to look so . . . hopeful.

He closed the distance between them, standing in front of her. Her skin looked smooth and impossibly soft in the moonlight. "Good evening."

Layla's eyes flew open and she startled, splashing her drink. "Oh!" Something fell off her lap and landed in the grass. The former peace in her expression melted away, replaced by a mask of calm, cool indifference. She was good at that mask. She didn't used to be. He remembered how her face used to be like an open book, with every emotion easy to read. If it weren't for the rapid rise and fall of her chest showing her agitation, Sebastian might've been fooled.

She set her drink on the step beside her. "You startled me."

"I didn't mean to." He bent to retrieve her cell phone in the grass and handed it to her.

She silently took it, watching him from beneath thick, dark lashes. She reminded him of a startled deer, preparing to bolt.

He took a seat on the end of the step, leaning against the opposite railing. "Why aren't you inside enjoying the party?"

Layla's back straightened. "I just needed to check messages, and it was too noisy in there. I thought I'd come out here for some peace and quiet." From the look on her face, it was clear he'd disturbed her peace.

Sebastian's mouth curved at one corner. "I didn't mean to interrupt. Do you want me to leave?"

She squared her shoulders and lifted her chin. "Not at all. I was just about to go back inside, anyway."

He watched as she nervously brushed invisible lint off her skirt. She was clearly unsettled, so he fought for something to say to put her at ease. "I hear you're a top real estate agent now. A force to be reckoned with, they say."

She looked uncomfortable with the praise. "Who says that?"

"My sources," he said mysteriously.

"Spying on me, Dr. Harrington?"

"Absolutely not," he said with mock severity. "Do I look like a spy?"

She glanced sideways at him. Sebastian could feel her gaze traveling over him, and it made his pulse pick up. "Wears all black. Lurks in the shadows. Sneaks up on people in the dark." She shrugged. "If the shoe fits."

He pressed a finger to his ear, pretending to speak into a hidden mic. "She's onto me. Yeah, our cover's blown. Can you send a cleanup crew to the garden at the community center?"

Layla pursed her lips, a soft blush visible on her cheeks. He could tell she was trying not to smile. An unexpected warmth bloomed inside him.

"Someone I met inside sang your praises," Sebastian admitted. "A guy named Albert from your office."

"Ah." Layla lifted her drink and took another sip. "Good old Albert. He's my boss."

"He seems very . . . enthusiastic," Sebastian offered. He remembered Albert's booming voice and hearty laughter. The man was very happy to talk about his business, and the people who worked there.

"Albert eats, sleeps, and breathes Pine Cove Real Estate," Layla explained with a reluctant smile. "He's always looking for ways to expand the business through advertising, and he expects everyone on the team to be fully invested in the community." She shook her head and sighed. "Last year's mandatory holiday activity was a disaster. He made us all go Christmas caroling door-to-door."

"That doesn't sound too bad."

She shot him a look. "Dressed as reindeer."

Sebastian raised a brow. "I see."

"Be glad you *didn't* see. It started raining that night, and our antlers were made of papier-mâché. Within minutes, they were crumpling on our heads, and our faces were covered in craft paint. We looked like extras from the set of *The Walking Dead.*"

Sebastian chuckled.

"It's only funny in retrospect," she assured him.

"I'll make sure to be on the lookout for a singing herd of zombie reindeer."

"No, this year we're participating in the tree lighting ceremony, so it shouldn't be as bad." She flashed him a genuine smile. With her bright eyes and the dimple in her left cheek, she looked so much like the girl he remembered.

He smiled back. If only . . .

Layla suddenly seemed to catch herself. Her humor faded, and she quickly stood. "Well, I should head back."

"Wait." He rose to stand beside her.

She paused.

"I—" He cleared his throat. What could he say? How long had he chastised himself for the mistake that happened years ago? There was so much he wanted to say, but he needed time. "I just wanted to tell you I'm sorry."

She blinked up at him, the cool mask back in place. "For what?"

"Back in high school." He took a step closer. "I never meant to hurt your feelings. That day when—"

"Oh, that." Layla waved a hand. "That was so long ago. Really, Dr. Harrington. I barely remember!"

He swallowed hard. "Please call me Sebastian."

She kept nodding, then turned to leave again.

"Come to dinner with me," he said, surprising himself. He hadn't planned on asking her out, but he hoped she'd say yes. He liked the idea of spending more time with her, and it would give him a better chance to explain things.

"Sorry, I already ate."

"It doesn't have to be tonight," he said quietly. She looked disturbed, but he had to try. "How about later this week?"

"Oh." Her gaze shifted around the garden, never quite landing on him. "I'm just super busy this week, so I don't have a lot of time."

"Dessert, then?" What the hell was wrong with him? Clearly, she wanted to blow him off, and he should just let it go.

"I . . ." She shook her head, as if she were trying to think of a polite way to refuse.

He found it oddly endearing, even though disappointment settled over him because he knew she'd turn him down. Layla had always been a kind person and could never be rude to anyone, even if they deserved it, like he had.

"I don't like dessert," she blurted. "Sweet things. They just don't appeal to me. But thanks, anyway!" She waved quickly and then marched back inside.

Sebastian watched her go, a wave of amusement mixing with the disappointment. He distinctly remembered her friend Kat at the pet shelter saying Layla had a sweet tooth. He slid his hands into his pockets and continued walking through the garden. Layla Gentry was elusive as ever, but things were different now. He wasn't the same person he used to be. She might not realize it yet, but . . . A slow smile spread across his face. He'd just have to show her.

Chapter Four

"I can't believe I agreed to exercise at stupid o'clock in the morning," Mindy groaned as they trudged from the parking lot toward the Waterfront Gym early on Sunday. "Remind me again why we're doing this."

Layla hoisted her yoga bag over her shoulder, side-stepping a patch of ice on the sidewalk. It was shaping up to be a gorgeous winter day with clear skies, but the biting wind coming in off the ocean made it necessary to bundle up in fleece jackets and knit caps. "We're doing this so we can eat our weight in Christmas cookies with zero guilt, remember?"

"I haven't worked out in weeks," Mindy grumbled. "My body's going to revolt."

"You'll be fine. Muscle has memory."

"I'm pretty sure mine has amnesia." Mindy scowled down at her shoe and bent to tie the trailing laces. "Besides, it just seems wrong to do hot yoga half asleep. Dangerous, even, with all those pretzel poses and the sweaty yoga mats. A person could slip and hurt themselves. I'm not sure it should be legal at this hour."

They made their way toward the building on the far corner of Front Street, Layla trying not to laugh as Mindy gave a very energetic explanation about why she had no energy. The Waterfront Gym was a large, two-story facility with free weights and treadmills on the bottom floor, and rooms for spin classes and yoga on the second floor.

Halfway down the street, the delicious scents of fresh-roasted coffee and warm pastries wafted through the air.

"Let's skip it today and go there, instead." Mindy pointed to Fairy Cakes bakery. It was a beautiful little pastry shop and café with legendary cupcakes and fabulous coffee, owned by Emma Holloway, who was rumored to bake sweet charms and spells into her cupcakes. Most people thought of Emma's magic as nothing more than delicious fun, like wishing on a star or tossing a coin in a fountain, but some of the towns-folk wholeheartedly believed in it. Layla was more of a realist, but she never faulted the fanciful locals who did believe. Why not? Life wasn't always flowers and rainbows, she knew that better than anybody. If a person wanted to believe in a few sweet charms, good for them.

Mindy pointed again and gave Layla a pitiful expression, batting her eyes.

"Are you kidding me?" Layla jammed her hands onto her hips. "We said we were sticking to the plan this time. Balls to the wall, remember? Work out or die?"

"I don't know." Mindy slowed to a stop in front of the bakery window. "I'm cool with dying as long as I can get one of those blueberry muffins, first." She gasped. "Look! They have salted caramel mochas with homemade whipped cream!"

"No," Layla said, slowing to stand beside her friend. She watched a young couple exit the bakery with flaky pastries topped with chopped nuts and dusted in powdered sugar. "Were those toasted hazelnuts?"

"I think they were," Mindy said with a sigh.

"Still." Layla took a deep breath and let it out fast. "We're not weaklings. We didn't drag ourselves out of bed this early to skip the workout and have delicious treats instead. That would just be . . ." She watched another person leave the bakery with a steaming hot cocoa heaped with whipped cream and chocolate shavings. "Bad."

"Right," Mindy said weakly.

"Crazy."

"Uh-huh."

"Nuts," Layla insisted.

Mindy gave her the side eye. "Toasted, though. *Toasted* hazelnuts."

They both gravitated closer to the window until they were staring through the glass like starving street urchins.

Layla's mouth watered at the decadent scents floating in the air around them.

"So." Mindy paused. "Should I get us a table, or . . . ?"

"Hurry," Layla said, pushing Mindy toward the door.

Fifteen minutes later, they were seated at a small bistro table near the front window, blissfully sipping their drinks and chatting away. Emma had insisted on pairing their coffees with freshly baked cinnamon rolls, on the house.

"This is divine," Layla said, licking gooey cinnamon and sugar off her finger.

Mindy grinned like a kid on Christmas morning. "So much better than sweating miserably in a dark room with a bunch of morning masochists."

"You're not wrong." Layla scooped a dollop of

whipped cream from her mocha, savoring the rich flavors of French vanilla drizzled with buttery, salted caramel. What could be more mouthwateringly delicious than this?

The front door opened, and Layla's eyes flew wide.

Sebastian Harrington breezed through the door like the god of the rising sun. With the early morning light behind him, he practically glowed around the edges. He looked much different than he did last night at the party. Instead of a dark designer suit, he was wearing charcoal gray sweats, a black T-shirt, and running shoes. His hair was mussed like he'd just freshly showered, and he looked slightly rumpled, gloriously rugged, and disturbingly . . . hot.

Layla licked her lips and tried not to stare.

Mindy's back was to the door, so she kept chatting away, completely unaware that her scorching hot client had entered the building.

Layla pretended to follow along with Mindy's story as she watched Sebastian order a coffee to go. He didn't even ask for cream or sugar. Just plain, black coffee like a straight-up, no-frills manly man.

Mindy abruptly stopped talking. "Layla, are you listening to me?"

"Mmm-hmm."

"So you think I should get 'Fries Before Guys' tattooed on my forehead?"

"Sure." Layla took another sip of her drink as Sebastian dropped several dollar bills into the tip jar. That was generous of him. Interesting.

"I knew it," Mindy said. "You haven't heard a word I've said. What are you—" She spun around in her chair to glance behind her. Then she gasped. "Oh, my gosh, it's *him*. That's my new client I told you about." She waved her hand and called out, "Sebastian!"

He glanced over his shoulder. Surprise flitted across his face as he spotted them near the front window. He gave them a crooked smile, which somehow added to his attractiveness. Not that Layla cared or anything. It was just an observation.

"Good morning," he said.

Layla felt heat rise in her face, and she bit the inside of her cheek. What was wrong with her? It's not like she'd never seen a hot guy before, and she already knew Sebastian could be charming when he wanted to be. She also knew he could be a total jerk when he wanted to be, so she just needed to remember that. Really focus on that memory. Because this new side of him was throwing her off.

"Good morning, yourself," Mindy gushed. She quickly introduced them.

Sebastian gave Layla a secret smile. "We've met."

"So what are you up to today?" Mindy asked, eyeing his workout clothes in blatant appreciation as she licked her spoon. Layla barely refrained from rolling her eyes. Mindy was not subtle.

He mussed his hair with one hand. Layla tried hard to ignore the way his arm muscles bunched and flexed with the movement, drawing his T-shirt tight across his lean torso. "Just hitting the gym, then heading back to my apartment to take my dog for a run."

"That's nice." Mindy sighed, her gaze traveling down his chest and lower, lingering a little too long.

Okay, time to reel in Mindy the Maneater. Layla kicked her friend under the table.

"Ow—I mean, oh!" Mindy jerked upright in her chair. "Us too. At the gym. Hot yoga. Work out or die, right, Layla? That's us!"

Sebastian nodded politely, but Layla didn't miss the humor that flashed across his face. He gestured to the half-mangled cinnamon rolls and melted whipped cream. "Looks like a great way to unwind."

Mindy giggled. "We couldn't resist."

Layla slumped a little lower in her chair. She could feel the heat rising up the back of her neck. This was the part where Sebastian pointed out that she supposedly didn't like sweets. Then he could gloat about catching her in the lie she told him last night. She pretended to wipe crumbs off the table and waited for him to call her on it. Waited. And waited.

When Mindy started talking about the housing market, Layla stole a quick glance at him.

He winked.

Her heart did a little hop-skip. Once again, Sebastian surprised her. After last night, she'd left the party feeling flustered and more than a little confused. His gentle teasing had gotten to her, and she didn't know how to navigate around it. This new side of him was different. He seemed more grounded, and everything he said felt genuinely kind. A tiny part of her was intrigued by the changes in him, but the logical part of her brain refused to go there. Layla didn't get where she was today by allowing for flights of fancy, and she needed to remember that.

"Dr. Harrington," Emma suddenly called from behind the register. "If you linger beneath what hangs above, you'll soon be falling deep in love."

They all looked toward the pastry counter. Emma Holloway's lovely face lit with merriment as she pointed above the doorway. Another sprig of mistletoe hung from the ceiling with bright red ribbon. This time, Sebastian was standing under it.

"It's everywhere!" Mindy said. "We have some of that at our office, too. It's from Juliette Holloway's florist shop. She's Emma's cousin, and her superpower is growing plants and mixing up magic spells. What do you think, Sebastian?" Mindy asked. "Feel like falling in love?"

He grinned and slid on a pair of mirrored sunglasses. "I'm already there."

Layla couldn't see his eyes, but she sensed he was looking at her. She concentrated on stirring her mocha. Had to get those chocolate shavings mixed in just right. Super important.

"You *are*?" Mindy asked.

"Sure." He swung open the front door. "I'm back on Pine Cove Island, surrounded by all you wonderful people, celebrating the holidays and looking forward to bringing in the New Year. What's not to love?"

With a final wave, he took off down the street.

"Ho ho ho!" Santa roared right into Layla's eardrum the following evening.

She winced and pasted a smile on her face as she bent to fill her basket with more candy canes. Her boss, Albert, was a little overzealous in his role as Santa Claus for the annual tree lighting ceremony, but he played the part well, and the kids seemed to love him. With Albert's hearty laugh and ruddy complexion, he was practically typecast for the job.

Layla, on the other hand, got the short end of the stick. Everyone in the office had pulled straws to see who had to be Santa's elf, and she'd been the unlucky winner. But Layla was a good sport, so she'd graciously thrown herself into the role. She'd decided if she had to be an elf, then she was going to be the best-dressed elf this side of the North Pole.

She smoothed her red velvet skater dress and admired her new black stiletto boots. Even on sale, they'd been pricey. But, hey. Life was a gift, right? Sometimes you just have to wrap yourself well. With the green-and-white striped tights and sparkly holly berry wreath in her hair, she felt pretty good about her outfit. At least in this gig, she got to wear things she liked. It was way better than donning antlers and prancing around in the rain like last year, so she wasn't complaining.

Gazing across the crowd at the petting zoo, she thanked her lucky stars she didn't have to work that gig. It looked like a muddy madhouse over there.

"Layla," Albert stage-whispered through his beard after the last kid wandered away. "When does Santa get to take a break?"

Layla checked her watch. "Ten more minutes and you're home free, Albert."

He nodded as a mother and her three little kids approached. "Ho ho ho! Who do we have here?" he boomed.

The littlest kid began to cry.

Layla took a deep breath and checked her watch again. Just a few more minutes and she could grab a hot buttered rum from the drink station and get off her aching feet. As much as she loved her new boots, she'd barely had a chance to break them in, so they weren't all that comfortable. She scanned the crowd for familiar faces, spotting her friend Kat over near the petting zoo. All the animals came from Kat's farm where she and her husband, Jordan, ran an animal sanctuary. Jordan was one of Layla's oldest friends, and she was thrilled when he'd moved back to the island and married Kat. They were perfect for each other.

The waterfront lawn was packed with families and kids. There was a face painting station set up near the gazebo, a band playing holiday music, and another tent serving food with a cookie decorating station. Layla was just admiring an adorable little boy in a Santa hat that was too big for his head, when she saw something that made her stomach drop.

The little boy in the Santa hat ran straight up to a tall, laughing man in jeans and a forest green sweater. *Sebastian.*

He scooped the kid up and twirled him in a circle, then settled him onto his broad shoulders. A pretty young woman stood beside them, beaming at Sebastian like he hung the moon. The three of them were beautiful together. Picture perfect. They looked like one of those happy families in the black-and-white stock images that came inside Layla's sparkly picture frames.

A thick pang of disappointment filled her. Ridiculous! Why should it matter to her if Sebastian had a family? She didn't care. Of course she didn't. But as she watched them make their way toward the line for Santa Claus, her disappointment turned into a sharp bite of annoyance. What a jerk! Just last night, he'd followed her out into the garden and asked her out to dinner. And he'd winked at her this morning. Acting all charming and flirty . . . how *could* he?

Layla struggled to look cheerful as she passed out candy canes to the kids. Did Sebastian's pretty wife know he was oozing his way around town, trailing false charm wherever he went? Maybe she was used to it by now, the poor thing.

The woman's gaze settled on Layla, her dark hair curling around her friendly face. The smile she gave Layla was nothing but genuine. She turned and said something to Sebastian, and he bent to whisper in her ear. Layla gritted her teeth as she watched the woman pat his arm, kiss the little boy, then wave good-bye.

Sebastian stayed in line for Santa, with the boy perched happily on his shoulders. The minutes seemed to tick by at a glacial speed. Layla hoped he wouldn't notice her standing near Santa's sleigh. She pretended to check out the two-story Christmas tree on the lawn behind them. When they finally approached, she kept her face down and bent to fill the basket with more candy.

Albert roared his greetings from the North Pole.

The little boy let out a peal of laughter as Sebastian swung him down to meet Santa and get his picture taken.

A couple more minutes ticked by, and Layla steeled herself to deal with the inevitable.

"You're an elf?" a small voice asked her. His little boy was looking at her in confusion, and she couldn't help but smile. He was a beautiful child, with dark hair and big brown eyes.

"Yup," Layla said quickly. "Would you like a candy cane?"

The little boy ignored that. "But elves are boys."

Layla was acutely aware of Sebastian standing behind him. He placed a large hand on the little boy's shoulder.

"Some elves are, um, girls," Layla said lamely, without looking at Sebastian.

"But elves are small," the little boy insisted. "And they have pointy shoes with jingle bells." He stared at her black stiletto boots, clearly suspicious.

"Not all elves, Charlie," Sebastian said. "Sometimes if you're really lucky, you get to meet one like her."

Charlie tilted his head and looked at Layla thoughtfully. "Girl elves are lucky?"

"Yeah," Sebastian said. "Especially the ones who wear naughty boots."

Layla tried to keep her expression neutral, but it

wasn't easy. He was flirting with her in front of his son.
The nerve!

"Layla, this is my nephew Charlie," Sebastian said
warmly. "Charlie, meet Layla of the North Pole."

She blinked. "Your nephew?" she managed, glancing between them.

"Yup. It's date night for my sister Olivia and her
husband, so I'm on babysitting duty." He ruffled Charlie's hair.

"Hey, I'm not a baby," Charlie said indignantly. "I'm
five already."

"That's right," Sebastian said. "We're just two guys
hanging out. No babies in sight." He raised his hand,
and Charlie gave him a high five.

Wow. Sebastian just went from super schmuck to
superhero in the blink of an eye. Layla felt like she was
on an emotional teacup ride, spinning from one ex-
treme to the other.

"My dad's taking my mom out to dinner," Charlie
told Layla matter-of-factly as he eyed the candy. "Then
he's taking her to pound town for dessert."

"Charlie!" Sebastian's voice was thick with barely
restrained laughter. "Who told you that?"

"I heard him telling my mom," Charlie said absently, digging through her basket of candy canes. "I
hope they bring me back some pound cake."

Layla slapped a hand over her mouth.

Sebastian shook his head at Layla, his blue eyes
sparkling with humor.

She grinned, happy that she'd been wrong about
Sebastian having a wife and son. Not wanting to exam-
ine that emotion too closely, she turned her attention
back to the little boy. "Did you tell Santa what you
wanted for Christmas?"

"Yup." Charlie's face fell. "But I'm not gonna get it."

"Why do you say that?"

"Because my mom says no pets allowed in the house." He finally selected a strawberry-flavored candy cane. "And giraffes are too hard to potty train."

"Yes, I can see how that might be difficult." Layla lowered herself so she was at eye level with Charlie. "But do you know there's an animal sanctuary over on Griffin Road? My friend Kat runs it, and she has a very cool miniature donkey named Waffles, and a one-eyed goat named Lulabelle. Maybe you could go visit one of these days. She might even let you feed them. I can put in a good word for you."

Charlie's face lit up. "Can we go now, Uncle Seb?"

"I'm pretty sure the animal sanctuary's closed for the day," Sebastian told him. "But I promise to take you there soon."

Charlie hooted with glee, then pointed his candy cane at Layla. "Can she come?"

Sebastian's warm gaze settled on her. "She can if she wants." His voice was rich and smooth, and something about it sounded almost decadent. Like he was standing there offering up her favorite dessert on a silver platter, and all she had to do was reach out and take a big bite.

Layla had to look away, because, apparently, the more charm he used, the more brain cells she lost. For a split second, she actually considered saying yes. She gave Charlie an apologetic smile. "I'm sorry. I won't be able to go with you."

Charlie batted his eyelashes, which, paired with the angelic face and the oversize Santa hat, was some powerful stuff. Five years old, and he'd already mastered the art of puppy-dog eyes. "Why not?"

Because as much as I hate to admit it, your hottie uncle

gets me all flustered, and he makes me feel like I'm flying out of orbit into unknown territory. "Um, I have to work some extra shifts at the North Pole."

Charlie's sweet face grew very solemn. "Is it because of your naughty boots?"

"I—"

"Ho ho ho!" Albert boomed. "I'm heading out to feed the reindeer," he told Layla. "I'll be back in half an hour."

She waved good-bye to Santa as he waddled off toward the volunteer building.

"If you're on a break, want to walk with us?" Sebastian asked. "We're heading over to the refreshment tent."

Layla paused, considering it. Her knee-jerk reaction was to say no, but it was an innocent request. She was headed in that direction anyway. "Okay." She set her candy canes behind Santa's sleigh. "I was planning to get a hot buttered rum."

The three of them meandered through the crowd, Charlie darting back and forth between the activity tents. His childish exuberance was contagious, and Layla couldn't help laughing when he ran squealing for the petting zoo.

"Charlie, wait," Sebastian called. "We need to get drinks, first."

The little boy was already entering the goat pen, patting the goats and chatting excitedly with the other kids.

"Why don't you go," Layla said. "I'll keep an eye on him."

Sebastian nodded, then took off toward the refreshments. Layla leaned against the fence as she watched Charlie. He was young, but it was clear he had that same charisma his uncle had. It looked like he'd already made a couple of new friends.

"Oh, good. I've found you!"

Layla turned to see Mindy breaking free from the crowd, speeding toward her like a sparkly Christmas comet. Her bright gold holiday sweater had a reindeer wearing sunglasses and the words "Sleighin' It" across the top in blinking twinkle lights. "I've been looking everywhere for you." Mindy's face was flushed with worry, and she seemed distracted. "Listen, I have to talk to you."

"What's going on?" Layla searched Mindy's face in concern. She'd never seen her friend so frazzled.

"My mom just called from Kansas, and we have a family emergency. My dad had a stroke."

"Oh, my God."

"He's in the hospital, and my mom's not handling it well, so I need to take the next flight out tomorrow morning."

"I'm so sorry." Layla wrapped an arm around her friend and gave her a tight squeeze. "Is there anything I can do to help? Do you have someone to watch Pickle?" Layla didn't know how well her foster kitten would get along with Mindy's excitable Chihuahua, but if she had to make it work, she would.

"No, but thank you. Jay's taking Pickle while I'm gone, but I need something else," Mindy said. "I need you to take Sebastian."

Layla frowned. Take him? Take him where? Her overactive imagination chose this moment to kick into high gear. There were all sorts of places they could go. Dinner, for example. Home. Pound town. *Enough!* She forcibly shoved those ridiculous thoughts aside. "What do you mean?"

"I won't be able to show him houses, so I need to

cut him loose as a client. I'm giving you Sebastian Harrington. If you want him."

Before Layla could speak, a deep voice interrupted them.

"Throwing me away so soon?" Sebastian teased Mindy as he handed Layla a hot buttered rum. "Was it something I said?"

Mindy turned beet red. "Oh, not at all! I was just coming to find you next. I'm so sorry, but I've got a family emergency and I'll need to fly back home to Kansas tomorrow morning."

Sebastian looked concerned. "I hope it's nothing too serious."

"My dad had a stroke, so I'm heading there to help my mom."

"I'm sorry to hear that."

"I'm not sure how long I'll be gone, so I'm afraid I have to transfer you to another real estate agent. But I already talked to Albert about it, and we both agree Layla's perfect for you." She glanced at Layla. "I can e-mail you his information, if that works for you both?" She turned back to Sebastian. "I'm so sorry to spring this on you, but Albert and I just thought, since Layla's famous for finding people their dream homes . . ." She trailed off and looked hopefully at the two of them.

Sebastian raised a dark brow at Layla. She couldn't read his expression because she was too busy managing her own. Helping Sebastian go house hunting was not a good idea. Even if he was a perfect gentleman, it was going to force her to be in close contact with him, which only meant more opportunities to feel flustered and unsettled. Layla hated feeling that way, and he seemed to bring that emotion out of her every time they met. Like right now, for instance.

He waited patiently for her to respond.

Layla opened her mouth, but nothing came out. She was having trouble forming her thoughts.

Mindy looked pleadingly at Layla.

"I don't want to cause problems," Sebastian said. "Especially at this time of year when everyone's so busy. Why don't I head back into the office tomorrow and maybe Albert can set me up with someone—"

"No," Layla blurted. "I can help you."

"Are you sure?" he asked. "It's okay if you don't have time."

"It's totally fine," Layla said, nodding vigorously to prove just how totally okay it was. She could suck it up. It wasn't that big of a deal. If anything, this was good because she could use the commission if she ended up making another sale. The extra money would be a nice windfall, and she could use it to help her mom with bills. "Why don't I go over your requirements this week, and we can set up a time to view some of the available listings?"

He studied her for a moment, and Layla got the feeling he could see her internal struggle. She threw up a shield by giving him a cheery smile. She could tell he wasn't exactly buying it, but he'd play along.

"All right," he finally said.

Mindy erupted with sighs of relief and encouraging chatter about Layla's ability to match people with great homes. As she and Sebastian talked, Layla focused on Charlie and the kids petting the barn animals.

Her friend Kat stood in the midst of all the animals with her cousins Emma and Juliette. They made a striking trio, with Kat's bright red hair, Emma's curly blond ringlets, and Juliette's long dark locks. Even though they all looked so different, there was a distinct bond between them that couldn't be denied. They were more than just friends; they were family.

Kat caught Layla's attention and waved. Then she saw Sebastian standing beside Layla, and Kat gave her The Look. The one with the wiggly eyebrows.

Layla pressed her lips together and shook her head. *Solid no, Kat. So, don't even start with me.*

Kat just gave her a sassy grin and crossed her arms, as if to say, *We'll see.* Emma and Juliette watched their silent interaction with amused interest.

A strange breeze suddenly swirled through the crowd, caressing Layla's cheeks, kissing her eyelashes, and stirring the fine hair near her temples. She brushed the back of her neck and glanced around, no idea what she was searching for. She had the oddest feeling that change was in the air. Yet another reason to feel unsettled. Change was unpredictable, and unless Layla had carefully planned and orchestrated it herself, she didn't care for it.

She sipped her hot buttered rum, letting the sweet, rich flavor soothe her senses as she stole a glance at the man standing beside her. He was deep in conversation with Mindy, but his cerulean gaze flicked to hers, as if a part of him was tuned in to an invisible wavelength that only they shared. The wind blew a wave of dark hair across his handsome face, and Layla had the sudden urge to reach out and brush it back. *What the heck?* She peered into her drink, wondering just how much rum was in it.

When Charlie called out to them, Layla was grateful for the distraction. Anything to keep her attention from Sebastian and the pull he seemed to have on her. That odd breeze swirled around them again, but this time she ignored it.

Chapter Five

The following week flew by, and Layla still hadn't called Sebastian to discuss house hunting. Every time she planned to do it, she found reasons to keep her from making contact. It wasn't that she was being a coward. Of course that wasn't it. She was just really busy. At least, that's what she told herself until Wednesday evening rolled around. By then, it couldn't be avoided.

Layla stretched out on her sofa with Toonces purring in her lap. It had only taken the kitten two days to settle in to her routine. A couple of times, he'd tried to run outside when she opened the door, but now he seemed pretty content just to lord over her house. She had to admit it was nice having the little furball around. He snuggled deeper as she scratched him behind the ears.

When her cell phone rang, she reached for it and answered, careful not to disturb him.

"Hey, foster mama," Kat said on the other end. "How's our little guy doing?"

"He thinks he owns the place. This morning I woke

to him meowing in my face. He wouldn't stop until I dragged myself to the kitchen to feed him."

"I knew you guys would get along," Kat said happily. "Listen, I have a favor to ask."

"If you want me to take in one of your miniature donkeys, the answer's no. I don't care how many margaritas you ply me with."

"Nothing like that," Kat assured her. "I need you to run Toonces by the veterinary clinic tomorrow morning because he's due for a couple of shots. I made the appointment weeks ago and totally forgot."

Layla stood up, letting the kitten slide onto the sofa cushion like a melted marshmallow. "Oh, I don't think I—"

"It should only take twenty minutes, tops."

Layla bit back a groan. Sebastian would probably be there. "Why can't your favors be easy ones, like 'Hey, can I use your mixer?' or 'Can I borrow a cup of sugar?'"

"Please," Kat scoffed. "As if I'd bother baking when I've got Emma in my family."

"True," Layla had to admit. "I ate one of her cinnamon rolls last Sunday, and I swear I heard angels singing."

"So do you think you could swing it? I'm sorry to ask, but I have puppy training class to teach at that time."

Layla eyed the kitten, who was slumped in a boneless, purring heap on her sofa. She wasn't sure she was ready to see Sebastian. But would she ever feel ready? Besides, Toonces needed shots, and she was responsible for him, even if it was only for a little while.

As if he knew he was the subject of her thoughts, the kitten lifted his head and meowed at her.

She leaned over and smoothed the fur above his nose.

He nudged her hand, then licked it with his sand-paper tongue.

Fine, then. Gripping her cell phone tighter, Layla made her decision. "Yeah, okay. I'll take him in." It wouldn't be a problem because she had to talk to Sebastian anyway. Maybe this was a good thing. They'd talk about kitten stuff, then maybe set up a meeting time to look at houses, and that would be that. Purely professional, all business. If there was one thing Layla knew how to do, it was stick to business.

The veterinary clinic on Griffin Road was a bright white building with cheerful blue trim and two sepa-rate entrances, one for dogs and one for cats. When Layla pushed through the cat entrance with her pet carrier, the waiting room surprised her. She'd never owned a pet, so she hadn't been to a veterinary office before, but she fully expected it to look like a sterile doctor's office. Instead, the place had a cheerful, homey vibe. Two dark leather couches sat at one end of the room, flanked by turquoise end tables and potted plants. Framed art prints of cats added warmth and color to the walls, and a large ficus tree stood in the window. White twinkling lights were strung along the ceiling for the holidays, and colorful ornaments hung at different lengths above the reception desk.

"Good morning," a young woman called in a chip-per voice. She appeared to be in her early thirties, with wavy blond hair and a perfunctory smile. "You must be Dr. Harrington's eight o'clock appointment." She held out a pen with a plastic poinsettia flower taped to the end. "If you can just sign in, someone will be right with you."

Layla filled out the form, then settled on the end of the sofa. A few minutes later a vet tech in leopard print scrubs greeted them and showed them into a small room. Layla was scrutinizing a feline anatomy poster on the wall when she heard the door open.

Even though she was prepared to see Sebastian, it still knocked the wind out of her. Why did he have to be so perfectly handsome? Was it too much to ask for just one tiny flaw? In slacks and a collared shirt, he should've looked boring and basic, but no. Not him. Instead, with the sleeves rolled up his strong, tanned forearms, he looked like he could be lounging at a seaside resort in a magazine ad.

"Layla." His voice slid over her like a velvety caress, and he gave her a warm smile. "It's good to see you again."

"I've been meaning to call you about viewing some houses," she began in a clipped, professional tone. Because that was her. No-nonsense and all business. "It's just been a very busy week, but this weekend might be good if you want to view some properties."

"I'm ready whenever you have time," he assured her. Then he nodded to the pet carrier. "And who do we have here?"

"This is one of the kittens from the Daisy Meadows Pet Rescue." She opened the carrier door.

Toonces poked his nose out, and Sebastian's attention went straight to the gray tabby. He coaxed him onto the table, his large, powerful hands gently soothing the tiny cat. Layla suddenly wondered what it would be like to have Sebastian's big, strong hands on her. *Oh, what the?* Cheeks burning, she cleared her throat and focused on the kitten, who was now purring loudly.

"You're a good one, aren't you?" Sebastian said softly. "Of course you are."

Watching him interact with the kitten made Layla's heart feel all loose and fluttery, like the tail of a kite caught in the breeze. Sebastian was so tall and muscular, but the way he handled his tiny patient with such attention and gentleness proved how much he cared. She could tell just by looking at him that he loved his job. "When did you know you wanted to become a veterinarian?"

Sebastian glanced up at her in surprise.

D'oh! She gave herself a mental kick. Why did she ask him such a personal question? She was supposed to keep things strictly business. Where did that plan go? Apparently out the window after Dr. McHottie started sweet-talking a kitten.

"Sorry," she said quickly. "I know you're pressed for time, so you don't have to answer that."

"No, I don't mind." He eyed the ceiling for a moment, as if he was trying to collect his thoughts. "When I was a kid, I grew up with a West Highland terrier. He was a great dog, and even when he got old, he never lost that playful side he'd had as a puppy. One day after he'd just turned thirteen, I was out riding my bike and I witnessed him getting hit by a car. He died shortly after that, and I remember wishing I could've helped save him. I think that's the first time I decided I wanted to be a vet. And I've always loved animals, so . . ." He trailed off like the outcome was inevitable.

"I'm sorry that happened," she said quietly. "That couldn't have been easy with you being so young."

"It was tough. But I knew he'd lived a long, happy

life, so that helped. I think that's one of the toughest lessons for us, though. Welcoming a pet into your family, loving them, and then knowing you're going to have to say good-bye someday. Their lifespans are just so much shorter than ours; it doesn't seem fair. But that's one of the reasons I like what I do. If I can help pets be as healthy as possible, then I can influence the years they do have in a positive way."

Everything he just said struck her right through the heart. His reasons were so noble and beautiful. Now she just wanted to drop her chin into her hands and ask him a zillion more questions. She struggled for something to say to get her back on track. "Um, I wouldn't know firsthand, but I think I get what you mean. We didn't have a lot of space when I was growing up, and my mom was always at work, so I just never had any pets."

His expression held so much understanding and compassion, it made Layla uncomfortable. She looked away quickly. He already knew she'd grown up dirt poor. He and his buddies had even once teased her about it. Mercilessly. If he felt pity for her, she didn't care to see it. That part of her life was over and done. She rarely ever talked about her childhood. It surprised her that she did it now, and to him of all people.

He nodded to the kitten. "So is he your first pet?"

"Oh, he's not mine. I'm only fostering him until he gets a permanent home."

He gave her a dubious look. "Does he know that? Because in my experience, once a cat chooses you, that's it. They own you."

Layla reached out to pet the kitten, her hand gliding from his head all the way to the tip of his tail. Her fingers brushed Sebastian's, and she jerked her hand away.

If he noticed, he didn't show it. "What's his name?"

"Toonces." She wrinkled her nose. "I know it's weird."

"It's great," he said with a grin. "Like the driving cat."

"You've heard of it?"

"Of course. Didn't you ever watch old *SNL* reruns when you were a kid?"

Layla shrugged. She wasn't about to tell him she didn't grow up with a TV. Living in a run-down trailer meant making do without most things other kids took for granted. "I guess I just never saw that one."

"Well, we'll have to fix that, won't we?"

A tiny voice inside her liked that he said "we," but she shut it down fast. What was she thinking? It's not like she and Sebastian were going to get together for a TV marathon with popcorn and snuggly throw blankets. That would just be so . . . boring. She stole a quick glance at him. Now he was pulling out a stethoscope and listening to the kitten's heartbeat, which didn't make him look like a super-sexy doctor at all. Nope. No superpowers there. She tore her gaze away. *Boring.*

"All right." He lifted Toonces and held him close. "He appears to be in good health, so I'll just give him his shots and he'll be good to go."

Ten minutes later, Sebastian placed the kitten gently back in the pet carrier.

Layla reached out to pet Toonces one last time, her hand accidentally brushing across Sebastian's. This time, he clasped his warm hand over hers. He turned and gazed down at her with those fathomless, ocean-blue eyes. They were standing so close, his raw, masculine presence seemed stronger now that his attention was focused only on her. For the space of several heartbeats, neither of them said a word, but entire conversations seemed to ricochet in the air between them.

Suddenly, to her utter surprise, he bent his head and stole a kiss like a thief in the night. It was too brief and fleeting, and it ended far too fast. He'd barely brushed his lips against hers before it was over, and she didn't even get enough time to enjoy it.

Sebastian blinked, as though he'd even surprised himself. He let go of her hand and stepped away from the pet carrier, leaving a chill where his skin had warmed hers. Then he casually crossed his arms and leaned against the table. It irked her that he looked so completely at ease, because she felt like she was coming apart at the seams. "So, do you want to go out on Saturday?"

She froze. Go *out*? Like on a date? She spun away and pretended to dig through her purse to buy some time. There were a hundred reasons why that wasn't a good idea. Their messed-up history aside, he wasn't the type of guy she could ever just date lightly. Something told her if she fell in with Sebastian, there'd be no easy way to fall out. And Layla steered clear of those relationships. She liked her life calm, predictable, and easily managed. Guys like him didn't fit into that category. Before she had a chance to formulate a response, he derailed her train of thought.

"There are some houses I've checked out online," he continued. "If you have time on Saturday, I'd like to take a look at them."

Ah . . . He was talking about business. Her cheeks flushed at the ridiculous notion she'd been entertaining. Of course he wasn't asking her out on a date.

What's a tiny kiss between acquaintances? Apparently, not much.

"Yes," she said quickly. "I have time around ten o'clock in the morning on Saturday. Why don't you send me the listings you're interested in, and I'll arrange it?"

By the time she dropped Toonces off at her house later that morning, she'd thrown herself into work mode, convincing herself that all thoughts of Dr. McHottie were long forgotten. It wasn't until later that night in bed, staring at the ceiling, her mind began to wander back to their meeting at the veterinary clinic. Sebastian's warm smile and genuine concern for animals. His smooth, deep voice when he asked her to go out on Saturday. Those large, capable hands holding the kitten against his broad chest. *That barely-there kiss.* What the heck was that about?

Layla heaved a sigh and rolled onto her side. Here in the dark, she couldn't lie to herself any longer. She was developing an affliction—some kind of weird infatuation—for the very person who'd once made her life miserable. When she first ran into him at the Daisy Meadows Pet Rescue, her initial instincts had told her to run far and fast. But now that she was getting to know him again, it seemed like the old version of Sebastian no longer existed. A part of her wanted so much to believe he'd changed, but she'd never been a fool about men, and she couldn't start now.

Layla squeezed her eyes shut and willed herself to go to sleep.

Toonces jumped onto the bed and curled his little body next to hers. She absently reached out and stroked his soft fur. She had a few days to prepare for her Saturday meeting with Sebastian, and that was more than enough time to get her head on straight.

"More than enough time to get over this problem," she said to Toonces, who regarded her with an expression far too wise for his age. He twitched a whisker and glanced away.

"Thanks for the vote of confidence," she mumbled.

Chapter Six

The weather on Saturday morning was a shocking surprise. Layla trudged to her kitchen to make coffee, stopping to gape at the view through her living room window. The entire backyard was blanketed in over a foot of snow. An overnight storm had come in, and she'd slept right through it.

Pouring herself a bowl of cereal, she scrolled through her phone to check the weather forecast. Even more snow was expected over the next few days. She'd need to see about getting some chains for her tires. The wheels on her sedan were partially buried already. She couldn't remember the last time it had snowed this much. Heck, she didn't even have a proper snow shovel.

Layla finished her cereal and was just about to dial Sebastian to call off their meeting when her phone rang. *Speak of the devil.* She answered, still looking out at her sorry excuse for a driveway. "Hi, I was just about to call you."

"How's your driving situation?" Sebastian asked.

"It's not looking good. They've probably salted the main road, but I don't have a snow shovel to dig my car out of the snow. I think I'll need to reschedule our outing today."

"That won't be necessary. I can pick you up. My truck handles well in these conditions." Of course it did. Because in addition to being a hot veterinarian who looked like he should be snuggling kittens on a yacht in GQ magazine, he was also one of those "big strong men" her mother rambled on about. The kind who kept the serial killers from hiding out under the bed. The kind who went on off-road adventures in big manly trucks and probably chopped firewood in his spare time. Shirtless.

"Does that work for you?" he asked.

Um, yes. She took a gulp of coffee, burning her tongue and swearing under her breath.

"Layla?"

She jolted back to reality. "Yes! That'll work. Unless you'd rather schedule for another day?" Clearly, she still hadn't gotten her head on straight about him, so part of her wanted to postpone their meeting. But she couldn't think of a good enough reason to turn him down. They were planning to go to the same houses, after all, so it made sense to drive together.

"The weather report says it's going to stay this way until after Christmas, so I figure today's as good a day as any."

She gave him her address, got off the phone, and zoomed through her morning routine. If she spent a little extra time on her hair and makeup, that was just because it was important to look her best for work. At least, that's what she pretended as she added an extra layer of mascara and shimmied on her best skinny jeans. At ten fifteen, her doorbell rang.

The moment she opened it, she felt a rush of excitement at the sight of Sebastian on her doorstep. He was casually dressed in dark jeans and a navy fleece jacket, and his hair was delightfully wind-blown and messy, flopping over his eyes in a way that made him look wild and carefree.

"Hey," he said with a crooked smile.

She tried for mock annoyance, but her silly grin ruined it. "You're late."

"For a good reason." He glanced behind him. "It took a little longer than I expected."

Layla peered outside and gasped. Sebastian's truck was parked in front of her house with a snow shovel leaning against the truck bed. Her entire driveway was now cleared, and her car was no longer buried in snow.

"Oh, my God." She stared at him with a mixture of awe and appreciation. "I can't believe you did that."

He stuffed his hands into his pockets and shrugged. "I lived near Lake Tahoe for a while, so I'm used to this kind of weather—Whoa, there!"

A gray ball of fur streaked past Layla's feet, making a run for the front yard.

Sebastian lunged and scooped up Toonces just before he reached the porch steps.

"Thank you." Layla pressed a hand to her chest in relief. "That's the second time he's tried to run outside. He's determined to see what's out here."

Sebastian scratched the kitten under the chin. "Well, you know what they say about cats and curiosity."

"Exactly. Which is why I can't have him running off in this crazy weather. Thanks for grabbing him. And for shoveling the driveway. It would've taken me hours with my garden shovel."

"No problem," he said easily, still petting the now

purring Toonces, who looked right at home snuggled up under Sebastian's chin.

Layla realized she was staring at the two of them, and she gave herself a mental shake. "Come inside. I'll get you a cup of coffee for the road." Layla swung the door wide, and he stepped into her house. Her. House. Sebastian Harrington was in her home! If someone had told her this would happen a month ago, she'd have laughed in their face.

He left his snow-covered boots in the foyer, then followed her down the hall to the living room.

As Layla poured him a cup of coffee in the kitchen, she suddenly felt nervous about him being there. Even though she didn't have many visitors, she'd worked hard to make her place beautiful and comfortable, mixing upscale, traditional furniture pieces with a few eclectic accents. The main part of her house had an open floor plan, with a bar-height granite counter separating the kitchen from the living room. The lounge area had a comfy gray couch with cheerful throw pillows, two overstuffed armchairs, and a lively patterned rug. A large, colorful painting of the Seattle skyline hung on the wall, and the rest of the room was decorated in peaceful shades of blue and green.

"It's really nice in here," Sebastian said as he wandered around the living room. "But then it's yours, so I wouldn't have expected anything less."

Layla blushed at his casual compliment. It made her feel all warm and glowy inside, and she turned to the sink so he couldn't see how much it affected her. As much as she hated to admit it, his approval mattered.

He stopped in front of the console table, pausing to look at her collection of sparkling crystal frames. "No pictures in them?"

"Oh." She waved a hand self-consciously and handed him the coffee in a to-go mug. "I haven't had a chance to fill those yet. One of these days I'll get around to it."

He nodded, as if that was totally acceptable. Her mom and friends teased her about it all the time, so Layla was surprised he didn't think it was weird.

"It's a great collection," he said. "Even without the photos. It reminds me of you."

She tilted her head. "Why?"

Sebastian took a drink of coffee, studying the frames.

Layla came up beside him, twisting her hands together nervously. She felt like he was studying *her*.

"Because they're bright and sparkling and . . . hopeful," he finally said. "Like they're fine exactly as they are because they know something amazing is in store for them."

Somehow, he'd managed to put into words exactly how she felt about her collection, and she couldn't have said it better. It was the exact reason she loved to collect them. All the colors, and the way the crystals caught the light, just reminded her that someday she was going to fill them with memories as beautiful as the frames were. She managed a nervous laugh. "They're just frames."

"They suit you." He turned toward her, softly brushing a lock of hair back from her face. "Beautiful and a little mysterious."

Layla's mouth opened on a tiny exhale. She was floored. If he'd taken his coffee mug and clunked her over the head with it, she couldn't have been more stunned. It was too lovely and poetic. Is that really what he thought of her?

His gaze dropped to her mouth, and she felt it like a sensual lick against her lips. Her heart took off on a wild sprint. He was going to kiss her again, and she wanted it. Not just because he set her blood on fire when he looked at her like that. He seemed to understand her, to see right into the heart of her, when most people didn't.

Mreeow! Toonces trotted into the room, demanding attention.

Layla couldn't decide if she was grateful for the distraction or not. She walked into the kitchen and busied herself with the dishes until her heartbeat returned to normal.

Toonces wound his body around her ankles, meowing loudly.

"Okay, you greedy beast." Layla reached for the jar of cat treats on the counter, pulled one out, and dropped it into his food dish. "Even though you've already had one this morning."

"Your cat has you trained," Sebastian teased.

"He's not really mine, remember? I'm just fostering him."

"Uh-huh. And where does he sleep?"

"In my bed," Layla grumbled. "This morning he woke me up because he was wrapped around my head like a pair of headphones, purring in stereo."

"Like I said." He pointed at Toonces. "That's your cat."

"Come on," she said, shaking her head. "Let's get out of here and go find you a house."

They made their way outside to Sebastian's truck. He took her hand as they navigated around the patches of ice and knee-deep snow. She wondered if he was just trying to be helpful, or if he wanted to touch her the same way she found herself wanting to touch him.

He opened the passenger door for her, and Layla felt loose-limbed and jittery as she climbed inside. The interior smelled like leather and the same alluring scent that seemed to cling to his clothes and hair. Or was it his skin? He smelled like crisp evergreens and fresh air. Like a winter stroll through the woods on a bright, sunny day. Heat rose up the back of her neck. *Get it together, Layla!* What next? Giggling like a giddy teenager? She dug through her tote bag so she wouldn't have to look at him.

"There's another house I'd like to take a look at," he said as they pulled onto the main road. "It's right down this street, actually."

Layla clenched the straps of her tote bag tightly in her hands. She knew exactly which house he was talking about, because it's the one Mindy had mentioned earlier. The big, gorgeous place only a block away from Layla's house. It had been on the market for months because it was a luxury property, and the owners had just finished doing some renovations. But it was too close for comfort. "I think they might be doing some work on it," Layla said, hoping to throw him off. "But I'll check with the sellers next week. In the meantime, let's go to the house near Front Street first."

For the next two hours, Layla took him through the properties on her list. After the first house, she'd slipped into easy conversation with him, and by the time they made it to the third house, she'd completely forgotten to be nervous.

"This master bedroom has a gorgeous view of the backyard." She walked to the window overlooking a pool and an outdoor kitchen for entertaining. Then she searched the property map in her hand. "There's supposedly a swing set too, but I don't see it."

He came to stand beside her. "Maybe it's in the side yard."

"No, I checked. There are just a couple of vegetable planters out there. But still," she said brightly, turning on the sales charm, "I think this place has a lot of potential. It's great for entertaining, and depending on your future needs, it could really grow with you."

He cocked an eyebrow. "My future needs?"

"You know, for if you have a family. There are four bedrooms on this floor, plus a huge bonus room above the garage that's big enough for a playroom, or extra bunk beds, or whatever you might need."

He took the property map and nodded, his brow creasing in concentration. "Huh."

She looked at the map. "What is it?"

"Oh, I'm just trying to find the outdoor barracks." His mouth twitched. "You know, for my army of future children you seem to think I'll be having."

She rolled her eyes and took the page back. "Come on, there's one last room we haven't seen."

When Layla opened the door to the last room at the end of the hall, she blinked in confusion. "This is kind of weird."

Sebastian walked into the room behind her and whistled low. "That's a lot of red."

It really was. The entire room was like a punch to the face. She tried to think of a way to spin it in a positive light, but it wasn't easy. "I mean, red paint is okay in some cases. A nice brick shade for a kitchen or dining room, for example. But this . . ." She trailed off, frowning. The walls were padded channels of deep red velvet, and the shag carpet was the same shade of crimson. Decorative metal rings were anchored along the wall at intervals. "Maybe this was a movie room."

Sebastian eyed the mirrored ceiling where a large hook hung from the center beam. There was an odd look on his face, and he pressed his lips together like he was trying not to laugh. "I think it was definitely used for entertainment."

Layla checked the property layout, but the room was labeled as a bedroom, just like the others. She shrugged and shook her head. "Oh, well. People and their decorating choices. I remember one house where the owners painted all the interior walls Pepto-Bismol pink, with Hello Kitty murals in the dining room and kitchen." She walked to the window and peered out of the black blinds. "Anyway, this room has a great view of the side yard, and good closet space."

Sebastian tried to open the closet, but the handle was stuck. "I think it's locked."

She turned from the window. "No, all rooms should be fully accessible. Here, let me see." He stepped aside, and Layla gripped the handle, jiggling it. Nothing happened. "It shouldn't be locked," she muttered, twisting it harder. Suddenly the handle came off in her hand with a loud *pop*. "Well, great. That's just poorly secured. I'm sure they can reattach it." She used her finger to open the latch, swinging the door wide. "I'll just make a note of—"

The overstuffed closet exploded around her, and a body came flying out.

Layla let out an ear-piercing shriek and fell to the floor as a box tumbled after her.

"Layla!" Sebastian grabbed the body and ripped it off her, sending it flying across the room. But instead of rushing to help her up, he paused. Warm laughter bubbled up from deep in his chest.

She scowled. The "body" was a blow-up doll with painted yellow hair and a gaping mouth. Blinking, Layla focused on the contents of the closet surrounding her on the carpet. Heaps of skimpy costumes. A leather whip. Colorful rubber sex toys. Fur handcuffs. A wooden paddle in the shape of a heart. She jerked, struggling to get up, but her legs were tangled in a strappy leather contraption with long black ropes and metal hooks.

Sebastian held out his hand, and she grabbed it like a lifeline.

He lifted her off the floor as she shoved at the weird strappy thing, kicking it away like it was on fire. "What the ever-living hell?" she muttered.

His eyes twinkled with laughter. "I think you found the swing set."

Back in the car, Layla took a deep breath and let it out slowly, acutely aware that she was still red with embarrassment. She could practically feel the tips of her ears burning. Why couldn't it have been a pink closet full of Hello Kitty stuff? She cleared her throat and stared out at the snow blanketing the fields. "Well, that was fun. I'll be sure to tell the seller's agent to add kinky sex dungeon to the list of features."

"Hey, every pot has a lid," he said with a chuckle. "Some people might consider it a big plus. You sure you weren't just saving the best for last?"

She cringed and shifted on her seat.

"Come on, don't be embarrassed. It's not that big a deal."

"I'm just annoyed they didn't do a better job staging the house," she said, checking her nail polish. "I'm not embarrassed, Dr. Harrington."

"You sure?" He looked like he found her highly amusing. "Because you just called me Dr. Harrington, and if I remember correctly, we've kissed. So I think that puts us on a first-name basis with each other by now, don't you?"

Layla flushed, her heart bumping around in her rib cage at the mention of that elusive kiss they'd shared.

"People sometimes revert to formality when they're trying to distance themselves," he said conversationally.

"Oh, is that so?" She pulled a folder from her tote bag and pretended to flip through it. "I didn't realize you had a doctorate in psychology, *Seb*."

He tipped his head back and laughed, and she had to grit her teeth because it looked really good on him, with the playful spark in his eyes and the dimples. He was just too handsome for his own good. Or hers.

"Are you done?" she said, pulling out a pen. "Because I'm about to cross that house off your list of potential homes."

"All right, I'm done," he said. "And now I'm starving. It's past noon. How are you at cooking lunch?"

"Terrible. I've got Hot Pockets and wine."

Sebastian made a face. "You can cross that off your list, too. I've got a better idea."

Somehow, twenty minutes later, Layla found herself following Sebastian into the Pine Cove Country Club, a sparkling establishment with a palatial lobby and sweeping views of the golf course. When she was younger, she used to dream of belonging there, convinced that the country club was the epitome of success. Layla's mom used to tease her about it, reminding her that the elegant members with their fancy cars and seemingly perfect lives were just people with problems like everyone else. But Layla had been so sure if she could just get there, her life would be complete, and her problems would be solved. Now, she had absolutely no desire to golf, and even though she could probably afford a membership, she wasn't interested in one. The establishment had an air of old money and elitism, and while it didn't bother Layla anymore, it never failed to remind her of who she used to be—the poor kid from the trailer park who didn't belong.

The restaurant hostess seated them near a bay window in the main dining room, and Layla wondered how she'd arrived at this point in her day. When she woke up that morning, she'd planned to make her meeting with Sebastian as short as possible. And now, she was sitting across from him in a beautiful restaurant about to have lunch. With the crisp linen napkins, soft music, and sparkling chandeliers overhead, it almost felt romantic. Like they were on a date. She gripped her hands nervously in her lap as the server came to pour water and discuss the menu.

After they'd made their selections, Sebastian leaned back in his chair, regarding her thoughtfully. The silence stretched out for far too long.

She searched for something to say. "You golf?"

"Only when forced," he said. "My dad used to make me when I was a kid, but I never got into it. Give me a good hockey or football game any day."

"Yet, you're a member here," she said pointedly. "At a golf course."

"My family has a lifetime membership." Right. Of

course they did. If Layla remembered correctly, his parents had donated large sums of money to local establishments, and his mom used to be on the fund-raising committee. "I just come here for the pool and restaurant." He said it so casually, like it was nothing. Earlier when they were looking at houses, she'd almost forgotten that he was one of the shiny, happy people who'd been born with a silver spoon in his mouth. Or in his case, an entire shovel. His family was *loaded*.

The server arrived to pour wine and deliver a basket of bread. She sipped the cool, crisp chardonnay, hoping it would help ease her frazzled nerves.

He sat back in his chair, the picture of relaxed ease. "So. What are your plans for the holiday?"

"You're looking at it."

His mouth curved up. "Drink wine all day?"

She gave him a look. "I'll be working, as usual."

"No traditional holiday plans with your parents or trips to the tropics with your boyfriend?" He asked it so casually, in the same offhand way a person might ask about the weather.

"I'm not currently in a relationship," she told him. "Hence, that thing that happened between us you mentioned earlier."

An amused quirk of his lips. "Thing?"

"You know." She waved her hand. "The barely-there kiss."

"Barely there," he mused, watching her carefully.

She shrugged, feigning nonchalance. "It was over before it began, so I'm not sure it even counts."

His eyes glittered with heat and challenge. "I'll keep that in mind."

He was looking at her as if he had plans for next

time. Big, sexy plans. She fought to keep her voice casual. "Anyway, I don't do that whole Norman Rockwell holiday thing. My traditions are a little less conventional."

"Such as?" he prodded.

She looked away in exasperation. "You're very curious today."

"Hey, I'm just trying to understand you."

"Why?" She tilted her head and searched his face. If she was going to answer personal questions for him, then she deserved a decent answer.

"Because I think you're brilliant and beautiful, and you fascinate me. You always have."

Okay, that was way more than decent. It was wholly unexpected. He thought she was brilliant! And beautiful! Butterflies were cartwheeling in her stomach. This business meeting was going off the rails. The train had jumped the track, and she was now heading into unknown territory. She should be freaking out, except she wasn't.

His voice dropped a little lower. "I just really want to know you better."

Wow. She took another sip of wine, feeling as floaty as a helium balloon bouncing on a string. "There's not much to tell. It's only my mom and me during Christmas, so we just hang out at her place and watch *Miracle on 34th Street*. Neither of us are great cooks, so Mom usually makes a Twinkie tower, I bake a pizza, and we play Scrabble." She shrugged self-consciously. "That's about it."

He nodded, like everything she said was perfectly normal. "No brothers or sisters?"

She shook her head. "No dad, either. My mom was single, and he was never in the picture. She told me he was a silver-tongued devil who'd built her castles in the air and then forgot to bring a ladder. Nothing he ever promised came true, and eventually he left her before I was born. She worked all the time, two or three jobs just to make ends meet, so things were . . . different for us." Their trailer with the leaky roof was too small for a Christmas tree, and Layla remembered warming her hands over the candle on the Formica table and pretending it was a fireplace like in the storybooks. "Roast turkeys and homemade cookies weren't really a tradition in our house." She took another sip of wine, rubbing her fingernail over a crease in the tablecloth. "But no matter how bad it was, my mom always took Christmas day off to be with me. She'd bring home Twinkies and we'd just play games or go next door and watch movies with the neighbors." It was so weird. She should've felt uncomfortable sharing that with him, but for some reason, she didn't feel judged. Like she'd realized earlier that day, Sebastian was easy to talk to. "I bet that's pretty pathetic compared to your family."

"Not at all." His face grew pensive. "You'd be surprised how terrible the holidays could be in the Harrington household."

Layla's mouth opened in surprise.

"Don't get me wrong," he rushed to add. "My sister's family's great. She and her husband and my nephew Charlie have included me in everything since I moved back here. They've even managed to convince me that having a family is something to look forward to, which is a miracle, considering the way I grew up."

"The way you grew up?" That made no sense. He was raised in the lap of luxury, with doting parents who were pillars of the community. He had a sister and pets and trips to Disneyland. A giant house in a gated community and pool parties and a Porsche for his sixteenth birthday. "But your family was—"

"Things weren't as perfect as they seemed, Layla. My parents fought all the time. At first, when my sister and I were little, we were blissfully unaware of how bad things were getting, and we were distracted by the lies. But by the time we got older, we learned just how bad their relationship had become. The image they portrayed to the public was just a shiny veneer. A façade. The only thing they ever agreed on was keeping up appearances. But behind closed doors, they hated each other. They were so bitter, it got to the point where they used me and my sister to communicate because they refused to talk to each other. And if they ever did stoop that low, it often ended in screaming fits and broken dishes." He shook his head in disgust. "The tension in our house was unbearable. By the time I was a teenager, I spent more time sleeping over at friends' houses than I did at home."

Layla stared at him in disbelief. "But you were so . . ."

"Go ahead and say it. I was an ass."

"Well, you weren't my favorite person," Layla admitted.

Regret flashed across his face. "Layla—"

She briefly closed her eyes, unwilling to go there. "What I was going to say is that you seemed so confident and outgoing. You seemed to have everything you wanted."

He lifted his wineglass. "*Seemed.*" Took a drink and set it down. "But in reality, I was miserable. My home life was hell."

"I had no idea all that was going on with you," she said, shocked.

"No one did. I guess I was trying hard to keep up

appearances, too. But, hey." He gave her a smile that didn't reach his eyes. "I learned from the best."

"I'm sorry you went through that," she said softly.

"I'm sorry for a lot of things." He reached out and took her hand in both of his. So many emotions flickered across his face, Layla had to lower her gaze. It was too much to try to decipher, and she was still trying to process everything he'd told her.

The server brought their food out, and Layla reluctantly pulled her hand away. She immediately missed the warmth of his skin on hers. Through some kind of mutual, silent agreement, their conversation turned to work and easier topics. Layla poked at her grilled salmon, mulling over everything he'd revealed. All this time, she'd judged him for being such an arrogant jerk in high school, and while it didn't excuse his behavior, it made her understand him a little better.

"Where've you been living before this, and what made you decide to move back to Pine Cove Island?" she asked after the server had cleared their plates.

"When my parents went through their messy divorce, it tore our family apart. I ended up moving to the San Francisco Bay Area with my dad, and my sister stayed with my mom. It was tough because my sister and I didn't want to be separated, but we were caught up in their custody battle and they made us choose. Anyway, I ended up going to UC Davis for veterinary school, much to my father's disappointment. I think he never quite accepted my chosen profession, and always acted like it was just a passing phase. In his opinion, being a veterinarian was a huge step down from running the family business. Last year he had a stroke, and after he recovered, he decided to retire. He also decided it was time for me to step in and oversee our vineyards in

Napa and spearhead our family's wine company. But that's not what I wanted to do. I never wanted to follow in his footsteps. When I turned him down and told him I'd already made the decision to move back here where my sister lives, he was furious. He saw it as a form of betrayal and disowned me."

Layla sucked in a breath. She couldn't imagine how painful that must've been for him. Even through all the hard times, she and her mother had always remained close. She couldn't imagine what it would feel like to be disowned by someone you love. "I'm sorry."

"Don't be," he said with conviction. "My father was a bitter man, and he was unhappy for a lot of reasons. Walking away from him was one of the most difficult things I've ever done, but I've made my peace with it, and I'm grateful to be here. If anything, it's a relief to be out from under his constant judgment, and I love being near my sister and her family."

"Then I'm glad you're here," Layla said, meaning it. As surprising as it was, she enjoyed his company more than she ever would've believed possible. Guilt stabbed at her for how she'd judged him when he'd first arrived back on the island. She knew, better than anybody, how life's difficulties could shape a person, and she was genuinely glad to see him happy. Who knew?

"Now all I need is to find a good house, and I've no doubt you'll help me do that."

Layla suddenly thought about the house near hers. It met all his requirements. Open floor plan, huge, fenced backyard, and lots of room to grow. She'd be wrong to steer him away from that just because of some old grudge she'd held against him when they were kids.

She leaned forward and rested her elbows on the

table. "Look, I'm going to set up an appointment for you to view that house on my street. After talking with you today about your requirements, I think it might be perfect for you."

"It doesn't have any padded rooms, does it?"

"Not a single one."

"Okay, then." He gave her a warm, secret smile that made her feel all melty inside. "I'm glad you came to lunch with me today. We should do it again soon." Was he asking her out? Maybe he just meant they should go to lunch again the next time she took him house hunting.

"There's a restaurant called Haven on the waterfront that everyone keeps talking about. Would you like to go to dinner tomorrow night?"

Layla bit her bottom lip. He was really asking her out this time. Like, on a *date* date. Her toes curled in her boots, and she tried to find her voice. Now that she'd shared some of her past with him, she felt even more connected than before. Something had definitely shifted between them. It astonished her how much she wanted to be with him. As a general rule, she didn't date clients. Mixing business with pleasure was way too messy. Everyone knew that. But this felt different. She wanted the adventure with him.

"Okay," she said shyly. "That sounds good."

The server came back with dessert menus, and she politely listened to the man discuss things like warm apple crisp and chocolate ganache with pistachio brittle. Normally, she'd be all ears for that deliciousness, but she couldn't concentrate. The whole time, she was thinking about Sebastian and how the idea of going out with him made her heart swell with hope and optimism. Maybe this could actually work. Maybe they'd be really good together and they could make some beautiful memories to fill those empty picture frames.

Layla suddenly felt light-headed and nervous. Declining dessert, she scraped her chair back and stood. "I'll be right back." She walked out of the lavish dining room and across the lobby toward the bar. A harpist played peaceful holiday music beside a brightly lit Christmas tree, but Layla wasn't feeling peaceful at all. She pushed into the ladies' room and washed her hands, checked her hair, then stared at herself in the mirror. This was crazy. Sebastian Harrington just asked her out, and she said yes. A giddy thrill coursed through her body, and she felt a giggle bubbling up inside her.

Back in the lobby, she was making her way past the bar when someone grabbed her wrist. "Hold on, there, lady."

Layla spun around to see Keith Miller, Sebastian's old high school buddy, swaying in front of her with a glass of scotch. His ruddy complexion and glassy eyes made it clear he'd been drinking for a while.

Her stomach churned with distaste, and she yanked her hand away.

"I know you." His words were slurred. "You're little Layla Gentry."

She kept her face carefully blank. "Sorry, I don't remember you." She turned to go, but he quickly blocked her path. For a pudgy drunk guy, he moved fast.

"Sure you do," he insisted. "I'm The Hammer, remember? I played football for Pine Cove High." He looked incredibly proud of himself, like that one fact was his defining moment in life.

"Huh." She made a show of trying, but failing, to remember. "It doesn't ring a bell."

Keith began to laugh in that drunken way where

everything's funny. "We used to call you Sebastian's little mouse. Mousy Little Layla." His bleary gaze traveled down her body, stumbling over her chest, her hips, then stalling back at her chest again. "Damn, girl. You've changed."

"Funny," she said in a bored voice. "You haven't."

"Aha! So you do remember me." He cackled and polished off his drink. "Look here, doll. Get me another of these, will you?" He held his glass toward her and hollered to a man behind him. "Hey, Bobby, what're you drinking?"

"I don't work here," Layla said through gritted teeth. Typical of someone like Keith to just assume she was there to serve him. He'd always been a snob.

"No?" He blinked in surprise, hiccupped, then glanced forlornly into his empty glass. "What are you doing here at the club, then?"

"Having lunch." She spotted Sebastian heading out of the restaurant.

"You're having lunch *here*?" Keith chuckled under his breath. "Moving up in the world, eh, Mousy? Or trying, anyway."

She wasn't even going to dignify that with a response. Instead, she turned away and headed toward the lobby entrance. Arrogant jerk! Clearly, not everyone changed. Keith had been one of Sebastian's cronies, and he was one of the worst people she knew.

"Seb, my man!" Keith called, catching Sebastian on his way toward Layla. "Come and have a drink with us." The man named Bobby, and a couple of other people, including a pretty woman with bleached blond hair, surrounded Sebastian on all sides. He'd always had that magnetic charm that attracted a crowd.

Layla watched as he talked to them for a few moments. The blond woman laid a hand on Sebastian's arm, then tiptoed to whisper in his ear. He said something, and she tipped her head back and let out a tinkling laugh. Layla's skin felt hot and prickly. She crossed her arms and balled her hands into fists, mad at herself. She shouldn't waste her time being jealous. Sure, she'd agreed to go to dinner with him, but it's not like they were dating exclusively.

Keith gestured to Layla and said something to Sebastian under his breath, slapping him on the back. Sebastian shook his head, and Keith snickered. The blond woman glanced at Layla with cool, assessing eyes that showed barely concealed disapproval.

Like an avalanche, all Layla's old insecurities came rushing back to haunt her. She turned away and stared out at the circular driveway. What was she even doing here? She had much better things to do than stand around being insulted by idiots who no longer mattered in her life. She'd almost forgotten how catty they could be. The giddy, happy feeling she'd had earlier was now eclipsed by the realization that Sebastian was still a part of that crowd. No matter how much he seemed to have changed, it was clear he was completely at ease hanging out with Keith "The Hammer" Miller and the others.

Layla scrolled through her phone, silently berating herself. It made her mad that she could come so far, but one snarky comment had the power to make her feel like Mousy Little Layla all over again. She glared out at the snow-covered driveway, trying not to remember how insecure she used to be, with her shabby life and her shiny dreams.

"Sorry about that," Sebastian said, coming up behind her. "I got roped into Keith trying to reminisce about old times."

"Fun," Layla said lightly.

"About as much fun as a root canal."

She ignored his joke, because she couldn't be sure if he was just saying that to make her feel better. On the way home, Layla wasn't up for conversation. Instead, she pretended to read through e-mails.

When he finally pulled into her driveway, she was already opening the door to hop out.

He laid a hand lightly on her arm. "Layla, wait."

She pasted a polite smile on her face and turned back, gently pulling her arm away.

A crease formed between his brows. "Is everything okay?"

"Of course." Her voice sounded a little high-pitched and not very convincing. She tried again. "I just have a lot of work to do, so I have to run."

"Can I call you later?"

"Why don't I just contact the sellers and shoot you an e-mail about that house?" she said brightly. "Hopefully, we can set up a time to view it soon."

"I meant, can I call you about dinner tomorrow."

"Oh, I'm sorry. I just remembered I have plans tomorrow night." Plans to watch Netflix and polish off the rest of the New York Super Fudge Chunk ice cream in the freezer, but he didn't need to know that.

Sebastian's forehead creased in confusion. Before he could respond, she hopped out of his truck, her boots squelching in the snow. "Thanks again for lunch!" Then she ran across her yard and up the porch steps.

Once inside, she leaned against her door and slid to the floor in a heap. She unlaced her snow-covered boots and leaned her head back, thumping it lightly against the door. "What was I thinking?" she said out loud. She hadn't been thinking, that was the problem. All this time, she'd just let herself *feel*, and whenever she was around him, things just felt right. The way he looked at her like she was the most important person in the world. The small things he did to show her he cared. The way he held her hand and the ease with which they shared their personal stories. She'd never felt that connection with anyone before, and it hurt knowing that she wasn't going to have it anymore. No matter how wonderful the idea was, logically, their worlds just didn't fit together.

Toonces came trotting into the foyer, already purring.

"I almost got pulled into Sebastian Harrington's tractor beam," she muttered.

He rubbed his furry head against her shin.

"But don't worry, I wised up just in time." A heavy mantle of disappointment settled over her like a dark storm cloud. She tried to shrug it off, but it was impossible. *Moving up in the world, eh, Mousy? Or trying, anyway.* Keith's sneering face and cruel words echoed in her head, and she pulled her knees up, hugging them to her chest. Why did it hurt? His mental growth was clearly stunted, so his rude comment shouldn't have bothered her as much as it did. She squeezed her eyes shut, but the image of Sebastian smiling down at the blond woman invaded her mind.

Enough. No more dwelling on something of no consequence. She and Sebastian needed to go back to just having a working relationship, and that's where it would stay. Rising with determination, she walked into the kitchen, made some hot tea, then settled onto the couch with her kitten. *Her* kitten. She smiled down at him. Over the past several days, she'd really gotten used to having him around. It was nice to have someone at home, looking forward to seeing her each day. Maybe she should adopt him. The more she thought about it, the more she felt it was the right thing to do.

"What do you think, Toonces?" She smoothed his soft fur. "Just you and me?"

He nudged her hand with his nose, purring louder.

Layla was beginning to feel better. "See? Who needs a man like him when I've got a fabulous cat like you?"

She reached for her phone on the end table, then dialed Kat's number to give her the good news.

Chapter Seven

Sebastian watched his nephew barreling down the hill behind his sister's house on Sunday afternoon. Charlie's squeal of delight rang out over the snowy meadow, his little face barely visible underneath his knit cap and fleece scarf. It was impossible not to be affected by the kid's sheer happiness, and once again, Sebastian found himself glad he came to visit.

Ever since his outing with Layla the day before, he'd been unable to shake his disappointment that something had gone wrong. She'd been so relaxed and easy to talk to at lunch. He'd been thrilled that she felt comfortable enough to open up to him about her past. When she'd made the comment about that "barely-there" kiss they'd shared, he'd wanted to reach across the table and drag her into his lap so he could kiss her thoroughly, over and over, until there was no doubt in her mind that it "counted." Ever since that moment back at the veterinary office, her soft mouth and sweet sigh had been all he could think about. And at the country club, when she'd agreed to go to dinner with him, he'd been elated. But then he'd run into Keith and some old acquaintances at the bar, and from that moment on, she'd grown quiet and distant. When she later backed out of their dinner plans, he'd felt it like a gut punch.

He shook his head and shoved his hands into the pockets of his fleece jacket. Maybe seeing Keith at the bar reminded Layla of old times. If that was the case, then it was no wonder she wanted to distance herself. Who could blame her? Keith, Bobby, and his clingy sister with the name Sebastian could never remember, had been their usual snarky, gossipy selves yesterday. Amazing how being gone for so many years put things into perspective. Those people Sebastian remembered from his past—the so-called friends he'd spent so much time with back then—were not even people he cared to be in the same room with now.

"Hey, broody." His sister came to stand beside him, nudging his shoulder with hers. "How come you're not sledding with your poor neglected nephew?" She handed him a cup of eggnog.

Sebastian took the drink and slung his arm over her shoulders. "Olivia, that kid is the least neglected child I know. He told me Santa Claus is visiting him for dinner tonight."

"It's true," she admitted. "Dan won a raffle at his office, so one of his coworkers is stopping by dressed as Santa." Dan was Olivia's devoted husband, and he was one of those dads who jumped headfirst into every festive occasion. He was the kind of dad who draped the house in glowing holiday lights every year and left reindeer prints in the snow for Charlie to discover on Christmas morning. In Sebastian's opinion, his sister could not have married a better man.

They watched Charlie's sled come to a stop at the bottom of the hill, snow flying in a wide arc as he hooted with glee. "Uncle Seb, watch me go again! And then let's go inside for more sugar cookies."

"Spoiled," Sebastian mumbled, waving enthusiastically at Charlie.

"Rotten," Olivia said with a laugh. "Dan would give him the world, if he could. He's such a sucker for Charlie's puppy dog eyes."

Sebastian squeezed her shoulder. "In that case, I understand he'll be getting a pet giraffe on Christmas morning. That should be interesting."

"Not happening," she declared. "But Charlie did ask for something else, and I'm happy to report he'll be getting that." She placed her hand on her belly and gave her brother a knowing smile.

Sebastian's face lit up. "Really?"

She nodded, her cheeks turning pink with happiness. "I'm three months along, so Charlie will have to wait a bit for his baby brother or sister, but we're going to tell him on Christmas morning."

Sebastian set his cup of eggnog on a tree stump, then threw his arms around her in a bear hug. She giggled as he spun her in a circle.

"I'm so happy for you, Sis," he said. "I think that's the best news I've heard all year."

"Now, what about you?" She crossed her arms in that bossy way she used to do when they were younger, and even though she was wearing rubber boots and standing in over a foot of snow, Sebastian could almost see her foot tapping impatiently.

"Happy to report I'm not pregnant," he announced.

She gave him a playful shove. "I can tell something's on your mind. You've got that faraway look you get whenever you're trying to solve a problem."

He picked up his eggnog and focused on Charlie's

little body lugging his sled to the top of the hill. "It's nothing."

"Uh-huh. Does this 'nothing' have a name?"

He stared off in the distance. "She does."

"Ah." His sister nodded. "Layla Gentry. You always did have a thing for her, even back during your wild child days."

"I asked her out to dinner tonight, but she turned me down." His chest tightened in disappointment. Saying it out loud made it somehow more real.

"So, now what are you going to do?"

"I don't know." If Layla didn't want to go out with him, he needed to respect that. He just wished he didn't feel so bleak and hopeless about it. "Nothing, I guess."

She gave him a long-suffering look. "Right. Clearly, you've tried hard. I think you should just give up and go live in the woods like a hermit."

"What do you expect me to do?" he asked in exasperation. "It's not like I can go *thunk* her over the head with a club and drag her back to my man cave."

"Yeah, that would be disastrous. Especially because I've seen your man cave, and the glowing neon beer sign is enough to scare even the bravest of souls."

"I got rid of that years ago."

"Then there may be hope for you yet," she said. "Maybe you could do something nice for her. Give her something she needs or help her in some way, to show her that you care."

"That's just it," he said. "Layla's such a powerhouse. She's taken care of herself for so long, I can't think of a single reason she'd need or want me."

"Then think of a kind gesture . . ."

He let out a frustrated breath. "If I can't come up with something, I'm screwed."

"Totally. Because it's not like you have your charm and good looks to fall back on. Hey, if she doesn't find you handsome, she should at least find you handy, right?" Olivia smacked him on the shoulder, cracking herself up.

He frowned. "How many of those eggnogs have you had?"

"Mom," Charlie called, dragging his sled toward them. "I think I need cookies."

"Okay. Bring your sled to the garage, and then we'll go inside and have hot chocolate, too."

Charlie did a fist pump and whooped with joy. His childlike enthusiasm was contagious, and they couldn't help laughing as he zipped toward the house.

"Spoiled," Sebastian said, shaking his head.

"Rotten," she agreed.

Chapter Eight

Layla sat at her office desk on Christmas Eve, staring glumly at the swirling snow outside. The place was quiet for three o'clock in the afternoon, as most people had either taken the day off or gone home early. She hadn't really needed to go to work, but she chose to get caught up on some paperwork to keep busy until she drove to her mom's place later that evening.

She sighed and leaned back in her chair, wishing she wasn't feeling so gloomy. Ever since her outing with Sebastian on Saturday, she couldn't seem to get him out of her head, but that was nothing new. After that brief kiss back at the veterinary clinic, all she could think about was doing it again. And again. When he'd asked her out on a date, she'd been so thrilled. But then that schmuck of a Hammer had cracked down on her, and she'd had to endure his snide comments. It threw her off, and she was still reeling. Deep down, Layla knew it wasn't Sebastian's fault. But that whole incident had reminded her of how she was always on the outside looking in. So what did she do? She shut down and ran home to hide and lick her wounds. Typical Layla. Never let anyone get too close.

She sighed again, leaning her head back to stare at the ceiling.

"Do you have asthma?" Jay's mischievous face popped over the wall of her cubicle. "Because I swear I can hear you sighing from across the office."

Layla rubbed her face and started closing down her computer. "I'm just tired. What are you still doing here? I thought everyone went home early."

Jay came around the corner and leaned against her desk. His boyish face now only held faint yellow traces of bruising from his adventures at the sports bar. With his red silk tie and crisply pressed shirt, he was back to his normal, dapper self. "I'm heading out now. My parents are having Christmas Eve dinner at their house tonight, and my brother's introducing his new mail order bride to the family."

She stopped with her laptop halfway into her bag. "Mail order bride?"

"Not really. I just say that to imply it's the only way he could get a woman to marry him. It gets him all riled up, and that makes it worth it."

"You're kind of evil. You know that, right?"

"Sibling rivalry," he said, grinning. "It's a thing. Oh, Mindy called the office earlier. Her dad's on his way to a full recovery, but she's going to stay in Kansas for another couple of weeks to help her mom."

"Good," Layla said with relief. "I'm glad he's going to be okay." She slung her laptop bag over her shoulder. "And now I'd better get on the road. My mom's expecting me this evening, although . . ." She glanced out the window. In the last ten minutes, the snow started falling heavily, and the wind had really picked up.

"The weather forecast says there's another big storm coming in," Jay said. "Come on, let's get out of here. I've got a brother to harass. Christmas cheer awaits!"

Layla pulled up to her house, wishing she'd bought a snow shovel at the hardware store. Even though Sebastian had shoveled the driveway a couple of days ago, the snow was piling up fast again, and the roads were becoming difficult to navigate.

She opened her door, dropped her keys on the hall table, and checked her phone for the zillionth time. No missed calls. No texts. Her heart squeezed when she thought of Sebastian. Of course he wouldn't be contacting her on Christmas Eve. Why would he? It's not like they were together. *But you could be,* a quiet voice inside her said. *You want to be.* She sighed and kicked off her shoes. She did want something more with him, but it would take a huge leap of faith on her part, and she wasn't sure she was brave enough to go there.

"Toonces," Layla sang out, heading to the kitchen to fix a cup of tea. "Shouldn't you be nagging me for dinner, right about now?" Odd that he didn't come running. Normally he greeted her at the door demanding attention. She turned her electric kettle on, then walked down the hall to her bedroom. After checking her bathroom, the hall bathroom, and her home office in the spare room, she still hadn't found him. A prickle of unease skittered down her spine.

She called for him again, clicking her tongue on the roof of her mouth a few times, but he still didn't come. In her mind, she tried to backtrack through her morning routine that day. She'd been in such a hurry to leave, but she'd forgotten her purse in the kitchen.

"Oh, no," Layla whispered. She remembered leaving the front door cracked open when she ran back to get her purse. If he'd slipped past her this morning, he could be outside somewhere right now, lost or hurt. *Or worse.*

Heart thumping in fear, she bolted to the front door, shoved her feet into a pair of rubber rain boots, and ran out into the yard.

"Toonces!" she cried, searching under the porch. "Where are you?" She circled the perimeter of her house, checking the foundation bushes and the hedges lining the front walkway. She wanted to look for paw prints in the snow, but it was futile. Any tracks he might've made would've been covered up within minutes because of the heavy snowfall.

Layla stumbled again through her yard, trying to figure out where a kitten would go to hide. He was so small. Fragile. What were the odds that a little cat could survive in this weather for several hours? Tears pricked the corners of her eyes as she called out to him. This was her fault for not paying closer attention. Guilt ate away at her as she circled the house once more. With no further luck, she unlatched her back gate and ran down the trail leading to the beach.

Halfway down, she came to an abrupt halt, panic seizing her throat so hard she gasped for breath. A lump of gray fur lay barely visible, wedged underneath an outcropping of rock. *Toonces.* It looked like he'd crawled under the rock to get out of the wind. Layla ripped her jacket off and ran to the bedraggled kitten. His body was cold and limp, and he wasn't responsive. Dread bubbled up inside her at the thought he might already be . . .

"Come on," Layla choked out. "Please wake up." *Please be okay. Please don't let me be the reason you don't get to grow up and have a happy life.* She squeezed her eyes shut. It was her responsibility to look out for him, and she'd let him slip away. How could she have been so careless?

Gently wrapping him in her jacket, she clutched him to her chest and ran back up the trail to the house.

In the foyer, she peeked at the bundled kitten in her arms. He still wasn't responding, but when she lay her hand on his cold body, his eyes flicked open for the briefest of moments. "Toonces." *Thank God.* But just how hurt was he? Was he dying? She had no idea what he needed or how to save him, but she knew exactly who could.

Layla's remorse stunned her into action. She didn't even think; she just grabbed her purse and keys, ran to her car, and pulled out onto the main road with Toonces bundled in her lap. She turned the windshield wipers on, wishing she could speed down the highway, but the snow was falling so hard and fast, she had to slow down for safety's sake. Heart slamming like a loose shutter in a windstorm, she turned the heater up full blast. If nothing else, at least she could keep him warm until she got to the veterinary clinic.

Call Sebastian. That's what she needed to do. She searched for her phone, but it was inside her purse, which she'd mindlessly tossed into the back seat in her haste to leave. Layla thumped her fist on the steering wheel and kept driving, praying the veterinary clinic would still be open. It was late afternoon on Christmas Eve, but medical offices still held regular business hours, didn't they?

Seventeen excruciating minutes later, Layla pulled into the Pine Cove Veterinary Clinic. The howling wind and snow was now blowing so fiercely, the parking lot looked like a white wasteland. No cars were parked in front of the clinic, but she refused to lose hope. Her car tires spun in place, but she gunned the engine and finally managed to pull up to the side of the building.

Layla gripped the bundled kitten tightly in her arms, grabbed her purse from the back seat, and ran the rest of the way. *Please, please be open.* She reached the front door and shoved at the handle, but the door was locked. With a cry of frustration, she banged on the glass, peering inside. No one was sitting at the reception desk.

"Is anyone in there?" She banged on the door over and over again. "I need help!" What if she was too late and no one came? Fear had her digging in her purse for her phone. She was just about to dial Sebastian's number when movement inside caught her attention.

"Sebastian," Layla cried, spotting him near the back door.

His handsome face lit with surprise, then he quickly strode to the front door and unlocked it. "Layla, what are you doing here? I was just closing up and heading out."

"I need your help," she choked out.

He glanced out at the empty parking lot. "How did you get here? There's a huge storm rolling in."

"I drove my car."

He looked shocked. "In this weather?"

"I had to." She swallowed the lump in her throat and held out her bundled jacket. "It's Toonces. He got past me this morning when I was leaving my house, and he's been outside all day. I found him down by the beach trail. He's not moving, and I don't know what to do." Her chest heaved, and she closed her eyes, fighting back the tears that had been threatening to fall for the past hour.

Sebastian's expression softened with concern, and he quickly took the kitten from her. "Come on. Let's take him in the back and have a look at him."

Layla followed Sebastian down the hall and through a door she hadn't noticed on her last visit. It led to a sterile room with a metal operating table in the center, huge magnifying lights overhead, and medical equipment lining the walls. Something about it seemed so cold and uninviting, which only added to her guilt. Toonces belonged back at home, cozy in her bed or snuggled on her lap. It seemed wrong for his small, motionless body to be on a cold metal table.

The minutes ticked by agonizingly slowly, and by the time Sebastian had given Toonces a thorough examination, Layla felt like a tightly stretched rubber band, about to snap at any moment.

Sebastian gave her a reassuring smile. "He has a moderate case of hypothermia, but no signs of broken bones or other problems. He must've found a good spot to hide out from the weather, because it's a miracle he isn't worse off than this. I'd say he's used up one of his nine lives today."

Layla anxiously twisted her hands together. "He's going to be okay, though, right?"

"Yes." He placed a warm hand on her shoulder. "I believe he'll make a full recovery."

"Thank God," Layla breathed.

Sebastian turned his full attention back to the kitten. He administered some fluids to keep him hydrated and wrapped him with a heating pad and blankets to help slowly raise his body temperature. Layla felt an ongoing buzz of adoration and respect as she watched Sebastian work. He was so caring and gentle, it made her want to throw her arms around him in gratitude. She couldn't have dreamed up a better hero to come to the rescue.

When the treatment was finally finished, Sebastian tucked Toonces into a cushioned pet bed surrounded by warm blankets. Then he placed the bed into a small crate and carried him out into the waiting room.

Layla made a quick call to her mother explaining the emergency, promising to visit tomorrow if the weather died down.

"But honey, what are you going to do if the storm doesn't let up soon?" her mother asked worriedly. "You could be trapped in that veterinary clinic alone and starving for days."

Layla rolled her eyes. "Mom, are you hearing yourself? I'm not lost in the Amazon jungle. The clinic is literally a mile away from the town hall, and we have full power here so we won't freeze to death."

"We?" Her mom paused, and Layla could practically hear her mother's gears spinning. "Who exactly is there with you? Please tell me you've got a big strong man there who can look out for you."

Layla glanced at Sebastian as he peered out of the front window. "Yes, Mom. That's exactly what I've got here."

Her mother gasped, then erupted into a hailstorm of rapid-fire questions. Was he single? Was he good-looking? Was he financially stable? Did he like to play board games?

"Yes, yes, yes, and I don't know," Layla answered in exasperation.

Sebastian turned and gave her a questioning look.

"Listen, Mom, I have to go. I'll call you as soon as the weather changes. Okay-bye-I-love-you!" She kissed the air and ended the call, flopping back onto the sofa.

He took a seat beside her, stretching out his long legs.

The storm raged outside, and the parking lot was no longer visible through the front window. All she could see was a blizzard of white. It was so fitting with her current mood, because her emotions were all over the place. A lot of it could be attributed to almost losing Toonces, but part of it was also because of Sebastian. As much as she'd tried to pretend there was nothing between them, she couldn't anymore. Her feelings for him had become too strong to ignore.

"I think we're going to be stuck here for a while," he said. "My truck's parked out back, but even though it can handle snow, there's no road visibility right now."

"I'm so sorry. You're trapped here on Christmas Eve because of me."

He smiled softly, and Layla shivered with physical awareness. He was close enough that she could see dark streaks of gray in his sapphire eyes.

"I'm glad I was able to help," he said. "And I'm happy to be here with you."

She bit her bottom lip. He was just so . . . everything. Kind. Genuine. Sincere. "Did you have big plans tonight?"

He tipped his head back, relaxing into the sofa. "I was supposed to head to my sister's house for dinner. My nephew Charlie was planning to make a gingerbread house, and I got roped into bringing the candy for it."

"Oh." Guilt pricked her skin. "I guess I messed up your family's plans, too."

"Not at all. The last thing Charlie needs is more candy," he said with a chuckle. "And I've already called my sister and told her to carry on without me. Luckily, she has my dog with her today, so I won't have to worry about him." His expression grew more serious, and he turned to face her. "Layla, listen. I'm glad you came. I wanted to talk to you about last Saturday. I can't help but think I must've done something to upset you."

"You didn't," she said quickly. "You were fine. It was me, really. I just . . . I started thinking about the past, and it started to get to me."

Pain flashed across his face. "I'm sorry. I never meant for any of that to happen."

She swallowed hard as memories came flooding back. She'd been a freshman in high school. A dirt-poor, quiet kid who tried very hard to fade into the background. She always felt like she had to put on a façade so people wouldn't know how hard she and her mom struggled to make ends meet. One of her friends, Jordan, was from the wrong side of the tracks, like her. They often talked about the future and how they planned to better their circumstances. Layla was a good student, and she was fiercely determined to someday have a better life. Getting her mother and herself out of that trailer park was all she ever thought about. The idea of having food on the table every day and a comfortable place to call home was the epitome of success, in her mind.

Sebastian had been a few years older than she was, so he shouldn't have paid her any attention, but for some reason, no matter how hard she tried to be invisible, he noticed her. Layla found it disconcerting, though sometimes a little flattering, that he went out of his way to say hello. He was cocky and arrogant, and not always very nice to people. She'd heard the rumors about his wild parties and his many girlfriends, so it hadn't made sense to her that he'd singled her out.

"You used to confuse me so much," she admitted.

"One day you'd try to talk to me, and you were almost nice. Then another day you'd look away like you couldn't stand the sight of me. I could never figure out why."

"Layla." He shook his head, then scrubbed his face with both hands. "Forgive me. I was an idiot back then. I was drawn to you, but I was too immature to handle everything I was feeling."

"Drawn to me?" Warmth crept up the back of her neck, scorching across her cheeks.

"Yes. You were this fascinating, mysterious person, and I couldn't figure you out. I knew you didn't have a lot, and your home life was difficult. People talked. Gossiped. I had an idea of how hard it must've been for you. And yet, there you were, every day . . ." He looked at her like she was the most precious, amazing thing he'd ever seen. "This exquisite, sparkling girl with so much optimism. You'd float through the sea of kids in the halls and you always stood out to me. You always seemed so happy and *hopeful*. Like you just knew better things were in store for you, and your life was going to someday be as beautiful as you were."

Layla blinked in surprise. She had no idea he'd thought that much about her at all.

"And there I was," he continued. "The kid who supposedly had it all. On the outside my life was just one big happy party, but inside I was miserable. My parents' marriage was falling apart, and the fighting was so bad I sometimes wanted to just run away." He shifted on the sofa, leaning a bit closer. "I wanted so badly to know you, to know your secret. I wanted to figure out what made you tick, figure out how you could be so content, when you had it so much worse than I did. Sometimes I felt like I was getting close to you, and I'd talk to you and think it was possible we could be friends. Maybe even more than friends. And then things at home would blow up and the bitterness would settle in, and I'd see your glowing face at school and I'd . . . resent you. I'd be mad that you'd somehow figured out how to be happy, when I couldn't seem to do it." He briefly squeezed his eyes shut. "Like I said, I was an idiot."

"That day of the fight," Layla said. "I thought you were coming to talk to me. You seemed like you were in a good mood."

He ran a hand across the back of his neck, his expression etched with regret. "Believe it or not, I was in a good mood that day. Things had quieted down at home, and I'd just been accepted to college. I was feeling hopeful, for once. And then I saw you sitting outside waiting for the bus. I finally got up the nerve to go sit beside you, but that's when Keith Miller and the rest of my so-called friends showed up. They'd already started drinking from a flask one of them snuck into the school, so they were even more obnoxious than usual. All of them were stupid drunk. Did you know that?"

She shook her head.

"Anyway, Keith's mom was friends with mine, and he'd just found out some news about my family. He came walking up to me, punched me on the shoulder, and said, 'Bummer about your parents getting a divorce, man. Come on, let's go do tequila shots.' The guys all joked like it was no big deal. But I was floored. I didn't even know my parents were getting a divorce. My mom had told Keith's mom before she'd even told me. So I stood there and played it off like it was nothing, even though I was boiling mad on the inside." A muscle ticked in his jaw. "And that's when they saw you sitting there."

Layla stared down at her hands in her lap. She twisted her fingers together, remembering the shame she'd felt when his friends started making fun of her hand-me-down clothes. Her shoes with the broken heel she'd glued back together that never stayed stuck. Her sweater with the hole in the sleeve that kept unraveling. Her thrift-store backpack with someone else's last name scribbled out in Sharpie pen. Keith grabbed her backpack and tossed it in the garbage can. They jeered and said it was a piece of trash. Then they said she was trailer trash, and she belonged in the garbage, too.

The memory of her intense shame welled up inside her. And the whole time his friends were bothering her, Sebastian just stood there glowering at the ground. His hands had been balled into fists, and she'd never seen him so angry. It was like his body was there, but his mind was far away. He never said a thing to defend her. Then one of the guys dragged the trash can over to her and acted like he was going to toss her in, too. That's when Sebastian snapped out of his daze. He started yelling at the kid. But by then, her friend Jordan saw what was happening. He came running up to defend her.

Jordan started punching Sebastian and his friends, and soon a full-fledged fight had broken out in front of the school. Kids started gathering around making bets and cheering. At one point, Sebastian shoved Jordan off him and Jordan fell against a broken chain-link fence. A piece of jagged wire gouged Jordan in the face, and he still had a visible scar from it.

Layla just remembered standing there in horror as one of her only friends bled on the pavement. By then, the principal came out to break things up, and he hauled the boys off to his office. When she finally pulled her backpack out of the garbage, she'd been so embarrassed with all those kids standing around watching her. She'd never forget that silent bus ride home. How she'd clutched her filthy backpack to her chest like a security blanket, crushed beneath everyone's stares and whispers about her being that "trash girl."

Days later in the hall, Sebastian had tried to approach her, but she never spoke to him again. If she saw him walking toward her, she turned and went the other way. Once, she found a note in her locker, a hastily scribbled apology from him, but she never acknowledged it.

"I'm so sorry for how things escalated that day." His voice was thick with remorse. "It's bothered me for longer than you know."

She glanced up at him, and for the first time she felt nothing but complete forgiveness and understanding. He'd been a troubled person back then, just like her. She reached out and placed her hand lightly on his. "You don't have to apologize to me anymore. I understand."

"About last Saturday. If I said or did something to bring those bad memories back, I swear I never meant to."

"It wasn't anything you did," she assured him. "Keith stopped me in the bar and made a comment that wasn't very kind, that's all."

He gripped her hand. "What did he say to you?"

Layla shrugged. "He just alluded to the fact that I didn't belong there."

Sebastian's expression darkened like a storm cloud covering the moon. His jaw was granite-hard, and he looked like he was about to breathe fire. "I'm going to strangle that smug assho—"

"You can't," Layla interrupted with a laugh.

"Sure, I can," he said with a scowl. "Knowing Keith, I'll probably have to get in line. I can't be the only person who wants to take him out."

"That may be true, but you're a doctor. Didn't you have to swear an oath to do no harm, or something?"

He narrowed his eyes. "The Veterinarian's Oath is for animals."

"Well, there you go. Keith's a total pig, so it has to apply."

Sebastian's mouth curved into a reluctant smile.

Like morning mist in sunlight, the past seemed to fade away, and all that mattered was them sharing this moment, together. Layla's stomach growled, and she laughed. "I'm starving. What time is it?"

He checked his phone. "Past dinnertime. I'll go see if there's anything in the kitchen. Don't get your hopes up. I think our office manager emptied it before she went home for the holiday."

A few minutes later, Sebastian came back with two coffee mugs, a carton of orange juice, and a bottle of champagne. "Here are our choices. We can have dog treats from the jar on the reception desk, or we can use this champagne someone gave me for Christmas to make rustic mimosas."

"Rustic?"

He held up the two coffee mugs. "We don't have proper champagne flutes in the office."

"Ah." She pretended to consider the options. "What flavor are the dog treats?"

"*Nope* flavored. Trust me."

"All right, fine. Let's be festive and go for the rustic mimosas."

He sat beside her and popped open the champagne.

She splashed orange juice into the mugs and held them out, giggling when he hastily poured the champagne and it spilled over the edges.

"A toast." Sebastian lifted his mug. It was hot pink with glittery paw prints. "To healthy cats."

"And to us," she said shyly, holding up her zebra-striped mug. She felt as if she were standing on the precipice of something big. The old Layla might've retreated, taken a step back to play it safe. But she didn't want to be that person anymore. Not with him. "To letting go of the past," she added.

"To us," he said huskily. "And to new beginnings."

She clunked her mug against his and took a sip. In spite of the unconventional delivery, the mimosa was one of the best she'd ever tasted. Maybe it was the Veuve Clicquot champagne. Or the fancy organic orange juice he'd swiped from the office fridge. She peeked at Sebastian from beneath her lashes. Or maybe it was just because of him.

Very slowly, he bent his head and took her mouth in a soft, searching kiss. Layla felt her limbs go weak, and her eyelids fluttered shut until all she could do was revel in the firm pressure and the slow, building heat. There was nothing "barely there" about this kiss. This one *counted.*

When he finally pulled away, Layla took a shaky breath, her insides curling with pleasure and the desire for more. A whole lot more.

His gaze lingered on her mouth, then slowly lifted to meet her eyes. "Magic mistletoe."

"What?" she breathed.

He pointed above them.

She tipped her head back and saw a sprig of mistletoe

hanging from the ceiling. "Juliette Holloway's specialty," she said softly.

"Yes. I'm not sure who hung it here, but it's all over the island. It seems like every time I walk into a place, someone shouts out the warning."

Layla smiled and repeated what she'd heard people say all season long. "If you linger beneath what hangs above, you'll soon be falling . . ." She trailed off and glanced shyly at Sebastian. She suddenly felt happy and giddy and hopeful. Was she falling in love? This had to be what it felt like. A joyful voice inside her sang out with a resounding, *Yes!*

"Do you know, I don't believe I ever stood a chance," he said quietly. "I think I loved you back when I was too young to know how to show it. And then when I saw you again for the first time in years, I realized my feelings for you hadn't changed."

Layla felt as if she were floating near the ceiling. He *loved* her. "I don't know if I believe in any of that Holloway magic."

All at once, he looked vulnerable and a little bit nervous.

She placed her hand on his chest and leaned closer, feeling the steady thump of his heart. "But I do know I believe in *you.*"

Relief then joy flashed across his face. He took his mimosa with hers and set them on the end table. "Layla." He said her name like it was a prayer as he gathered her into his arms. "I'm afraid I love you. Can you handle it?"

Happiness unfurled inside her, and she slid her hands up his chest, winding them around his neck. "Only if you can handle me loving you back. I might make a muddle of things, because I've never done it before."

"We'll figure it out together then," he whispered, lowering his head to kiss her again.

It started out softly at first. Just the barest pressure of his lips against hers, a tentative, unspoken question that Layla very much wanted to answer. She tilted her head and parted her lips, intoxicated by the sweet, heady taste of him, bright and tart from champagne, hot and decadent like her deepest fantasies. He slid one arm around the small of her back, the other hand sliding up under her hair to cradle the back of her head as he deepened the kiss.

She could practically feel the tension straining in his powerful muscles, like a low-level hum of electricity he was struggling to hold back. She'd seen him work with delicate, fragile creatures, and she knew how careful he could be, but she didn't want that. She wanted him to lose control, because with every passing second, she was losing control, too, and it didn't feel like falling at all.

It felt like flying.

It was exhilarating, and she wanted more of it. She tightened her arms around him and pressed closer, reveling in the feel of his hard body, the rasp of light stubble on his jaw, the woodsy, evergreen scent of him surrounding her until she could no longer think. On and on they kissed as the storm raged outside, but inside, neither of them noticed. They were swept up in a storm of their own making, and they wouldn't have wanted it any other way.

Chapter Nine

The fairy lights strung throughout Haven restaurant on the waterfront gave the entire establishment a sparkling, otherworldly glow. Gold and silver balloons with shiny ribbons hung from the ceiling, and round tables with crisp black tablecloths surrounded the large dance floor. Three-tiered platters of cupcakes and chocolate truffles were centered on each table, along with party hats, noisemakers, and scattered confetti. Layla couldn't have imagined a better venue for a New Year's Eve party.

"There you are," Kat said over a mouthful of cupcake. "It's almost midnight, and I've barely had a chance to talk to you. I swear, every time I've seen you tonight, you and Sebastian have been wrapped around each other." She made air quotes. "Dancing."

"What?" Layla said innocently. "We have been dancing."

Kat rolled her eyes and licked frosting off her finger. "If, by that, you mean barely swaying, mostly smooching, and whispering sweet nothings to each other? Then, yeah. You guys are excellent dancers. Practically professionals."

Layla blushed, but laughter bubbled up in her chest. "I've been kind of distracted."

The past week had been a whirlwind of exciting, new experiences. After the storm died down early on Christmas morning, Sebastian had driven Layla home where they'd made breakfast together. Then they'd spent the day visiting Layla's mom, who was ecstatic that her daughter had finally gone and found herself a "big strong man." Later, they'd visited his sister's family. Charlie had been thrilled to see Layla, and happy to see she was no longer doing penance at the North Pole for her naughty boots. In the week following the snowstorm, Layla and Sebastian had spent every moment they could together, and for the first time ever, Layla truly felt her life was complete. She used to think she had everything she needed, but now she realized she'd been missing the most important thing of all: *love.*

"I get it," Kat said with a happy sigh. "I mean, look at them. Could our guys be any hotter?"

Sebastian and Kat's husband, Jordan, stood on the other side of the room, deep in conversation. Both of them were striking in their tuxedos and black ties, but even though they were dressed to the nines, there was a bit of a wild aura about them that wasn't conventional. Kat's husband had unruly hair and odd golden eyes that made him look a bit like a wolf in sheep's clothing. And Sebastian . . . well. He was the epitome of tall, dark, and wickedly handsome, and when he gave her that secret smile—like the one he was giving her now—it made her insides swirl with delicious anticipation. He was like her own personal hurricane, sweeping her up and spinning her into a whirlwind of desire until she felt like she was losing control. And the best part? She didn't even care. She *liked* it.

Sebastian continued speaking to Jordan, but he didn't take his eyes off her. His glossy dark hair looked a little windblown, and Layla knew it was because she'd been running her hands through it all night. She grinned when Jordan said something and slapped Sebastian on the back. Clearly, Jordan held no grudge against him, even though Jordan was the kid who'd flown to her rescue all those years ago during that fight. Apparently, the past really was water under the bridge, and Layla was glad of it.

"Ladies and gentlemen," the DJ's voice boomed through the microphone. "It's almost time for the countdown!"

Excited cheers and happy laughter swelled through the crowd as people scattered to find their friends and loved ones.

Sebastian strode across the room toward Layla, not stopping until he'd wrapped his arms around her and pulled her close. "Hello, beautiful," he murmured, nuzzling her neck.

She shivered with pleasure and brushed her lips against his.

"Smile for the camera," someone sang out.

They turned and posed for the photographer, who snapped their picture and quickly moved on to the next group of revelers.

"That photo's going into one of my empty frames," Layla announced. "It's time I started filling those up with good memories."

Sebastian gave her a tight squeeze. "I wholeheartedly agree."

A waiter passed by with a tray of champagne, and Sebastian took two glasses, handed one to Layla, then led her outside onto the patio overlooking the marina.

Brightly lit sailboats and yachts dotted the harbor like sparkling jewels in the darkness.

An unexpected breeze swirled in off the ocean, surrounding them both and ruffling their hair, kissing their eyelashes and brushing over their skin. Layla shivered, once again filled with that strange sensation that change was in the air. Only this time, she was going to embrace it with open arms because it just felt *right*.

Sebastian drew her in for a hug, resting his forehead against hers. "It's almost a new year."

She closed her eyes and made a wish. "I hope it's a good one."

"It's going to be amazing," he said with conviction.

The crowd inside began to chant. "*Ten! Nine! Eight! Seven!*"

"How do you know?" she asked.

"*Six! Five! Four!*"

"I just do. Trust me."

"*Three! Two! One!*"

"Okay." She looped her arms around his neck.

"*Happy New Year!*" the crowd roared. Brilliant fireworks lit up the sky above the water.

Layla rose up on her toes to kiss him. He drew her tighter and deepened the kiss until she felt as if the whole world spun away and the only thing in the universe that existed was the two of them, together. It was the kind of kiss that made the fireworks pale in comparison. The kind of kiss that was far more intoxicating than all the glasses of champagne, and more heartfelt and hopeful than the lilting tune of "Auld Lang Syne" floating on the breeze around them.

"See?" Sebastian whispered against her mouth. "It's already perfect."

When he kissed her again, Layla knew from the top of her head to the tips of her sparkly stilettos that he was absolutely, gloriously, one-hundred-percent right. Here, in his arms, with the shiny new year ahead of them, nothing had ever felt better.

Missing Christmas

KATE CLAYBORN

Dear Readers,

Thank you for picking up a copy of *A Snowy Little Christmas*! Whether you are new to my books or not, I so hope you enjoy this story, which I absolutely loved writing.

Missing Christmas features characters who appear briefly in my debut, *Beginner's Luck*. In that book, the hero, Ben, must make a choice between his longtime business interests and his newfound love interest. His best friend, Jasper—the hero of *Missing Christmas*—tries (unsuccessfully) to sway him to the side of business. But of course, things aren't always what they seem, and Jasper's reasons for being so laser-focused on business have more to do with love than we might think. *Missing Christmas* stands alone, but if you want to learn more about Jasper, Kristen, and their friendship with Ben, be sure to pick up a copy of *Beginner's Luck*, available wherever eBooks are sold.

Kate Clayborn

Chapter One

JASPER

December 14

Here's the long and short of it: I kiss her *because* I miss her.

I know how it sounds. If she's close enough to kiss, she's not far away enough to miss.

But I've seen or talked to Kristen Fraser almost every day of the last six years, and I think, deep down, I have missed her for every single one of them.

Only I've never—not until tonight—dared to kiss her. With Kristen, I've always, always followed the rules.

It's not how I would've pictured it, my first kiss with her. That's probably because the only way I've ever allowed myself to picture it, in my weakest moments, is in scenarios that would never actually happen: Me and her, under a blanket of starlight, nothing fluorescent or LED or otherwise unnatural. The clothes between us soft and comfortable, easy to pull off—none of the tiny, tyrannical enforcers usually kept between us, belts and buttons and zippers. No phones ringing or computers pinging, no appointments or negotiations or closings.

Nowhere to be but with each other.

But maybe it's right, that it's this way. The end of an endless day in a small conference room, working on a recruit Kris has been pursuing for weeks, her first solo approach. The deadline firm, our last job before we close down the office tomorrow for the holidays. Three hours of calls, two in-person meetings with our client, four frantic hours of typing, each of us on our laptops staring at the same shared document, one hour of sipping coffee and staring anxiously between our phones, our computers, each other. The way our eyes locked when the call came in, the way unspoken words passed between us: *this is it*; *good luck*; *whatever happens, we did our best*; *I'm proud of you*; *I'm glad we're here together*. The way she'd tapped her knuckles on the table quietly when Dr. Nhung said he'd read the contract, the way I'd punched a fist in the air when he'd said yes. The way we'd both stood from our chairs while we each tried to sound casual, expressing our pleasure, our promises to finalize details soon.

It's the way we've always worked together. Fast, close, in sync.

Electric.

So when she presses end on the call, I *think* I know what will happen next. I think she'll set her hands on her hips and smile at me for a second or two, letting some of that electricity crackle out and away. I think she'll say something brief but celebratory, efficient but powerful. All business Kristen, more so now since we've opened this firm, and I'll love it but I'll get that familiar pang of *missing* her, and I'll clear my throat and gather my things and congratulate her and go home to have a drink.

Alone.

But she doesn't do that, she *isn't* any of that, not tonight. Instead she turns to face me, and even in the heels she wears she's got to look up at me, a disadvantage she's never much liked, though I think she knows by now—as smart and kind and capable and funny as she is—that it's the only one I've got over her. Her light brown hair, fine and straight, has started to sag a little from the tight ponytail she'd had it in when she'd entered this room this morning. Her gray-green eyes are tired but her smile is huge, so big I can see a flash of the bottom row of her teeth, a little crooked.

She closes her eyes and tips her head back and the noise she makes—it's a half laugh, half sigh, and I think I ought to sit right back down in my chair and take a deep breath to get over it but I can't do it; I can't sit down, because Kristen does the most unexpected thing.

She hugs me.

I make a noise, something between an *oh* and a *mmph*, and maybe someone else, someone who hasn't wondered about this exact feeling for years, would stand stiffly out of shock. Maybe that's what even I'd do in literally any other circumstance like this that didn't involve Kristen Fraser—Jasper with a heart of stone, Jasper who barely bothers with a handshake, Jasper who'd do anything for the job, who's always on to the next one. I don't even hug my family, not that any of them would try it.

But as soon as I feel her against me I wrap my arms around her, not like I've been wondering about it for years but like I've been *doing* it for years, and she's warm and soft and perfect and she says, "I *did* it" and

I can feel her breath against my skin and I say roughly, "You did," even as I'm tipping my hips back slightly so she doesn't feel what she does to me.

You are an absolute bastard, Sorenson, I'm telling myself, trying to ignore the way the edge of her ponytail is resting against the back of my hand, cool and smooth and perfect.

And then she pulls back but she stays holding on and she's just looking at me, right into my eyes, and her face is flushed in the exact way it gets every time we have a win together—the day we finally told our former boss we were going out on our own, the day we signed the lease on this space, the day we landed our first recruit under our new firm's name, the day we'd finally made enough money to hire an admin to run the office.

Her breath hitches and she says, "Jasper," and I have to close my eyes at the way it sounds. Breathy and surprised and *wanting*.

"Kris, I . . ."

My voice trails off when she moves a hand to my cheek, my evening stubble rough against her smooth palm. I open my eyes and she's watching that hand; she watches, almost dazedly, her own thumb as it moves to stroke over my cheekbone, and—holy hell. Unless I can move my lower half into the next state she's going to know about the situation down there, and I try to focus on other things while she works out, works off whatever this uncharacteristic form of affection is. There's a tinkling echo of holiday music coming from outside the conference room, something Carol must've left piping out of her computer speakers when she took off a couple hours ago. That alone ought to be enough to dull this buzz, since I hate this holiday. I hate that every year it takes me away from the things I'm best at and the people I care about the most.

I hate that it takes me away from this office.

From her.

"Jasper," she says again, and she moves that thumb enough to press it, lightly, on the curve of my bottom lip. I feel like I live a lifetime in that second of pressure, like I see every fantasy I'm not allowed to have about her. Starlight, soft clothes, silence. "Kiss me."

It's a demand she's given me, but I can hear something living beneath it, a little question in the words that makes my shoulders tighten. There can't be a question there; there can't. I've followed the rules for this, for us working together and being friends, starting this business together and making it a success. I can't ever have Kristen regretting me. I'd never recover from it.

"Kris," I say warningly, even though I don't let her go. I take a breath, gathering the will I need to stop this. It feels beyond my considerable, long-honed resources of restraint. Carol's computer speakers are tinnily piping out a version of "Let It Snow!" and I really, really hate that song.

"Do it," she says, and she knows why that would work. She knows I love a challenge.

But what she doesn't know is that I've always loved a chance to break the rules, and I'm so, so tired of following this one. The most important rule I've ever made for myself.

I've missed her for so long.

So I do it.

I press my mouth to hers.

Chapter Two

KRISTEN

December 15

It had felt like Christmas morning, kissing Jasper.

Like the thing you've been waiting and waiting for, lying in bed at night with wishes stacked up in your head. Like waking up extra early when it finally comes, the house dark and quiet and your ears straining to hear for someone else to stir, to give you permission to burst from your room and start the day's celebration. Like holding in your hand a perfectly wrapped present, your hands fairly trembling with excitement. *Is this the one?* you're thinking, holding it there. *Is this the one I really, really wanted?*

Like opening that present and finding—with a burst of irrepressible joy—that it absolutely is.

At my desk I let my eyes slide closed, blinking out the light from my computer screen, where I've been staring at the Nhung contract since I got here an hour ago. Going over it again like this—it's the kind of thing I might've done last night, once I'd heard the "yes" I've been working to get for months. Six weeks from now Dr. Nhung will be starting a five-year stint with Möller Metals, a job I'm certain will make him happy, and an agreement that will bring Jasper and me one of the biggest recruiting commissions we've gotten since we started up fourteen months ago. A good salary bump for Carol in the next quarter, enough money to make some improvements to the office we've been waiting on. I could've heard that yes and gone back to my office, e-mailed my contact at Möller, opened this document, and let myself feel proud of what I'd done.

Instead I'd asked Jasper to kiss me. I'd practically *dared* him to.

And *oh*. Kiss me he did. One hand in my hair, one arm wrapped around my waist, a rough sound in his throat—

The sharp ring of my phone stops me from reliving it—*again*—and even before I look down at the screen I know it's my older sister, and I know the lecture I'm about to get.

"Kris, you absolute hag," Kelly says, her voice strained, her breathing shallow. I can hear the thud of her feet on her treadmill. She's probably on mile four at least, her Bluetooth in her ear and her tablet in front of her face. Likely she's been answering e-mails since mile one. "I have been waiting for *hours*. Did you get him?"

I have a flash of my thumb on the curve of Jasper's lip. I cross my legs under my desk.

"I did."

"What the *hell*," she says, and I can hear her slap the stop button. "You said you'd call! I figured it went bad and you were off somewhere with Jasper drowning your sorrows."

"It didn't go bad," I lie.

Because it *did*. It did go bad, once the kiss had

stopped. One pause to catch my breath—who knows how long we'd stood there like that, arms around each other, lips and tongues tangling—and in that pause while I'd stared at him, taken him in and what we'd done, it'd been like a light had switched on in Jasper's head, the glazed, hungry look in his eyes before the kiss suddenly gone. He'd stepped away from me and said, "I shouldn't have."

He'd looked at me like he didn't know me at all.

I stand from the desk and walk to my door, peeking out before I close it to the small, dimly lit lobby outside. Carol won't be in for another hour, and Jasper—who is always here before me—still isn't in his office across the way.

I take a deep breath. "Kel, I messed up."

I try giving her an abbreviated version: a long day, a jolt of adrenaline, a huge achievement, a kiss I shouldn't have initiated, an awkward parting.

But I should've known that wouldn't work on my sister.

"Oh my *Goooooooooooooood*," she shouts, and I wince on her behalf. It's barely six a.m. in LA right now, and no way are Malik and their two kids out of bed yet. I shush her on instinct, but this doesn't work either.

"Freaking *finally*! What was it like?"

I can't say Christmas morning, obviously, unless I want Kelly to know how far gone I am, how far gone I've *been*. "What do you mean, *finally*?"

"Please. 'Jasper this, Jasper that.' He's all you ever talk about."

"We *work* together. We're business partners. Of course I talk about him."

She ignores me. "Plus he looks like a cologne ad come to life. God. Does he still have that scar at the corner of his mouth?"

"Uh, yes? Why would he not have it anymore?" I stifle the urge to tell her what that scar—a small, upward curving line that makes the right side of his mouth look slightly upturned, a tease for the smile he so rarely gives out—felt like against my tongue. I *love* that scar.

"Who knows. People here get stuff like that lasered off, or whatever. Anyway. What. Was. It. Like."

I slump into my chair again, turning it out to face the window. Early morning light bathes the glass-and-steel buildings of downtown Houston. Even from up here I can hear a swish of traffic on the surface streets below. It's supposed to be sixty-two degrees today. It doesn't feel like Christmas morning anymore at all.

"It can't happen again."

"Oh. You're going to play it this way, are you?"

"Kel. This is our business. We've worked so hard to get here. Being with Jasper—it goes against everything I know about professional life."

Kelly sighs, and I know part of her—the part of her that finished her law degree two years before I started mine, the part of her that spends ten to thirteen hours a day doing contracts for the second largest studio in Hollywood—knows exactly what I mean. Before Jasper and I started this firm, I spent five years working alongside him at a massive materials conglomerate here in Houston—him part of a scouting team for new tech and the talent that produced it, me doing human resources contracts for the hires he and our former colleague Ben would bring in. When I wasn't doing contracts, I was negotiating conflicts within the company—and more than a few of them came from romantic relationships turned sour. In my head there's a looping echo of things I've said to Jasper over the years—the frustration I expressed over two people in accounting whose relationship had gone so wrong that we'd had to rearrange the whole floor to prevent worse fallout. The anger over a VP who'd promoted a woman he'd been dating over someone far more qualified. *It's too messy to do these things at work,* I'd say, and the worst of it was, part of me knew I was saying it almost as a way to convince *myself.* To talk myself out of the things I already thought about Jasper.

"You're not his subordinate," Kelly says. "And he's not yours. You're partners."

"You know it's more complicated than that. I don't know what I was thinking."

"Maybe you were thinking you've been half in love with him since the day you met him."

Wrong. I'm pretty sure, much as I've tried to deny it, that I've been whole in love with him. Since he looked me straight in the eye, shook my hand, and asked me bluntly if I could help him write a restrictive covenant for a new hire on my first day of work. But I've never let it get in the way before.

Not like I did last night.

"I need to apologize to him. I sort of did, last night, but he couldn't leave fast enough." He hadn't even picked up his suit jacket. It's probably still draped over the back of his chair in the conference room. I press a hand to my forehead. "How could I do this? He's my best friend."

"Hey," Kelly says softly, hearing the quiver in my voice. "*I'm* your best friend."

I offer a small, wet laugh. "You know what I mean. He's my best friend *here.* We do everything together."

"No. You work together, and work has been your everything for too long." I can sense her changing her tactic. A born lawyer, Kelly is, and I always thought I was, too, until I started getting the itch for the recruiting side. "Maybe you're just getting your wires crossed. You're around him so much that you get confused sometimes. Like a work husband kind of thing."

I try not to feel a shudder of delight at that word— *husband*—in any way connected to Jasper. I try instead to cling desperately to what Kelly has said. Yes, maybe that's it—maybe these last months especially, when we've been working so closely to get this firm off the ground. The scouting trips we've taken and the close quarters in this office. Dinners and drinks with clients that sometimes stretched into wrap-up sessions between the two of us, my place or his, late-night desserts and laughter and the occasional baseball game . . .

"Maybe," I say, unconvincingly.

"Today's your last day, right? Before the holiday?"

"Yes. Yes, that's right. That's a great point." *Ugh.* What am I, on a conference call with my own sister? I turn back to my computer screen, see Jasper's office light is on now. I must not have heard him come in. "It'll be fine," I tell Kelly, and myself. "I'll speak to him today, and then we'll have a break from each other until after Christmas."

There's a pause, and I know Kelly's deciding whether to say something else about this; I know she wants to. But instead she says, "Can't wait to see you, peach."

I feel a warm comfort at her words. In a week we'll all be back in Michigan with my parents—she and Malik and my niece and nephew arrive the day before I do. We'll make cookies and sing carols off-key and I'll wrap presents and watch seven to ten Hallmark movies with Kelly.

Christmas will reset me; it always does. And it'll reset this thing with Jasper.

"Can't wait to see you, plum."

When we hang up, I feel better. I just need to get through this day, and that'll be easy. A quick, more prepared apology to Jasper. Follow-ups and final details on last night's deal. It'll be over before I know it.

My computer pings with a new message alert.

Jasper, efficient as always.

Conference room, he's written. *9 a.m. We've got a problem.*

Christmas feels so far away.

Chapter Three

JASPER

"Jasper. You are going to *love* this."

Carol bursts into the conference room at 8:56, where I've been sitting for a half hour, staring out the long wall of windows and trying to shake the sense memory of what I was doing the last time I was in here. I've got to get my head on straight in the four minutes before Kristen shows up and I break the news. If nothing else it's bad enough that she'll probably forget about the mess I made of last night, kissing her like that.

Kissing her at all.

"I mean, just you wait," Carol says, reliably immune to my brooding even on regular days. On the day before a holiday break? She seems to take it as an invitation. "This one is going to knock your socks off."

I blink up at her from where I'm sitting, and she's standing there, her ash blond hair Texas big, her brown eyes wide behind red-framed glasses with tiny rhinestones at the edges, a set of massive earrings that look like Christmas ornaments dancing at her ears. We hired—or rather, Kris hired—Carol six months ago, and since day one she has proudly displayed

her dogged devotion to holiday attire of all sorts—
Independence Day, Labor Day, International Beer
Day, whatever. She has also proudly displayed her devotion to showing each sweater or T-shirt or entire track-
suit to me, in spite of the fact that I can never think of
anything to say in response except, "Very nice, Carol,"
before going to my office and shutting the door.

She reaches a hand into the opposite sleeve of a
bright red cardigan sweater with half a Christmas tree
on either side of the front buttons, and after a few seconds of fumbling, the whole entire front of it lights up
in multicolored twinkling. I wince.

"This is a great sweater, Jasper," she says, ignoring
me. "I have a backup battery. I'm going to let it run all
day."

"Terrific," I say blandly, but in spite of myself—in
spite of the fact that I've had maybe thirteen minutes
of sleep since I left here last night and in spite of the
fact that I'm about to have an awful meeting with the
very person whose face kept me awake all night—I feel
a smile tug at my mouth. Most days, the soundtrack in
this office is Carol's loud laugh or her humming; she
treats every admin task like it's the newest and most interesting experience of her life, and sometimes when
she prepares travel packets for me she puts a glittery
smiley-face sticker on my agenda.

I hate it, but I also don't.

"Now what's all this about an emergency meeting?"
she says, her sweater still flashing as she settles into a
seat beside me. "Are you rethinking my idea to have a
holiday party for us? I could whip something up by
this afternoon. One of those nut-covered cheese ball
things, and—"

"No." I hear Kristen's door open down the hall and
my whole body clenches with nerves at the thought of

seeing her again. That furrow in her brow and that look in her eyes when she'd pulled away from our kiss—shock, confusion, and, my worst fear, regret. I felt like my whole body and brain had shut down at that look.

When she comes in she blinks in surprise at Carol, and that's when I realize I doubled down on my screwup by sending that e-mail, since clearly Kristen was expecting this meeting to be me and her alone, and she probably also thinks the problem I referred to is what happened between us. I can almost hear Ben scolding me. *You are terrible with women,* he'd say, in that friendly, warm tone he has, the one that comes so easy to him. What he'd really mean is: *You are terrible with people in general,* and he'd be right.

"Good morning," she says, more to Carol than to me, and for a couple minutes it's a lot of oohing and aahing over the sweater, cheerful exchanges about holiday plans.

I clear my throat in that way I have. Carol rolls her eyes but Kristen's snap to mine immediately, and I don't have a chance to arrange my insides against what happens when our gazes lock. I *held* her last night. Given the news I have to deliver, it should be the last thing on my mind.

"You remember the Dreyer job we closed three weeks ago?" I say, proud of myself for getting it out, getting back on firmer ground.

"Sure," Kristen says. "He's going to Dubai. Two years, and turning over his desalination patent."

"He's not."

She blinks, startled. "He's—he has to. He signed the contract."

I shake my head. "He says he'll pay the penalty. He

doesn't want to uproot his wife. They've got a grandkid coming."

Her eyes soften briefly before she looks down at her clasped hands. It only takes a couple of seconds, but I can feel it, when she registers what this means. We did the Dreyer job on behalf of GreenCorp, an environmental solutions firm. Getting Dreyer was a condition of them signing us for an exclusive recruiting contract. We lose Dreyer, we lose GreenCorp.

And GreenCorp is a huge part of our operating budget for next year.

Carol's sweater blinks obnoxiously in my periphery. We lose GreenCorp, we'll probably lose Carol, too. I think she knows, because she reaches into her sleeve and turns off the sweater.

"Okay," Kristen says. "Okay. It's only the fifteenth. You can get there Monday, spend the day. Change his mind."

"Can't. He's off the grid until Thursday afternoon." A hunting trip with his brother, he'd said, and I don't think he's lying, but I do think he's relieved he won't have to deal with me.

She nods, looks down at her tablet. "Friday, then. That's still three days before Christmas. You'll have time to get home to your—"

"I'm not going home."

It's so annoying that she's said it. I don't even really have a home back in west Texas. My family situation is a shambles, and maybe she doesn't know why, but she knows that it is. Last year she'd FaceTimed me on Christmas Eve with a flimsy excuse about needing a software code for her phone, her face flushed with the pleasure of being with her family, and maybe with an eggnog buzz. We both knew she'd been checking up on me, alone in my condo. *See you next week?* I remember her saying, her eyes on me steady and a little sad. *I miss you,* I'd wanted to say, but of course I hadn't.

She clears her throat. "Right, yes. I'm sorry."

"Kris." At the sound of my voice, she raises her eyes to me. "You know I can't do this on my own."

For a long second, we look at each other. In all the years we've worked together, we've come to know each other's weaknesses, and mine has always been the human stuff. I can talk all day about where a recruit's tech will land, give them stats about equipment they'll have, but I'm garbage at selling places, experiences, people, and obviously this is where the Dreyer job has fallen apart. When Ben and I worked as a team, he'd always handle that side of things, and he was unstoppable. Now it's Kristen who works these angles, and she's even better than Ben was. Thorough and detail-oriented, but never robotic or distant. Approachable but not overfamiliar, genuinely excited but not frenetic in her energy. And so, so *warm*.

I fist a hand against the table. *Don't think about how warm she is.*

"What if we set up a call?" she asks weakly. I don't even have to say anything. Carol turns her head toward Kristen and raises her hand slightly, like she's about to check her temperature. She thinks better of it and looks back at me with a question in her eyes. As many times as the three of us have sat together in this room, I'm sure Carol is thrown—not just at Kristen's passivity, but at the cool awkwardness between us. Kristen does not want to go anywhere with me, and my stomach twists in dread.

It's never been this way. Kris and I, we work as a team.

"A call isn't going to do it," I say grimly, and I realize

that Carol might also be thrown by my somber delivery. I'm not a cheerful guy, but this problem—it's exactly the kind of challenge that usually gets me focused, energized.

It's doing neither for me right now.

"I'm supposed to go to Michigan on—" Kristen says. She raises a hand to her forehead, her full lips compressed and turned down at the corners, and my chest feels tight. Looking at her face like that, I don't give a damn about the job, the firm. I'll pay Carol out of my savings, find her a new job. GreenCorp can get fucked, so long as Kristen has what she wants.

"But I guess I'll push it," she says, just as I'm about to open my mouth. "Carol, can we do some travel rearranging?"

She turns the sweater back on. "My favorite! How long do y'all need?"

"A day," I say firmly, even though I don't know if a day will do it. Ben once spent six days in rural Oregon to get someone to sign off on some 3-D printing tech our old boss was pissing his pants over. "I don't care what you do with my tickets, but Kristen needs to be on her way to Michigan Friday night."

"Jasper," Kristen says. "I can—"

"No," I say, and my voice sounds so flat. "We'll do it quickly. Treat it like a hiccup, and it will be one. A minor inconvenience."

I see the flash of hurt in her eyes. Carol looks back and forth between us, twinkle lights glinting off her glasses. I *am* terrible with people. It's only by some strange, inexplicable miracle that it's taken me this long to be terrible with Kris.

She stands from her chair, clutching her laptop to her chest. On instinct, I stand too, and now the sense memory of last night is even fresher. My hands clench in my pockets.

"Absolutely," she says, her voice curt, her eyes not meeting mine. "A minor inconvenience."

This time, she leaves the conference room first.

Chapter Four

KRISTEN

December 22

The first fight—the only *real* fight—Jasper and I ever had was about a kiss.

But not one between us.

It was over two years ago, not long after he'd first come to me about leaving our old company to join him and Ben in the venture that would eventually become our current firm. Ben had been away for an extended leave, but was working a metallurgist recruit our boss wanted badly enough to let Ben and Jasper out of the non-compete that was keeping them from starting their own firm. If Ben could close the deal, Jasper could do what he'd been working toward since the day I'd first met him—go out on his own.

But then, Ben kissed the recruit.

"She's a distraction," Jasper had said to me that summer day in my office, pacing in front of my desk, his jaw tight.

"He did the right thing," I'd told him calmly. "He's got feelings for her, and he told you he can't work with her. He's following the rules."

"He's forgetting about the *job*," he'd said, a little angrily, and I'd felt a jarring sense of discontinuity, a sinking, embarrassing sense of disappointment in myself. The night before, Jasper and I had ordered tacos from our favorite place and stayed at the office until ten, going over a contract while an Astros game streamed on my computer screen. It had been the most fun I'd had in months, and when I'd gone home, flushed with the pleasure of being around him—the tie-loosened, talkative Jasper it seemed no one else ever got to see but me—I'd thought, *Maybe I could ask him out sometime. Maybe me and Jasper, we could make it work.*

But seeing him like that—not even acknowledging that Ben, his best friend since their college days, had found someone he liked enough to jeopardize such a big job—had felt like a glass of cold water to the face, a reminder of how ridiculous it would be to break my professional boundaries for a man who so clearly didn't care about relationships. When I'd found out, not long after, that Jasper had nearly sabotaged things between Ben and Kit to get the deal, I'd told him to forget about the new firm, that I'd be staying put. I'd stood in his office with my hands on my hips and told him I'd never been so disappointed with someone in my life, and I hadn't even been exaggerating.

Of course we patched it up, eventually. He'd apologized to Ben, had apologized to me, and he'd done it sincerely, with genuine remorse in his voice and in his eyes. But for a while, it had strained things between us. Or at least, it had for me. It was my feelings for him—my feelings outside of friendship or collegiality—that had made me so completely disappointed, and I'd known it was unfair to him, unfair to our work together. I'd tried, after that, to keep a better distance. To keep work at work, to enjoy our friendship but not expect more from it. I'd even dated a little, though pretty unsuccessfully, and Jasper and I had gotten back into a good routine.

But I don't have much hope for that routine as I prep for our trip.

Because I *kissed* him.

How do you reestablish a routine after that?

Through e-mail we agree to meet at the airport, an early indicator of how awkward it will be, since our buildings are barely a half mile from each other and we normally would've shared a car. By the time I get to the gate I'm flustered and feeling sorry for myself— the security line long and irritating, but also full of reminders of where I was meant to be flying today. I see a young woman carrying a tote bag full of wrapped gifts and feel a pang of envy; I see a family—the parents harried-looking but the kids, wearing matching snowman sweatshirts, giddy and energetic—and think about Kelly and Malik and the kids.

Jasper's sitting in the spot he always prefers at a gate—end of a row, facing a window. He never works right before a flight, at least not in any of the obvious ways. He puts his phone away in the front pocket of his bag and reads a book, usually a paperback he's bought from one of the airport shops. "You're overpaying," I always tease. "Go to the bookstore next time." And he always smiles and says, "Too much choice at the bookstore."

I wish he had a paperback right now, so I'd know how to open this conversation, our first face-to-face since last week. Instead I sit beside him and settle for a neutral "Good morning," and for a long minute I think the only thing he'll say back is his quiet repetition of the same. But finally, he speaks.

"I know we need to talk about it," he says. He keeps

his eyes ahead, staring out into the predawn dark, the white body of plane huge and stark. "I've been thinking about how to talk about it."

Despite the fact that I've never had to talk to Jasper about something like this between us, I know, from all the years I've worked with him and been his friend, what this means. It's how he approaches any problem he has to solve—a quiet retreating while he works it out, understands all he can. A forceful returning once he has the answer, an unyielding commitment to seeing it through.

But since he doesn't say anything else, I guess he still doesn't have an answer.

"Jasper."

He drops his eyes from the window, looks over at me.

"I am so sorry. I know the kiss was awkward, and—"

"That's not the word I'd use for it," he says, his voice sharp.

I swallow. "It's not?"

"No. It was the best kiss of my life."

"Oh." *Oh*. It's the only thing I can say, think. My brain feels like it's been put through one of the wind turbines of that plane out there. *The best kiss of his life*.

He clears his throat. "But I know the rules here. I know why we have them, and I know they're important to you."

"I'm the one who broke them." It's the thing he doesn't seem to have worked out. He's acting like the kiss was all his, and I don't like it. I don't like the way it takes away my agency, makes us unequal. I open my mouth to protest, thinking of Kelly's words to me—that Jasper and I are partners, not boss and employee—but Jasper speaks before I can.

"I can't lose this," he says, staring down at where his

hands rest loosely clasped in his lap. "I don't know what I'd do."

He's said it so seriously, with such *feeling*, and for a split second I let it echo through me, some ringing holiday bell of hope. But then I remember. Jasper's *this*, the *this* he can't lose—it's the job. It's always going to be the job. He'd done as much as tell me so himself, back when we'd had that fight about Ben.

"Good morning to everyone in the boarding area," comes a too-loud, slightly crackly voice over the gate speakers, and both Jasper and I raise our heads. "We'll now start boarding at Gate A6 for Flight 2124 to Boston, starting with first class and business class—"

"That's us," Jasper says, shifting his hand to his bag.

"That's you," I tell him, relieved. I need some space after that exchange, that reminder.

His brow furrows in confusion.

"Carol said, remember? There was only one business class seat on this flight. I told her to give me coach."

"I"—he blinks down at his ticket—"I don't remember that. I would remember that."

He looks so confused, and frankly, I get it. He *would* remember that. When it comes to the business, he remembers every detail.

"It's no big deal." It's under four hours to Boston, and it's not like I don't have work—or my incredibly painful interpersonal issues with my colleague—to distract me.

"You'll take my seat."

"No, I won't."

"Kris," he says, swiping a hand across his face. The gesture is so vulnerable, so unlike him. I have such an aching feeling of longing that I have to look away. "I don't want to argue."

"So don't," I say, too sharply. "You're six foot four, Jasper. I'm not taking your legroom."

"I'll be fine."

"You won't be. You'll be cranky and uncomfortable. Just get on the plane. Take a nap. I'll see you when we land."

He stands, and I think maybe he's relented, but instead of heading to the boarding lane he walks to the ticket counter. The woman not swiping passes looks up at him and after a stunned blink, she smiles. I resist the urge to snort knowingly. She's going to do her best, even in spite of the fact that she's wearing a jingle bell necklace and elf hat, but Jasper is probably not going to notice. His mind is so one-track, all the time. If he went up to that counter to try to get a second business-class seat, then that's literally all he's thinking about. I once saw a waitress undo two buttons of her shirt while he asked her about the dinner special and his eyes didn't stray once while he ordered the rockfish. I still remember the exact, slightly befuddled way he'd said, "What?" when he looked back at me after she'd walked away.

She makes a few keystrokes on her computer and they exchange a few words, Jasper turning to nod his head my way at one point. *Ugh.* Now we seem like *those* people. Like we're so important, we just *have* to be in business class. I pretend to be interested in my phone.

"Here."

A ticket appears in front of me. I look up at Jasper. "There's no way."

Forget that the ticket agent thought he was handsome; even a face like Jasper's doesn't make a new business-class seat appear on a full flight three days before Christmas.

"I switched our tickets."

"Jasper, I said I didn't—"

"I can't be comfortable," he says bluntly, still holding out the ticket. "I can't be comfortable if you're not. Just take it, please."

When I look up at him, I hear that holiday bell again. All the years I've known him and I've never seen emotion like this on his face, something so desperate and yearning. I know, I *know* I shouldn't hear it, but I do.

I reach out a hand and take the ticket.

But I don't look at him when I walk away.

Chapter Five

JASPER

I know it's over before we even knock on the door.

When Kristen and I met Gil Dreyer six weeks ago, we did it at his office, a nondescript building ninety minutes outside of Boston. The space where Gil did his work was as rumpled and unexpected as the man himself. No one would expect the most advanced desalination tech the world has seen in years to come out of that lab, and no one would expect that a man with a bachelor's degree in philosophy and absolutely zero employment history in advanced scientific fields would be the one to develop it. It hadn't been an easy sell, getting him to GreenCorp, but in that cramped, messy, dated office, we'd had an advantage.

But there's no advantage in driving up the winding gravel driveway leading to the Dreyer home, which is, in fact, more like a rustic, snow-covered country compound. We lucked out in missing a heavy fall a couple of days ago, so the roads were mostly clear, flanked by dirty, packed drifts, but out here the snow is mostly bright white and smooth.

Frankly, it looks like Christmas Town, also known as my personal nightmare, and judging from Kris's face—which had mostly been stoic throughout our drive—her personal charm factory. It's midafternoon, so the lights aren't on, but through the light snowfall we can see them strung up everywhere—winding around the trees flanking the drive, lining the roof-line of a small red and white cottage that's got a massive mulberry wreath on its door, woven around the columns on a front porch that lines the entirety of the tidy ranch house with smaller red-ribboned wreaths hung on every window, white candles on every sill. There's an actual Christmas tree in the front yard. Fully fucking decorated.

This man is not going to go pick up from here and move after the first of the year.

"Oh!" Kristen says, which, disappointingly, is a much more enthusiastic *oh* than the one I got for telling her she'd given me the best kiss of my life. When I look over at her she's got her hands clasped together, leaning forward in her seat so she can see better. I follow her gaze and see a young couple walking around the side of the house, a massive basket swinging between them, full of what looks to me like literal boughs of holly.

I am in hell.

"He knows we're coming, right?" I say, more to myself than to Kristen. Carol had confirmed it all late Thursday afternoon, once Gil was back from his trip, and I'd followed up with a call that evening. He'd warned me there wasn't much of a point, that he'd made his decision, but I'd insisted. "We're in town for another meeting," I'd lied. "We'll just make a quick stop by." He'd chuckled and said he and Romina wouldn't mind the company.

Before Kris can answer me, the man himself has stepped out onto the porch, wearing a green cable-knit sweater and jeans with a hole in the knee; he's got one hand holding a mug of something steaming and the other stroking the length of his steel-gray beard. Behind him, a short, dark-haired, bespectacled woman in a red sweatshirt follows, also holding a mug. She raises a hand and waves enthusiastically.

Kristen says, "They're like Mr. and Mrs. Claus!" and I shoot her a look. She smiles sheepishly, pink washing her cheeks. She's always so *pretty*.

Out on the porch we shake hands, meet the two holly-gatherers—Tanner and Allison—who turn out to be Gil and Romina's son and daughter-in-law. Tanner pats Gil's shoulder and says to me, "You're the one trying to take my genius old man away from us," but he's got a smiling, easy demeanor about him that tells me he knows we've got no real shot at this, either.

"Kristen and I, yes," I correct him. Beside me, Kris shifts her body slightly so her arm presses lightly, almost imperceptibly against mine. That's not a thank-you; it's a warning, or at least a reminder. It's not the time to be corrective, she's saying. Touches like this— they're normal for us on the job, a way we've learned to communicate with other people in the room. But I'm feeling them all wrong now, my brain and body scrambled, one sending misguided messages to the other.

"This is beautiful," Kristen says, smiling and looking out over the white expanse of land. "Whether we convince you or not, Gil, this is quite a sight. Thanks for letting us drop by."

Gil and Romina beam at her, both of them almost tripping over each other's words to offer information. Gil says he'd give her a tour if it weren't for "those fancy shoes" she's wearing, and Romina points out the cottage, a former garage, which they've been renovating

in case "certain someones"—Tanner and Allison smile—
want to spend extended time on the property for "oh,
any reason at all!" I'm guessing this means we're not
supposed to talk directly about the grandkid on the
way, and my suspicion is confirmed when Kristen only
gives a smiling, knowing look to Romina, as if they're
old friends.

I trust whatever she's doing, though, and so when
we move into the house and Kris completely avoids
talking business, I follow her lead. I sit at the small
round table in the eat-in kitchen that only has
room for four, a relief since I don't expect Tanner
and Allison—who retreat down a narrow hallway—are
going to be much help, and I avoid getting out any of
the materials Kristen and I brought. I take a mug
from Romina and pretend to enjoy what tastes to me
like hot apple juice; I fake the sweet tooth I don't
really have and eat a frosted cookie in the shape of a
candy cane.

I feel the distance between me and Kristen like it's
a wall.

"Now, Gil, I know you said you've made up your
mind," she says eventually, and I sit forward in my
chair, letting her take the lead, both because it's the
best option for this and because I need to get my brain
back online.

She's good; she's always good—she makes it a conversation, not a pitch. She doesn't assume the con-
cerns they have; she asks about them, and each one
she's got an answer for—a contract revision that offers
more time off, paid flights back here, more options for
working remotely. She asks whether funding for stew-
ardship of this property while they're away would
help—a regular groundskeeper, updated security sys-
tems, whatever. But just like I can feel the wall between

me and her, I can feel the wall Gil and Romina are putting up between themselves and us.

I feel tense, slightly desperate, and it's unlike me. Sure, I'm intense about work, but this—*emotion.* I feel all inside out, same as I've felt since the kiss. Losing this job feels like losing her, especially now that I know how she felt about that kiss.

Awkward, she'd said.

"Your grandchild," I say quietly, in deference to the privacy Tanner and Allison seemed to want. "The two years you spend over there—it would be doing something good for your grandchild."

I can feel Kristen's eyes on me. This is unexpected. I don't usually do family stuff.

"How do you figure?" Romina says. She's got a look on her face like I'm a robber baron, sitting here on a pile of cash I've hoarded for myself.

"It's not about the money, because of course you know about the money you stand to get here. Private schools, college, whatever you'd want—you know already you could do all that."

Gil looks up, eyebrows raised. Maybe it's *not* over.

"It's about the tech. It could change the world, make it a safer place for your grandchildren, all of them. Fresh, drinkable water for huge numbers of people from water that could otherwise kill them? You know how much this helps the world, Gil. And you're doing it in a way that doesn't ruin the—"

"I know," Gil says, and Romina purses her lips. He rubs a hand over his beard and under the table, Kristen moves so that her foot touches mine. I strain to get that brain-body synapse working right. *That was good,* she's saying, and it makes my heart grow two sizes.

I let it sit, something I learned from Kris. For the

first time I notice there's holiday music coming from somewhere. I distract myself by wondering if Gil and Romina are in some kind of "torture Jasper" pact with Carol.

"It's not just the grandkid," Gil says after a long minute. He stares into his cup, and I see the doubt written all over his face. Beside him, Romina clasps her hands, and he takes a deep breath. "It's that I don't want to miss a second of seeing my son be a father. Can't wait to see him be great at it." He smiles, looks over at Romina, chuckles slightly. "Can't wait to see him mess up at it, either."

I blink across the table, struck dumb. Of course I'd miss *this* part of the equation, this kind of unconditional family affection. Of course I have no answer for it.

"I know you don't have kids of your own," he says. "But you can imagine how I feel."

"No, sir," I say sharply, honestly, and I know as soon as it's out of my mouth, it's an error. It's the wrong tone, too personal. Beside me, Kristen's gone stiff, but I don't stop the end of my sentence. "I can't."

There's a heavy silence. I've ruined the mood, the possibility. I've ruined the job, if the way Kristen is standing from her seat is any indication.

"I think it'd be a good idea for Jasper and me to get settled in our hotel." She's said this so smoothly, as though there's some nearby hotel we've booked. We haven't—she's flying this evening and I've got a room in Boston for the next three nights, because why the hell not. But that's how bad I've messed it up—getting out of here for a debrief is necessary. "Would you be up for an early dinner in town?"

Romina looks at her, seeming grateful. But then

she chuckles. "I guess that means you haven't heard," she says. "I don't think we'll be getting out much this evening."

And that's when the first gust of wind roars outside.

Chapter Six

KRISTEN

A ground blizzard.

A *freak* ground blizzard.

Starting even earlier than Gil and Romina had heard about.

I'm sitting stiffly on their plaid-upholstered couch, staring at the muted television screen. The fact that there's barely any reporting from the Boston stations on what's happening outside says everything about how isolated we are out here. Gil says ground blizzards don't come around much in this part of the country, but their small town is unusually flat, and there's not many tree lines surrounding the main roads. If there's good news, Romina says, it's that it'll probably be over by midnight, and so long as there's no other weather in the area, the roads will probably be clear by tomorrow afternoon.

Outside, the wind steadily howls, the windows shaking with it, white swaths of snow whipping by. Inside, it's almost as tense: on my lap, my phone lights up with texts from Kelly and my mom, who are now, given my quick update, afraid I might not make it to Michigan at all. In the kitchen, Tanner and Allison speak in

hushed tones to each other as they make dinner. Gil
and Romina disappeared about ten minutes ago,
probably because of what's happening behind me—
Jasper, pacing the length of the couch, on his phone,
his tone rigidly, falsely controlled.

The bad weather feels like compounding interest,
piling on top of the tension Jasper's carried with him
all day—this morning at the airport, the quiet drive
here, his reaction to this house, this family. His frank,
almost desolate reply to Gil at the table. If there's any
advantage to what's happened here, it's that I'll have
more time to figure out what's really going on with
him. Whatever else is strained between us, we're
friends, and I don't like seeing him this way.

"Your website says you're the best car service in the
state of Massachusetts," he's saying. "You don't have a
single car in your fleet that could get the job done?"

"Jasper," I say quietly, but I don't think he hears me.
I told him not to bother with this, that he'd only need
to take one look outside to see all he'd need to know
about our chances, but he'd insisted.

"I've got four and a half hours to get my partner on
a flight. I will pay you whatever you want. Up front,
I'll pay you. A bonus if you get her there on time.
Anything."

I move around to the back of the couch, stand at
one end so I can intercept him when he makes his inevitable turn. He's got his head down, so I reach out,
set a hand on his forearm. It stops him in his tracks.

"It's fine," I whisper. "Really. I'll rebook for tomorrow."

His jaw clenches and he mutters a grudging "Thank
you for your time" into his phone before hanging up.
He looks so defeated, and I can't help it—I move my
hand, stroke his arm lightly. He took off his jacket

before he made the call, rolled up his shirtsleeves as though he was about to get into a fistfight, so I'm touching his bare, warm skin, the muscles beneath corded and firm. I feel like my swallow could be heard on another planet, and that damned bell is ringing somewhere around my heart.

"I'm ruining your Christmas," he says quietly, keeping his voice low and looking briefly over my shoulder to make sure Tanner and Allison aren't listening.

"You're not ruining it."

"You'd be with your family right now, if it weren't for me."

He blinks down at where my hand rests on his skin, but he doesn't move. I don't either.

"If it weren't for the job," I say, keeping my voice hushed too.

"Right. The job."

"Jasper. What happened in there?"

He shrugs. "I'm off my game."

"Because of me."

He looks at me miserably. I think about lifting my hand from his arm, bringing it up to his face. I'd push the brown hair that's fallen over his brow off his forehead. I'd let myself feel the sandpaper texture of his jaw, like I did last week. It'd feel like Christmas again, and God knows, I'm really missing Christmas right now.

"Because of *me*," he says.

A fresh, angry gust of wind rattles through the house, and I startle where I stand.

Immediately Jasper sets his large, warm hand over mine, and it should be friendly, comforting, not unlike casual ways we've touched before in the midst of a tense meeting, or a turbulent flight, whatever. But now it feels so intimate—Jasper's skin beneath and above my hand, a miniature version of the embrace we had a week ago.

"I'll fix this," he says, his features set in a familiar way. This determination—it's at least more recognizable.

"Plane tickets are one thing. It's not like you can control the weather," I tease.

His mouth—scar-side, my favorite—lifts slightly in a smile, and my own lips curve in mirrored pleasure. While we stand like that I think of how fervently Jasper has been clinging to control since this morning. As much as he hates that I'm missing my family Christmas, I hate that he's feeling so lost and out of sorts.

"We'll make the best of it," I say, squeezing his arm slightly, and he nods. Between us, a small shift has taken place: we feel more on the same team, more like the Jasper and Kristen who order late-night food and watch baseball. "We'll have fun."

"Well, we've found some things!" calls Romina's chipper voice, interrupting our hushed conversation. She's emerging from the basement door down the hall, Gil coming up behind her, his hands full. "We've got boots here that should work for you both, and we've just put some extra linens in the wash, so once those are ready we'll take them out to the cottage, and—"

"Oh, fun!" chimes Allison, wiping her hands on a towel. "It'll be nice for you two to stay out there."

"The—?"

Gil speaks up, cutting off my question. "We'd have you in here, of course, but we've only got two bedrooms, and it seems silly for Tanner and Alli to pack up all their things—"

"No, no," I say. "This is very generous of you."

"It's a bit rough-and-ready out there," says Romina.

"But the heat works, and you've got a small galley kitchen, and the bed is brand-new. . . ."

Jasper coughs. "The bed." He repeats it rather than asks it. His hand is still warm over mine, warmer than before.

Romina's eyes drop to where we've been holding on to each other, then she looks back up. "Oh," she says, her face flushing. "Are you not—"

"You're not?" says Gil. "I thought you were married."

"*Married?*" I squeak. Jasper and I practically yank our hands away from each other. We stand like two teenagers who've been caught right in the middle of the most awkward game of Seven Minutes in Heaven. Seven Minutes in Tense Conversation With a Coworker You're in Love With.

"We're not married," Jasper says.

"Huh," Gil says, his expression pleasantly confused. "Not sure where I got the idea, I guess."

I feel, rather than see, Tanner and Allison watching this sideshow. But I'm focused on the way Romina's face falls. She looks around the living space, her brow furrowed. It's a lovely, well-maintained home, but it's clear it was built long ago, before it seemed like everyone wanted houses big enough where they'd never really have to see one another. In this front area of the house, everything overlooks something else—kitchen to living room, living room to small dining room—and I'm sure the back, down that narrow hallway, is little more than two bedrooms and a single bathroom between them. It's not all that different from the house I grew up in, the house I'd be crammed into with my parents and my sister and her family, had everything gone to plan.

"But it's fine!" I say, my voice overly cheerful. "It's totally fine. The cottage sounds amazing! Like a special Christmas treat." I am as good at this farce as I am because of all the holiday movies I watch, obviously. Kelly would be very proud.

I don't know if my answer means Romina assumes Jasper and I are together, or if she's just so relieved to have a solution that she doesn't press the point any further. Gil's holding the two pairs of boots and looking back and forth between Jasper and me like he's trying to solve an equation.

"How about some dinner while we wait?" Romina says, clapping her hands together and smiling, already shuffling into the kitchen.

And it seems me and Jasper, we're in sync again, at least on the outside, because neither of us seems to be able to do anything but stand mutely and nod, half smiles on our faces while we try to act unruffled by this change of plan.

I only wish I knew if we're in sync on the inside. If he's thinking as much about that Christmas cottage bed as I am.

Chapter Seven

JASPER

You can't really avoid the bed in a place this small.

It's one room, the cottage—not unlike the hotel room I'd have been staying in tonight, had things gone to plan—and while it's true that there's some unfinished details about it, mostly Gil and Romina had been underselling it. It's warm and obviously freshly painted; the line of cabinets that form the small galley kitchen are bright white and brand-new; the love seat and coffee table only look gently used.

And the bed—yeah, it's also brand-new, not even made up, which is why I've got an armful of snow-dusted sheets and blankets when I step farther into the room behind Kristen. We'd insisted on coming out here alone after the meal, assuring the Dreyers we didn't want them facing the wind unnecessarily. It'd been a good decision—not just because the wind was, in fact, worryingly powerful, Kristen's body leaning into mine as we'd walked, both of us trying to shield her face from the whipping snow, but because it's better that none of them see the way Kristen and I seem newly frozen in place by that bed.

I think it's a full-size.

"I could take the love seat," she says.

"Oh, sure. Let's have this argument again," I deadpan.

And for the second time in a week, she surprises me.

She laughs.

"Oh my God," she says through a gust of it. "This is really ridiculous. We're *snowed in*." She laughs again. "We're snowed in and I—I *kissed* you!"

"Kris," I say, still standing there with those blankets, watching her laugh and feeling my heart lurch happily in my chest at the sight of it. "Are you all right?"

She's braced herself on the love seat as she nods, leaning forward slightly with her laughter, her hair dusted with snowflakes, her cheeks flushed pink again, and I feel myself smiling too.

"There's only one bed," I say, and she practically howls.

"Gil thought we were *married*." She presses a hand to her chest. "What would Carol say?"

"She'd probably plan an office party. She'd wear a wedding-themed sweater. She'd put 'Going to the Chapel' on her computer speakers."

She has to sit on the arm of the love seat after that, wiping her eyes. It's the best part of my day, seeing her laugh like that. I should set down the blankets, but I can't. If anything, I hold them tighter to my chest, the wet of the melting snow sinking through the fabric of my coat.

But after a few seconds she quiets, her face falling at the same time she moves to the side, sitting fully on the cushion now. Her eyes drift to the window—it's nearly nine, full dark, but the drifting snow, combined with what I worry is some fresh snowfall on its own— gives the outdoors an almost eerie lightness.

"It doesn't look good for tomorrow, does it?"

I move on instinct, setting the stack of linens on the bed and stripping off my coat before coming around to sit beside her. It's a small piece of furniture, suited to the space but not so much to either one of us, who're both above average in height, and definitely not so much if we're trying to avoid more of the physical contact that had seemed—at least to me—to fill up the Dreyers' living room with pheromones.

"Maybe it'll clear." I watch the space where the cream wool of her coat presses against the starched blue cotton of my shirt.

She purses her lips, her expression doubtful. She sits forward, takes off her coat, and tosses it over the arm before settling again. Back at the house, she'd been the one trying to cheer me, to contain my frustration about my having gotten us into this mess. But now that she doesn't have to put a face on for anyone, I can see how upset she is. It hurts to see her this way, but it's also a reminder. Kris can show me this because—even in spite of the way it's been between us since that kiss—we're friends. We're that close; we know each other that well.

"Hey." I nudge her lightly with my shoulder. "Tell me what you'd be doing. If you were with your family right now, I mean."

She rolls her head my way, looks up at me through dark-lashed eyes, her mascara a little smudgy. She gives a halfhearted shrug. "The usual stuff."

"What's the usual stuff?"

"You don't like Christmas. I saw you drink that hot cider. You made this face." She pulls her lips to the side, scrunches her nose slightly. This time, I laugh.

"I didn't."

"You did. You only kept drinking it to wash down the cookie."

"It was dry!" I nudge her again, and the *missing*, it's less now, the way it always is when we spend time together this way. As more than colleagues. "Anyway, I want to know. The usual stuff."

Kris takes a deep breath, and the action sinks her closer to me, her head almost resting on my shoulder. "Well, we'd make cookies. They're my grandmother's recipe, sour cream sugar cookies, with vanilla frosting. They're not dry at all."

I shift, pushing myself farther into the seat, resting my own head against the back of the cushions. "Cookies, all right. I'd try them."

She snorts, and it sounds like the rare times she's gotten a little tipsy around me—one late-night delay at an airport bar, one too many beers during a ballgame. "My dad's a singer, did you know that?"

"I did." She told me once, not long after we first met, out at a bar in Houston with Ben. He may have asked all the questions, but I remember all the answers. Mac Fraser. Classically trained at a conservatory somewhere in Ohio. Now, singing for fun in an eighties cover band, playing on Thursday nights at some dive bar outside of Lansing. His favorite song is "Eye of the Tiger."

"So we sing, usually on Christmas Eve. Most of us are terrible, but he and Malik are so good they drown the rest of us out."

"Singing," I say. "Sounds awful, but okay. What else?"

"Kelly and I, we watch Hallmark movies. A *lot* of them. You know what Hallmark movies are?" She too pushes back into the cushions, sets her feet—narrow and high-arched in the black tights that wrap her long, shapely legs—on the edge of the coffee table. I've already forgotten the question, which is okay because she keeps talking.

"Basically, one hundred and twenty minutes of pure sugar, right into your eyeballs. Cupcake shops, Christmas parades, some zany dog with a jingle bell collar. Happily ever afters. They are *great*."

"Oh, yeah," I say. "Sounds like it."

She nudges me this time, but doesn't pull back after she leans. She's fully resting against me, her head heavy on my shoulder. "Lots of snowed-in scenarios in these movies. You wouldn't believe it."

I shrug. "Guess I would, now."

She laughs, quieter now, and we settle into silence. The restless sleep of the last week, the early morning, the travel, the stress of everything from the day—I can feel it catching up to me, maybe to both of us. My eyes droop slightly, the weight of her body warm and comforting. There's only a couple of lights on in here, one above the kitchen sink, one small, shaded fixture beside the bed I'm still trying not to think about.

"Jasper," she says.

"Mmm?" I know I should get up, know I should deal with that bed, convince her to get in there alone. But it feels so good here, quiet words between us and soft cushions beneath our bodies. So close to my fantasy that I wonder if I'm already dreaming.

"How come you don't go home? For the holidays, I mean?"

I resist the urge to shift, to move away from her, though my eyes blink open, and I stare up at the still ceiling fan above us. I clear my throat. "I'm not welcome there."

I feel her head tip to look at me, but I keep my eyes

on the ceiling. I think she'll ask me why, but she chooses
a different tack, a smarter one—one that's more likely
to keep me talking. "What'd you used to do, then?
When you were welcome?"

I take a deep breath, closing my eyes again. It's
been so long since I've been there for a Christmas,
almost seventeen years. "Mostly we celebrated Christmas
Eve." Too many chores to do in the mornings, no
matter what day it was. "My dad's brothers and their
families would come out to the ranch. All fifteen of my
cousins."

"Wow," Kris says. "Must've been fun."

My lips tug into a smile, in spite of myself. "Could
be, yeah. We made a lot of trouble." No running in the
house, no snacks before dinner, no shaking the packages,
no going out to the stables. Every rule, we broke,
and almost always I'd be the ringleader. Because back
then, that's what I was used to being.

"We'd have a big barbecue dinner, and pineapple
cake my aunt Sarah used to make. Then church."

"Sounds nice."

"It was," I admit.

"Do you miss it?"

I don't let myself miss it, I think. *I only ever let myself
miss you.*

"No."

We're quiet again for long minutes, and I wonder if
Kristen's dozed off, if maybe I'm dozing a little too,
feeling the time stretch unusually with fatigue, pleasure
in her body next to mine.

"What are we going to do about the job?" she whispers
finally, and her voice sounds so worried. *The job.*
This one with the Dreyers, the firm in general. The job
has always been between us, but for once I don't want
the reminder. This night—the close of a long day at

work, ending with quiet talk about our families—it feels simple, natural. Natural in a way that makes me think about the other layers Kris and I could have between us, if only I could stop being so afraid of what would happen if it went wrong.

So this time, I do the unexpected thing. I move my hand from where it rests on my thigh and reach for hers, linking our fingers together. I hear her breath catch slightly, but before I can wonder if I've made a mistake, she squeezes my hand slightly, her cool palm pressing against mine.

"We'll worry about it tomorrow." I squeeze back.

I fall asleep thinking about Christmases—past, present, future.

Chapter Eight

KRISTEN

December 23

I wake up alone.

I'm curled on the love seat, a pillow tucked under my head and a blanket from the pile Jasper brought in last night draped over me. I sit up quickly, looking toward the bed, knowing already I'll find it unmade—if Jasper had woken up in the night, he would've made it. And he would've insisted that, at the very least, *I* get in.

So we must've . . . slept together?

I rub a hand over my eyes, my hair. I'm not surprised that I was dead to the world last night—Kelly and I shared a room until she left for college, and she could literally spend an entire night loudly making playlists on her computer without me waking up—but I am surprised I was comfortable enough to fall asleep in my clothes, my makeup. I probably look like the Crypt Keeper, but I can't summon the energy to care.

I know already that I'm not getting to Michigan today. I grew up on the west side of the Upper Peninsula, which means I *know* snow. I know the sound of its silence outside, the muffled quality to the air, even when you're inside. I know the way the light changes, whether it's gray—like it is now—or sunny. I even know the smell of it when it's freshly fallen.

So I know it's snowed more while I was sleeping.

I grab my phone from the coffee table, see Jasper's watch and phone there, pause briefly to listen for him moving around in the bathroom. But—nothing. He's brought our bags in; they sit right by the cottage's front door, so he must be dressed and at the Dreyers', probably using the extra time to work on Gil. I'd be mad, him on the job without me, but I can't help thinking about the way he spoke last night, the way he talked about his family's Christmases past. The way we'd sunk into each other, talking quietly, Jasper saying things he's never said before. I didn't even know he'd grown up on a ranch. Maybe he's escaping a bit, working on the job, reestablishing some boundaries, and I certainly can understand that.

Even if I do still feel that holiday bell in my heart.

I stand and walk over to my bag, my body stiff with sleep, and take a quick glance at my phone. The screen is stacked with texts, nearly all of them from the airline: *DELAY, DELAY, DELAY, CANCELLATION.*

But the most recent one is from Kelly, a single line.

Your Jasper is lovely.

I stare down at it, my brows crinkling in confusion. Kelly met Jasper a couple of times when she's been in Houston for visits, and obviously—as she reminded me last week—I talk about him a good deal. But I'm not sure what's prompted—

Just then, the door opens, nearly hitting me in the face. "Oh!"

"Holy shit!" says Jasper, stumbling slightly across the threshold as he tries to keep hold of the various brightly colored tote bags in his hand while catching the door. "I'm sorry!"

I step back, reaching a hand out to stop him dropping his haul. "What—?"

He steadies himself, pulling the bags slightly closer to his body, like he's trying to hide something. His cheeks are reddened—maybe from the cold, maybe from embarrassment, and my lips press together in an effort to suppress my smile.

"I was at the house. Gil and Romina's house, I mean."

"Yes. I figured that."

He's got snow all up the shins of his jeans, and he lowers the bags to the floor gently and then turns back to the open door, reaching outside to haul in a box. When it's in, he closes out the cold, the wind, the world—and for a second we stand there in the quiet. Me in a wrinkled skirt and blouse, stockinged feet and day-old hair and makeup; Jasper in jeans and boots, a thermal and a heavy coat, like he's natural to this place.

"I called your sister," he says.

I blink at him.

"She sent me the recipe for the cookies." He looks down at the stack of bags. "Romina didn't have everything, but she had most of it, and the oven here is small, but she said there's a cookie sheet in here that'll fit." He crouches down, pulls the box between us, and opens the lid. "She gave us this tree. It's small and fake but it's got lights on it already."

"Jasper, is this . . ." I trail off, my throat thick with emotion.

He stands, and he is holding the ugliest artificial tree I have ever seen. It's not plugged in, obviously, but I can see that the lights he referred to are, in fact, fiber-optic threads imitating pine needles. I love this hideous, slightly crooked tree. I love that he got it for me.

"It's not going to be like home," he says. "But just in case you can't get out tomorrow, I don't want you to miss—"

"Christmas."

He shrugs. The red on his cheeks isn't from the cold. "Yeah."

The smile I was holding in, it's irrepressible now. Probably my crooked bottom teeth are showing. "I need to put on my pajamas!" I blurt.

Jasper frowns at me, confused. "You just woke up."

"I know, but on Christmas, it's pajamas all day. Baking in pajamas, movies in pajamas." I bend down, unzip my bag.

"I don't have pajamas."

I laugh distractedly, pushing past a couple of sweaters to what I'm looking for. "What do you mean, you—oh."

His mouth curves up again on one side, his expression sheepish.

"You can just wear that, then." I gesture at his current attire, which is absurd. Like I'm a schoolmarm granting permission. All I can think about is Jasper, no pajamas, and that bed. The holiday bell is ringing somewhere different at the moment.

"Thanks," he says, his smile fuller now. "How about you change, and I'll get us set up?"

I mutter a flustered agreement and grab my bag of toiletries before ducking into the small bathroom.

When I come out twenty minutes later—the quick shower and teeth-brushing doing wonders to make me feel more human and less embarrassed—Jasper's put the tree in the center of a small café table to the side of the kitchen, has set out ingredients and cooking supplies over the small counter space. He's staring down at the screen of his phone, reading something.

"Ta-da!" I say, throwing my arms wide. It's silly, but now I'm determined to be silly. I promised Jasper we'd have fun, and he's made an effort, too. We're doing this thing, a friendly snowed-in Christmas at our lost recruit's guest cottage, so I might as well go for broke.

He looks up and for a second he only stares, lips parted and eyebrows raised. "Are those—"

"Snowmen? Yes! Yes, they are." I point to a spot on my thigh. "Frosty, right here."

"Wow. Did Carol give you those?"

"No, my mom did. But my mom's a lot like Carol. Is there coffee?"

I step into the kitchen area, and Jasper points to a Keurig hidden behind a stack of mixing bowls, a cup of steaming brew already prepared. Despite the fact that I'm wearing flannel pants and an oversize sweatshirt, and that I'm pretty sure Jasper is reading my grandmother's cookie recipe rather than his usual news feed, this moment is familiar, like mornings in the office where we meet up to go over our days.

"Says here we have to start with the sour cream mixture," he says, brow furrowed. I sip my coffee, peek over his shoulder to read the e-mail my sister's sent, and this is familiar, too—me and Jasper, working on a project together. Within minutes we're swept up in the rhythm that's been absent from our interactions lately. He's arranging tools and ingredients, I'm doing assembly; he scoops balls of batter onto a cookie sheet while I start on the icing.

And all the while, we talk easily. Some about work and some about life—Ben's recent proposal to Kit, my eldest niece's ballet class, the new high-rise that's being built not far from our office, the burger place we ate at a few months ago that neither of us can remember the name of. It's the kind of conversation that's made it feel, for years, like Jasper is, truly, one of my best friends. That it's not just work that brings us together.

"I don't think these are right," he says. I look up from stirring more powdered sugar into my buttercream. Beside me, Jasper is bent over, peering through the glass door of the apartment-size oven. "Look how much they're growing. They're gonna stick together."

I shift, crouching beside him. "They're not. That's just what happens when they bake. They'll slow down."

He frowns. "I don't like it."

I laugh, returning to my post. "Okay. Well, I'm telling you, it's going to work out. You can't tell dough what to do."

"Hm." When he stands, he leans on the counter right beside the oven, as though he wants to be close enough to keep checking on them. I duck my head, hiding another smile, stirring my icing. After a few seconds, he clears his throat. "The Dreyers said they have a big meal for Christmas Eve. A lunch."

"Oh?" My smile dims, the thought of my family pointed at the mention of something like this—another family's traditions, another family's gathering.

"They said we're welcome. If—you know. If we're still here."

I stop stirring, set the bowl aside. It's the perfect texture right now, just like my grandmother's, and I don't want to overmix it. I look toward the window, where the snow is steadily falling. "I think we're still going to be here." I try to sound sanguine about it, but I can hear the disappointment in my voice.

"Kris, I really am sorry."

"It's not your fault. It's the job, you know? Who knows, maybe we can make some progress."

He looks down at his feet, shakes his head slightly. I've sucked all the silliness right out of the room, mentioning the job, and I didn't mean to.

"Listen, of course I'm disappointed about my family. But this"—I wave a hand vaguely around the room—"it's sort of nice, you know?"

He looks up at me, a question in his eyes. My *this*—it's not the job. But I'm not sure how to make a start at telling him.

I smooth the front of my sweatshirt, notice some flour dust here and there, and I concentrate on brushing it off while I speak. "You know, every year, at Christmas, when we're away from work for so long, I—I miss you, you know?"

He doesn't say anything, for long enough that I finally have to look up at him. He stands still as a statue, his arms crossed over his chest. The posture is cold, but the way one of his hands grips the opposite elbow, the way his eyes are fixed on me, the way he's pulled his bottom lip, scar-side, slightly in—all of it is warm, warm, warm.

"You miss me?" There's something in his voice I haven't really heard before. Half surprise, half wonder. Like looking under the tree on Christmas morning.

I lift my shoulders, let them fall. "I do."

After another long pause, he speaks again, his voice low, tentative. "They said we could come over tonight, too. If we wanted."

The air between us crackles, like that moment just

before I asked for his kiss. But I'm not going down that road again, not without an invitation.

"I don't mind staying in," I tell him.

He nods, bends, and checks the cookies again. When he straightens, he fixes me with another warm look. "Good," he says. "We've got movies to watch, anyway."

Chapter Nine

JASPER

"Unbelievable!" I shout, waving a hand in the direction of my laptop. "He's in a Santa suit, not a ski mask! How does she not recognize him?"

Kristen laughs, keeping her eyes on the screen while the aforementioned man wraps his arms around the short, plucky woman who has spent the last ninety minutes not making the extremely obvious connection between her quiet doctor neighbor and the Santa who's been doing visits to the children's hospital wing where she works as an events planner. "But let me guess," Kristen says. "You've got no problem with Superman."

I frown as the two people on-screen kiss—chaste, close-mouthed, and not for longer than four seconds. Over the course of several movies, I have learned that this is the only type of acceptable kiss, and embarrassingly, each time I see one, I think of how unchaste Kris and I had been about it on our first try.

"Superman's different," I grumble, shifting on the love seat.

"Here comes the big reveal." We're quiet as the man

tugs down his beard and lowers his eyes, looking sheepish about his identity.

"Seems like a consent issue, if you ask me," I say.

"You know, I think you like these movies."

No, I think. *I like watching these movies with you.*

I like everything about this day with her. When I'd woken up this morning, it'd been barely five a.m., and Kristen and I had moved in the night—my back pressed against the arm of the love seat, ass to the edge of the cushions, feet still resting on the floor. Her curled beside me, feet tucked up and head resting on my chest. She sleeps so heavily, and she snores, too, which would probably mortify her to know. I'd watched the snow outside the window and thought: *this*.

This is what Christmas morning is supposed to feel like.

But soon enough I'd remembered it's not what Christmas morning feels like to her, so I'd gently disentangled myself and gotten to work. The cookie recipe from her sister, the massive assist from the Dreyers, a cable password borrowed from Ben and Kit for the movies, and my own determination to get it right. Somewhere in the back of my mind the job is kicking around; I'd thought about it all through my snowy walk back and forth to the Dreyers'. But in the cottage, I set it aside. For Kristen. For her Christmas.

On-screen, what's happening is what I've learned is the "low moment"—the couple is about to split. The lady who can't recognize her neighbor's eyes, cheeks, teeth, or voice is walking down what I'm pretty sure is the same Main Street set from the previous movie, a single tear tracking down her face. I've looked sadder than this after cutting my face shaving, so probably it's only another few minutes before we get the promised *happily ever after*.

I sneak a peek over at Kris. She's got both hands

wrapped around a cup of hot chocolate, her brows furrowed in concern. She does this every time, even though it always works out, and for a few seconds I get lost in the expressions that pass over her face as the music swells—Doctor Santa, I'm guessing, is about to make a speech. Another chaste kiss is coming, I'm sure.

"That was a good one," Kris says, when the credits roll. She looks over at me. "Don't make that face!"

I school my expression. "I liked it. Very uplifting."

She snorts, takes a sip of her cocoa. This plus the cookies—she smells like a bag of sugar, probably, and despite my general lack of a sweet tooth, I've never wanted to taste something more. I stand from the couch, holding out a hand for her mug. "Want a refill?" I ask, distracting myself. "Then we can watch another."

She looks up at me, one eyebrow raised. "It's almost midnight. Four's not enough?" I can tell by the way she's said it—four's enough for her for now, and she's got something else in mind. Something I'm guessing I won't like.

"I'm not doing the singing," I say, trying for a joke.

She doesn't take the bait. "I kind of thought we should talk about yesterday. What happened in the kitchen, I mean."

I sit down again, try to keep my face neutral. "I told you. I was off my game."

"But what Gil said bothered you. I *know* you, Jasper."

I sigh, stare down at my hands. "I know you do."

"Does it—is it something to do with what you told me last night? About how you're not welcome at home anymore?"

"Kris—"

"Tell me," she says, and the *way* she says it. Exactly like that last challenge she put to me, with the same weight behind it. She sets her mug on the table, closes the lid of the laptop. Shifts on the love seat so she's facing me, her knees hugged to her chest and her arms wrapped around her snowman-covered legs. With the laptop closed most of the light in the cottage is from the garish fiber-optic tree. I take a deep breath, something thudding inside me at what this might reveal to her. Where it'll lead.

"Gil—the way he is with Tanner—that's very different from how my dad was with me."

"Yeah?"

I nod. "My dad—all he ever wanted was for me to take over his ranch. No matter the cost—school, fun, whatever. Drove me crazy, working for him."

"Working for—?" Kris says, clearly confused at the way I've described it.

"Mean as hell, he was. About chores, about everything. When I got into science I'd try to bring him stuff, stuff I'd read about agricultural management, but . . ." I trail off, thinking about the way he'd once knocked a book from my hands, right into a trough of water. He'd probably have pushed me in too, but I was bigger by then.

"Well," Kris says stiffly. "He must regret it now. He must be proud of what you've done."

"He hates what I've done. He threw me out when he found out I got into college."

"*What?*"

I shrug, passing on the details of that day—Dad stuffing my things in garbage bags, yelling. Mom watching, saying nothing. He told me if I hated my life so much on the ranch I could take the bags and what was in my truck and never come back. It wasn't so bad that he'd said it; he'd always had a temper.

It was so bad that he'd meant it.

"Listen, there were lots of things he wanted for me that I didn't want. The ranch, yeah. But even when I was younger. He wanted me to play football; I didn't. He wanted me to take out a girl from a nearby ranch; I didn't. He wanted me working every second I was free—no studying, no books, nothing. Everything I did back then, it was against his rules."

"How could he throw you out?"

"Easy. We didn't get along. I pushed all his buttons." Signing up for science fairs. Taking the PSATs. Being in AP courses. "He thought something was wrong with me."

"Wrong how?"

"Not sure, really. I wasn't into the same things he was. He couldn't understand me, and I can't say I blame him. Everyone in my family, they've all done the same sorts of things. I'm an outlier."

"What about your mom?"

"She's all right, but she didn't much understand me either. I think it was a relief for her. We all get along better now, see each other a couple of times a year for a dinner out or something. They've both said they're sorry for how it all happened, but I don't think they're sorry it did. My dad's got one of my cousins in at the ranch now, and that makes him happy. They still don't invite me back."

"Jasper." Her voice is full of sadness. Way more than event planner lady.

"I wasn't an easy kid. Once I knew what I wanted—I'd do anything to get it, break any rules he set, no matter how mad it made him. I was determined."

"You're still like that. Determined."

"Best and worst thing about me. That's what Ben says."

"I don't see how it's the worst thing."

I give her a look that says, *yeah, right.* "I almost ruined my friendship with him—with *you*—so I could start the firm. I was so determined for us to get out on our own I couldn't see straight." After a few years at Beaumont, I'd felt like I was twitching every day under the thumb of my various bosses, like being back on that ranch.

"You figured it out, though. You apologized."

I smile at her. "You helped."

She smiles back softly. Looks down at the space between us.

"Back then, I guess I felt—I'd given up so much for my career. My family, my—" I break off. *My feelings for you,* is what I want to say, and I realize that this is why I was afraid of this conversation. I swallow. "I had to make it work, getting out of the non-compete. I had to get us out on our own, be in charge of myself. Or else—what had all that suffering, all that loss been for?"

For a few seconds neither of us says anything, and in the silence I realize—that's the best way I've ever explained it, what came over me a couple of years ago. I ought to call Ben, make sure I tell him, too. We're okay now, me and him, but I owe him more. Those first couple of years away from the ranch especially— at the college my dad had so hated the idea of—Ben had been my family.

I feel her shift, her feet curling slightly into the cushion before relaxing, and I know she's working up to something.

"Is that why the kiss was such a bad idea?" she finally

asks, almost a whisper. "Because of the risk to the business? To everything you'd sacrificed for?"

I look over at her, my heart kicking up into an uneven rhythm. This night, even more than last—the darkness, her quiet voice and everything I've just told her, those ridiculous pajamas she's wearing—it's so close to those fantasies of my sad, secret heart. The borrowed tree is the starlight; her soothing voice is the silence. She's the softness, no matter what she's wearing.

"You've always said," I begin, gripping my thigh too tightly, feeling my restraint dull second by second. "You've always said things can go wrong when—"

"I know what I've said."

I look over at her, see her lips compressed in frustration, determination. As much determination as I've ever had.

"That night, when we stopped, you seemed like you regretted it. You looked . . . startled."

"I *was* startled," she says. "Weren't you? Did you expect it to be like that?"

"Yes," I say without hesitation. "I mean, I didn't expect it to happen. But I expected it to be like that, if it ever did happen."

"You did?"

"Kristen. I always did."

She blinks. She's shocked, I'm sure, but I'm not taking this back, not now, not with the way she's looking at me. The day's blown over me, like a drift of the snow outside. Unstoppable. Covering and muffling everything that keeps me away from her.

"Remember what I told you about *my* Christmases?" I ask her, my voice low, and she nods. Both of us have leaned in, closing the space between us.

"Making trouble," she whispers, and I think I can feel the puff of breath on my lips.

"Let's do that, now," I say, almost against her lips—and *God*. Thank God.

She kisses me.

Chapter Ten

KRISTEN

December 24

It's the best Christmas tradition, this one. The one I didn't even know I was missing. After midnight, now Christmas Eve. Kissing Jasper.

Jasper kisses me like he's been making this kind of trouble with me for years, and within seconds of our lips touching I'm in his lap, and it's so fast, so hot, so natural that I don't know if I crawled over or if he pulled me. I only know the way we feel together—our lips and tongues tangling, his fingers pushed through my hair, holding one side of it back, his other arm wrapped tight around my lower back, pressing me close to him. Between our layers of clothes I can feel how hard he is beneath me, everywhere—the strong arms that hold me, the broad chest I'm held against, the muscled thighs supporting me, the thick length between those thighs that I feel desperate to rub against.

I bite at his lip, scar-side, and he grunts. "Damn," he breathes out.

"How did you get this?" I whisper, darting my tongue against it.

"I don't remember," he says, the words muffled against my neck, where he starts kissing. "A fence, maybe." He lets out another frustrated exhale. "This sweatshirt is enormous."

I tip my head back, exposing more skin, and he rewards me with a slow lick up the side of my neck, and—yeah. This sweatshirt *is* enormous, and too warm, and my breasts ache with the need to be closer to his chest, his hands, his mouth.

"Not"—I pause, gasp as he nibbles at the spot he's just licked, try to get my motor skills under control enough to find the hem of this thing so I can get it off—"the sexiest lingerie, I guess," I finish breathily. I have never been this turned on, ever. I hope he doesn't think I'm having an asthma attack.

"It's the sexiest thing," he says, moving my hands away, pushing his own under the hem, his hands hot and calloused on my skin. "I love this sweatshirt." His hands rise up, tracing either side of my spine, then the bottom edge of the pullover bra I'm wearing. "It's so *soft*."

"Wait until you feel what's underneath," I tease, and I feel his smile on the skin of my neck.

"You *are* trouble," he says, and then his hands work fast, pulling the sweatshirt and the bra off all at once, and for a few seconds he stares, his face dumbstruck— a slow blink of his eyes, his lips parted. His hold on me is firm, his big hands on either side of my rib cage, and that feels so good, to be held like this by Jasper. To be looked at like this by Jasper.

"You're beautiful," he breathes. "Feels like I'm un-wrapping you."

"My turn," I say, and the rest of our clothes come off

like that—like presents under a tree, like we can't decide how long to pause and admire the gift we've got in front of us before we start thinking about what we still have waiting.

When we're both down to just our underwear, me back to straddling Jasper's lap, his hands caressing all over my skin and mine clutching at his biceps, shoulders, and hair, Jasper pulls his lips back from mine, moving one hand up my arm and pausing when he reaches my neck, so sensitive to his touch that I shiver. He looks at me, his expression serious, his eyes searching, the lights from the tree winking across his skin gorgeously.

"Kris," he whispers. "Is this okay?" I realize he's waiting to see whatever he thought he saw the last time we kissed. Me regretting, or me startled, whatever.

"It's better than okay. It's . . ." I lean forward, kiss him again, sink into his warmth, feel the vibration of the moan he makes against my chest. My senses feel overloaded, not just from the way he touches me, or from the way he looks and sounds and tastes. It's everything about this day—the comfort I'd felt, lolling around in pajamas, like I would have at home. The glow of that ridiculous color-changing tree, the smell of the cookies baking, the familiar, cheerful instrumental holiday music in the movies we watched. All the things he's done for me today.

"*Christmas*," I finish, and that's when he stands, his hands holding the backs of my thighs as he maneuvers us around the love seat. I absolutely regret every time I have teased him for insisting on gym time for himself during our work trips. Gym time is great; gym time should have a hallowed shrine built in its honor.

He puts me down gently, swipes most of the sheets and blankets off the bed, keeping one that he drapes

over the mattress before coming back to me, wrapping
me in his arms to move me farther onto the now
half-made bed. "We should've taken care of this," he
murmurs, but I stop his mouth with mine. This bed
had frozen us both over last night, and I don't want
that happening again.

I don't know how long we spend like that—minutes, hours—spread out with him on top of me, kissing
like it's what we need to stay alive, our skin growing
warm, fevered, our hands clutching and desperate.

"Jasper," I breathe, clenching my fingers in his hair,
pulling him up from where he has just spent an incredibly satisfying few minutes. "Please tell me you
have a condom. *Please.*"

It's his turn to look startled, and he practically jolts
away from me, moving back to the love seat and bend-
ing to pick up his pants off the floor. I watch as he
clumsily yanks his wallet from the back pocket, tossing
the pants like he's angry at them, and I put a hand
over my mouth to hide my smile, and also to hide the
howl of sadness that will surely come out of my mouth
if he doesn't find a condom in there.

But he's victorious, a foil wrapper held between his
fingers and a triumphant smile on his face that dims
momentarily while he stalks over to the little Christmas
tree, holding the square package underneath one of
the fiber-optic branches and squinting.

The fact that he has to check the expiration—it is
ludicrously gratifying to me, even though I know I've
got no business wondering.

"Thank God," he says, coming back to me, standing
at the foot of the bed. "What if I'd had to go to the
house and ask that Tanner guy for a condom?" He
bends and kisses my stomach, the skin there quivering
with the laugh I let out.

"Probably he wouldn't have had one." I gasp at the feel of Jasper licking upward. He hasn't even un-wrapped the condom and I feel dangerously, embar-rassingly close to the edge, his tongue doing incredible things to me. "Because—of the baby?"

"Hmm." He kisses across my collarbone, and I'm so flushed with heat and anticipation. All at once it's hit-ting me, even more so than before—I have wanted this with Jasper for so long. I have loved him for so long, and I'm so relieved to be doing this finally that I hardly know what to do with all this feeling. Somewhere, kick-ing around in the deep recesses of my mind, is the knowledge that we haven't dealt with work—that inside this cottage Jasper has been all mine, but out in the world, it's always the job for him first, and I don't know what that means for tomorrow.

But I don't pay attention to those deep recesses, not right now. I have to keep talking to distract myself. "Gil and Romina seem pretty connected, though. Maybe he'd have one."

He laughs now, pulls away and looks down at me. "Kristen. If you want us to keep going here, you'd better get that image out of my head."

For a second we stay like that, smiling at each other like coconspirators in this trouble we're making to-gether. The moment is so easy and simple and happy, and then I realize that all I need to do with this over-flowing feeling I have is to . . . hang on to it. To enjoy it and celebrate it like the holiday it is.

I reach down, tuck my thumbs in the edge of my plain cotton boy shorts, and push them down.

He leans back and watches.

"Better image," he says, his voice rough, and then he's tearing open that foil square, and it's nothing like how it's always been before for me—nothing like when

I avert my eyes for this part, worrying that it'll feel too routine, too pragmatic, something that will spoil the mood. Nothing like when I stiffen slightly at that first press between my legs, the intimacy of joining with another person always somewhat awkward for me. Nothing like those moments where a fleeting thought—about work, about bills or laundry, or, most often, about Jasper—will tug at my mind, distracting me from what I'm doing, the person I'm with.

With Jasper, I watch everything. I feel everything. I focus on everything.

And nothing, *nothing*, has ever felt better.

Chapter Eleven

JASPER

This time, I wake up long after five a.m. The sun's up, the sky bright from the reflection of the snow, and I can hear a soft dripping, melting off the edges of the cottage's roof. Outside, the air is still, and no snow is falling.

I'll bet she can fly out later today. She'll get to her family; she won't miss their whole Christmas, and I'm glad.

I close my eyes again, breathe in the smell of her hair, feel the warm curve of her back against my chest, block out the sun and the day for a little longer. I've got a thousand feelings rushing through my blood: the hot, insistent desire that kept us up almost all night, finding new ways to make each other feel good once we'd used our one, blessed condom. The warm, settled assurance of my love for her. The creeping anxiety about what today will bring, when we have to face the Dreyers at their Christmas lunch, and when Kristen will get on a plane to her family.

But the thing I notice most is the absence of a feeling.

This morning, for the first morning in six years, I don't miss her.

Instinctively, my arm tightens around her waist, and I feel her stir and stretch, a movement that presses her ass against my lap. "Careful there, darlin'," I murmur. I feel like I can hear my dick cursing me out about the condom situation.

Kristen turns in my arms, her hair a messy tangle over her eyes and her smile sleepy. "You sound like a cowboy, calling me that."

I smooth the hair from her face, kiss her nose. "Guess I used to be one, sort of."

"I like it." She leans in to kiss me—brief and close-mouthed, a holiday movie kiss, and there's something to be said for a kiss like this. It's a happily-ever-after kiss, the kind of kiss that assumes there'll be a bunch more after.

Still, I stroke the backs of my fingers down her chest, over her stomach. Feel her shudder in pleasure and twist her body against the sheets.

Sometime in the middle of the night, exhausted and satisfied, we'd stumbled from the bed, gathered the rest of the linens and made it up properly, smiling goofily and getting into a ridiculous, good-natured argument about which side should face down on the flat sheet. It'd been strange, after all we'd done together, to have that single domestic moment be so crystallizing for me. But when I'd lain down next to her afterward, the sheets cool and clean, I'd made a decision. Today I'd do everything I could to get Gil to change his mind, to show Kris that we could still work together, be successful. To keep the firm together—us in our office, Carol our admin, all our plans staying on track. To make it so she'd never regret being with me, no matter what rules we've broken here.

It's that determination that gets me moving.

I give her another brief kiss, roll over, and grab my

phone from the nightstand. It's later than I thought, only an hour before the lunch is supposed to start. "I want to look over some things from GreenCorp before we get over there," I tell her. "You want to shower, or . . . ?"

She's quiet behind me, and when I look over at her, she's tugged the sheet up over her skin, turned onto her back. After a few seconds she shifts, keeping the sheet pressed to her chest while she sits up, her other arm reaching for her own phone. She clears her throat delicately. "You can go ahead," she says. I open my mouth to clarify that I meant it as an invitation, something we could do together. But she speaks before I can. "I should look at flights for later, see what's going on there."

I don't like the way her face has shuttered, the way she's tapping away at the phone. I reach back to set a hand on her leg. "You okay?"

Tell me you don't regret it.

She looks up at me, the light in her eyes dimmed but her smile in place.

"I'm good." She leans forward to kiss me again, quick like before. It doesn't feel so *happily ever after* this time but I try to trust her, to trust *this*. I can make this work with her. I can show her how good it'll be.

When I come out of the shower she's pulling clothes from her suitcase, holding them to her while she walks toward the bathroom. She smiles as she passes but also tells me she's on standby for a flight out tonight. I tell her I'm happy, and I *am*—but tension ratchets up inside me. If she goes tonight, and we don't have this job settled, what's she going to think about this, about us? About how we'll be able to do the job and do *this*, when this has only just started? What happens when Christmas is over and we're back in Houston, the place where we set all those boundaries that have kept us apart?

While she showers I open my laptop, which starts up where we left it, credits rolling over a version of "Here Comes Santa Claus"—annoyingly on the nose. I read over everything I've got on GreenCorp, on Gil's patent. I'm deep in it when she comes out, dressed in a pair of jeans and a heavy cream sweater, her hair down, no makeup. She looks over at where I sit on the bed in nothing but my boxer briefs, and I set the computer aside. I'd like to go over to her, or have her come over to me, feel the texture of that sweater all over my skin—

"Don't put on your work clothes," she says. "It's a family meal. We don't want to make them uncomfortable."

Her tone is so different than it was just a half hour ago. But maybe she's just feeling the way I'm feeling. This is a good tip about the job, one I probably wouldn't think of myself, and isn't that what's always made us such a good team?

"Yeah, of course," I say, and stand to get dressed.

I'm still uneasy when we pull the door closed behind us twenty minutes later. I've got the cookies we made yesterday, and Kris is clutching a small gift bag in one hand, a set of note cards she'd been planning to give to an aunt she'll be seeing the day after Christmas. The sun is blinding, the snow so white it feels like there's nowhere comfortable to look, and we mostly squint our way across the expanse of yard that takes us to the ranch house. I hold the tray of cookies tightly in one hand, keep my other at the ready as we trudge through the snow, in case Kris slips.

But she knows snow better than I do, and she doesn't need me at all.

On the porch we both stamp our feet, knocking off excess powder. As I watch her, eyes cast down and mouth free of her easy smile, I decide I don't want to ignore that uneasy feeling. Something's gone wrong enough that it's got me missing her again. And I've already decided: I can't go back to that.

So when she lifts her hand to knock, I say her name.

She turns to look at me, her eyes flat and her mouth in a line.

"What are we doing here?" she asks.

I slide my eyes to the door. "The lunch?"

"Is this for the job, or is it for Christmas?"

"I . . ." I swallow, not sure what to say. Isn't it both? Isn't part of what I'm trying to give her for this Christmas some assurance about the job? I realize, with a sinking sense of dread, how ill-equipped I am to handle this newness between us. Six years and all I've practiced with her is the *missing* part, and I feel the depths of my ignorance like a slap to the face.

"It's the job," she says.

"Of course it's the job." I'm frustrated with myself, with her, with everything that's not us in that cottage. "We have to—"

Just then, the front door opens. Gil's standing there, holding the same mug, wearing the same green sweater, except this time I think it's turned inside out. "Pretty cold out here just to be standing around," he says.

"Gil," Kristen says, shoving the gift bag in his hand unceremoniously, but keeping a false smile pasted on her face. "Could you excuse me for a few minutes? I think I forgot something back at the cottage."

For once I'm not the one who's done the socially awkward thing in a business interaction, and while what I want is to simply drop this tray of cookies and follow her, it's so out of character for Kristen that I feel a protective instinct to mitigate the embarrassment I know she'll have later. I turn to Gil, still working out what I'll say to excuse myself.

"That Christmas stuff didn't work then?" Gil asks. He's sipping from his mug, watching her stomp through the snow.

"Work for what?"

He shrugs. "I was wrong about you being married to her. But you want to be, right?"

"I—" I look away, watch Kris's retreating form. Yeah, I want to be, but I'm not telling Gil that first. Hell, I'm not telling Kris that until we manage at least a few months in a functional relationship; I'm not a barbarian, or a doctor in a Santa suit. "How'd you know that?"

He takes another sip of his drink. Inside, I can hear his family laughing, pots and pans clanging.

"That look on your face when you came around here yesterday morning. That's about what my face looked like for the whole first month I knew Romina, trying to get her to like me. She thought I was ridiculous."

"Kristen doesn't think I'm ridiculous." Wait, does she? "Also I've known her for six years, not a month."

Gil laughs. "You *are* ridiculous, then."

I am, I think. But I say, "It's because we wor—"

"Uh-huh," Gil says, not letting me finish. "You know Romina was pretty worried about me changing my mind about the GreenCorp thing."

I blink in surprise, both at the change of subject and at this admission, since I'd been working under the assumption, especially after that scene at the table yesterday, that it'd been Romina who hadn't wanted to go. Any other day, maybe, and I'd be focused on this as a new piece of information related to the job. I'd be thinking, *Change tactics. Work harder on Romina, and Romina will work on our behalf.*

But right now, all I want is for Gil to stop talking long enough for me to go after Kris without it seeming rude.

"Guess she thinks like you, about the difference it could make. She's worried I'll regret it later."

I tighten my hand on the tray I'm holding, my eyes going back to Kristen. "You don't think you will?"

He sets down his mug on the arm of the wooden bench by the front door and reaches out to take the cookies. "Nah. I'll find a way, with the tech. I pretty much try to put things in the right order in my life, and if I've got my wife and kid in the top two places, everything else tends to work out all right in the end."

"I'm in love with her," I say. That's the right order. I feel it in my bones.

"Right." He picks up the mug again, gestures it in her direction. She's almost to the cottage door. "What's all this, then?"

This, I think to myself, *is the low moment.*

And then I step off the porch and go after her.

Chapter Twelve

KRISTEN

Halfway to the cottage, and I know I've made a mistake.

I shouldn't have run, and I know it. First of all, there's the matter of how it must've looked to Gil, especially given my flimsy excuse, and he's probably back in his house right now shrugging and giving a *look* to Romina, one of those married people *something's-going-on-there* silent communications that'll surely make it even more awkward when I do go back. For the family Christmas lunch they were kind enough to invite us to in the first place.

Second of all, I know Jasper will follow me back here. I *know* he will, and then we'll have to have this conversation, the one I should've insisted on having this morning. I should've set an alarm to wake up early, should've made a list of points to cover. In what universe would I have thought it was a good idea to try to work with him, to attempt a more challenging than usual recruiting conversation after such a monumental shift in our personal relationship? The *morning* after? I *know* better. I know that at the very least you have to identify the boundaries, set the rules—

"Kris," Jasper calls from behind me, right as I'm getting to the cottage's tiny porch threshold.

Third of all, Jasper followed me back here looking like this.

Focused. Determined. Ambitious. Jasper on the job.

I stop short of opening the door, instead standing my ground on the porch, raising a hand to shade my brow from the sun. It's better than doing this inside there, inside the place where I woke up with a chorus of holiday bells ringing in my heart, thinking I'd finally seen and been with the real Jasper, the Jasper who wouldn't risk a relationship for a job. But then he'd rolled over and gotten to work, and everything inside of me had gone cold and silent, and I haven't been thinking straight since.

"I just need a minute," I say, and he takes a step closer and slightly to the side, the perfect spot to block the sun from my eyes. I drop my hand and try not to fall more in love with him, which is hopeless.

Now that I can see him better I can see that his determination is a little frayed around the edges, his hair mussed and his cheeks flushed, his eyes wide with concern.

I'm about to tell him not to worry about it, to go back to Gil, to count on me being ready to do the job. I'll say I got my period and need a tampon or something; that always makes men disappear into thin air.

But instead Jasper blurts, "I want to be in each other's top places."

A clump of snow from the roofline plops onto his shoulder.

"What?"

"That's what Gil said, about the job." He's breathing a little heavy, and I know from gym time and now also from sex time that it's not from exertion. "He puts his wife and kid in the top place, and then he makes everything else work. I think we can do that, me and you."

"Jasper—"

"So what if we lose this job? That doesn't have to be because of this, of what happened between us. Or maybe it does, but it doesn't matter. We'll find a way. We'll do what we have to do with the firm. We can keep Carol, lose the office space, downsize for a while—"

"*What?*"

"Listen, I know what you're thinking."

"You clearly do not know what I'm thinking. You think I'm worried about losing the job?"

Another small clump of snow falls from the roof, lands on the right side of his head, but he simply brushes it off and keeps going. "No—I mean, not this one, specifically. I think maybe you think Gil's doing the right thing, staying here. But I also know you broke your rules with me last week and last night, and I don't want you to think I'll let it mess up us working together. I *won't.* I thought if we could convince the Dreyers, you'd see that we could handle this."

I blink at him. A tiny chime in my chest. "What's the *this?*" I ask him.

He stares at me, the snow on his shoulder sliding down. "The . . . *this?*"

"What's the *this* we're handling? And back in the airport, when I said I was sorry about the kiss—you told me you couldn't lose this. What's the *this?*"

His brow is furrowed in confusion. "I meant that I couldn't lose us. I couldn't lose me and you, together."

"On the job?"

He takes another step forward, shakes his head. "God, I have messed this up," he says, more to himself than to me. "No. Kris, no. I'd lose the business tomorrow, if it meant staying with you, being with you. As friends, as—as what we were last night. Anything."

"You've always put the job first. In your top place."

"I've made mistakes about that in the past. I know I have. But Kris, with you—I thought you'd think it was a bad idea, to try with me. So I made a rule for myself. I'd never let my feelings for you get in the way of just—getting to be with you. Be around you every day, at work. It's the best thing I've got, having that with you, and I couldn't lose it."

I'm sure the bell is ringing; I'm sure it is. But all I can hear is the sound of my heart beating.

"Why—" My voice is a little shaky, like the timbre of the bell after it's been rung. "Why did you think you'd lose it?"

"Any reason, really. You decide it's a mistake, because of work—which would be fair enough, given everything you've seen. Or one of us messes up at it, and we can't make our way back together. Or—even if you'd decided you had felt that way about me, maybe your feelings would change eventually."

"Or maybe *your* feelings would change," I say.

He gives me a long, determined look. A *Jasper-on-the-job* look. "My feelings wouldn't change."

I roll my eyes, look down at my borrowed boots. One night, and he's suddenly got all the confidence in the world about the way he feels. "Okay."

"Kristen." He waits. Waits for me to look back in those determined eyes. "They wouldn't. They won't. They haven't, not in all the six years I've known you. They have never changed."

"Six years?" It's almost a whisper.

"Six years." His voice is clear. Not loud, but not quiet, either. "Every day. I guess I should say—they have changed. Because when I first met you, I thought you were smart and kind and beautiful and completely out of my league, and every day that passed I knew that more and more, and I've been in love with you for that long, and yesterday was the best day and the best night of my life, even if it did ruin your Christmas."

"Jasper." It is a whisper now, pressed out through tears gathering in my throat, and because I know the next part will be too, I reach out and grab the front of his coat, pull him under the porch overhang with me, just as another clump of snow falls, this time hitting the ground. "You didn't ruin my Christmas."

He ducks his head, places his hands over mine.

"I'm in love with you, too," I say, and then he looks up, meets my eyes briefly before closing his in what seems to be plain, simple relief.

"People's feelings," he says quietly, tipping his head down and resting his forehead against mine. "People who loved me, once. My family. Their feelings changed. I've been afraid of that, with you. Afraid of trying, for what I might lose. The job—it felt like the only way I could have you in my life."

I move my hands from his coat, bring them up to his cold cheeks, feel him wrap his arms tight around my waist. "I've loved you a long time too. And I was afraid too. Of not being . . . in your top place, I guess. I didn't think I could ever handle that. Being with you, but always knowing the job would be more important."

He lifts his head, but keeps me close. "You're in the top place. Forever. I'm telling you, it doesn't matter about the Dreyers. We can go back there, and you'll see. I won't say a damn word about the patent. I'll sing a Christmas song with them, whatever you want. I don't care."

I shake my head, a tear-soaked laugh in my throat.

"You don't have to sing," I say, and then we're kissing, my back against the door of the cottage, Jasper broad and strong and hungry against me, his arms lifting me those few inches we need to be level. It's cold and bright and perfect, a Christmas morning kiss, and the only reason I break it is because I can't stop from smiling in perfect happiness.

"Kris," he whispers to me, right against my lips. "I *missed* you."

I somehow know what he means, know what it means to him to admit it, and I hold him tighter, pressing my mouth to his again, and he smiles now, that scar-side of his mouth tipping away from mine first, until he's got to simply hold me, pressing his smile into the cold strands of my hair.

"Jasper," I say, tipping my chin up so he'll hear me. "Come to Michigan."

I feel his smile widen. "Yeah?"

I nod. "As soon as we can get on a flight together. I don't want you to miss it."

We both pull back then, just enough so we can smile at each other. Jasper lifts a hand, swipes his thumb gently across my cheek, catching a few stray tears. I don't think he'd mind knowing his eyes are a little shiny too. All of a sudden I see Christmases stretch out in front of us, years of cookie making and movie watching and kissing past midnight.

"We'll have to talk about it, you know," I say, placing my hands on his chest. Even through his coat I think I can feel the holiday bell of his heart. "How to make sure it works between us. We'll have to lay some ground rules for—this. This relationship, and our relationship at work."

He leans back, smiling down at me before leaning down to give me a quick, soft kiss.

"Kris," he says, his voice husky, his eyes soft. "That's not going to be a problem." Another kiss, this one more lingering. "I'm good at following rules, when it comes to you."

Epilogue

JASPER

December 25
One Year Later

Kristen's parents live in a tiny ranch house, barely three bedrooms, and the barely is because the third one is basically a thin-walled closet, hardly enough room for the futon Kris and I have been sleeping on for the last three nights to be unfolded. My back hurts, I'm sex-deprived, and last night I stayed up until three a.m. helping Kris's brother-in-law build a dollhouse for his daughters.

I am having the best time.

"Okay, last one," Kris says, passing me yet another pot from the stove. I don't remember there even being enough food options on the dining table this evening for this many dirty dishes, but I haven't much minded the escape, Kris and me alone in the small kitchen while the rest of the family relaxes and digests in the other room. It's been fun, my second official Fraser family Christmas, but it's been noisy, too, and hasn't allowed for much privacy. Later tonight Kris and I will drive over to Traverse City, where we've rented a cottage right on the lake. Our Christmas gift to each other, and a private continuation of a tradition we started last year at the Dreyers'.

"I'm getting good at this," I tell Kristen, scrubbing at a spot of stuck-on potatoes. "Your mom is gonna love me."

Kris makes a clucking noise. "Please. She already loves you."

I smile down at my soapy hands. She's said it casually, jokingly, but the truth is—I think her mom *does* love me. I think her whole family does, and I'm as proud of that as anything I've ever done, especially since it made it easier to ask them—two nights ago while Kristen built a snowman with her nieces—for their blessing about a particular question I'm planning to ask Kris soon.

Tonight soon, if I have my way. I'll be breaking a promise to her, saying the cottage was the only gift for the holiday this year, but I've got a feeling she won't mind.

"I talked to Carol," Kris says, interrupting my thoughts. "She opened our package. She says it's her new favorite."

"I can only hope her family put on sunglasses before she turned it on."

Kris laughs, swats me with a towel. Keeping Carol on after the Dreyer deal lapsed hadn't been easy, exactly. We'd had to downsize, moving into a space with only one private office, but as it turned out Kris and I liked sharing, and we'll probably re-up the lease, even though we're back—way back, thanks to a new deal we've recently made for Gil Dreyer that'll keep him and his patent in Massachusetts—in the green. But it'd been worth it. Worth it to keep Carol, who still hums and plays annoying music all day. Worth it to be with

Kris side by side, working together better than we ever have before.

Just as I'm rinsing, the screen of my phone lights up on the windowsill above the sink. I'd ignore it, but once I see the name I'm flicking my hands dry. "You mind?" I ask Kris, showing her the screen.

She grabs the pot I've just washed, leans over to give me a kiss. "Nope. Tell him hi."

I duck out, down the hallway into the closet-bedroom.

"Merry Christmas, man," Ben says when I answer.

"Hey, same to you. How you guys doing?"

"Hi, Jasper," comes Kit's voice through the phone, somewhat at a distance. "Ben, tell him hi!"

"I heard her. Tell her Merry Christmas," I say.

"Same to Kris. I can't talk long," Ben says. "We're on our way to my dad's place for dinner. He's trying to fry a turkey. I gotta get there before something goes real wrong."

A year ago, this might've hurt a little, hearing Ben talk about his family holiday plans. But not long after Kris and I got together, I realized something. All that missing I did—for her, for us—it had a whole lot to do with what I've been missing since I was seventeen years old, on my own and learning what it was like not to have a home. And what she and I have between us now is everything I knew I was missing and also everything I didn't know I was.

Including Christmas.

"Right," I say. "I think I've got to go sing some carols or something." In the living room, I can hear Kristen's mom playing scales on the small piano they have by the back door.

There's silence on the line for a few seconds. "What the shit did you just say?"

I laugh. "It's a Fraser tradition."

"Did I call the right number?"

I laugh. "I'm a changed man. I wore a Santa suit for Kristen's nieces yesterday." That'd been a hit. With the nieces, first, who squealed in delight and clapped when I'd come in the front door with a bag of presents, and then later with Kristen, who'd shoved me into this bedroom, pulled down my fake beard, and kissed me in a way that was entirely inappropriate for a television movie.

"I'm happy for you, bud," Ben says.

I clear my throat. "Me too. Thanks for calling."

When we hang up I head back into the living room. The kids are sitting on either side of their grandmother, wiggling excitedly on the piano bench. Malik and Mac are looking through a book of holiday songs. Kelly's on the couch with one of the disgusting cocktails she got me to try yesterday, some salted caramel thing that made my eyes water with the sweetness.

"Jasper," she says, patting the spot next to her. "I need you to tell me more about those solar panels I can get for our house."

Kelly is into tech, probably even more so than Kris is, and whenever we talk she's grilling me about the latest thing we're chasing down at the firm. "Thank God she goes to you now," Kristen said to me a few months ago after Kelly and I hung up from a long call about a new household generator. "She wants so much detail!"

But I like detail, and I like Kelly and Malik and their kids, and I like anything that makes Kristen press her body close to mine on our couch at home in Houston, cuddling close enough to kiss my neck, to tell me how glad she is that I get along so well with her family.

I'm headed to Kelly when Kristen makes her way in

from the kitchen, her cheeks flushed from the warmer temperature in there. "How's Ben?" she asks, sliding an arm around my waist as I put mine around her shoulders.

"Good. He says Merry Christmas."

She smiles and pats my back. "You ready to get out of here for the night?"

My brow furrows as I look down at her. "But what about the—uh." I use my free hand to gesture to the piano. "The carols?"

"Wellllll," Kris says, stretching out the word. "It's just that we've had a *lot* of family time." She sneaks a hand under my shirt, tracing her fingertips across my lower back. "Sleeping in that very small room. And our cottage for the night is . . ."

"You're right," I say quickly. "Let's leave. Now." Suddenly the Fraser house feels like an extremely tiny, painfully loud torture chamber.

"Hey!" Kelly yells from the couch. "Are you two trying to leave now?"

Kristen winks at me before looking to her sister. "Yeah, I think we're going to call it a night."

"No!" says Kelly, pointing her drink at us.

"Ah, Kell," says Malik. "Let 'em go. They've got a little drive ahead." Forget Ben; Malik is my new best friend. When Kris isn't looking he makes a totally obvious gesture at his wedding band.

Kelly gives her husband an exasperated look. "But we have to sing!" she says, and in her tone I can hear exactly what Kris is always telling me about Kelly from their younger years, how bossy she always was. "It's the *rules*!"

Kristen laughs and looks up at me. "Kel," she says, keeping her knowing, sparkling eyes on me. "Me and Jasper, we're going to have to break that rule this year."

I smile down at her, hold her tighter around the waist as I bend my head to whisper in her ear. She smells so good; she *is* so good, everything about her. "Making trouble, Kris?"

She shivers, clutches at the sweatshirt I'm wearing. Then she tips her head back to give me a kiss. "Of course," she says, smiling that big, bottom-teeth-crooked smile that makes every one of my days feel like a holiday. "It's a Christmas tradition."

And when I bend to press my lips against hers, I know it's a Christmas tradition I won't ever have to miss again.

First, to readers: thank you for reading! Having the opportunity to revisit the Chance of a Lifetime universe for this novella was a pure delight, and I hope those of you who know that series enjoyed this return trip.

I am incredibly lucky to work with two brilliant and inspiring women in bringing my books into the world. To Esi Sogah, my editor, thank you for asking me to be a part of this collection, and for shaping this story into its final form. To Taylor Haggerty, my agent, thank you for believing in me and encouraging to take this opportunity. You two are the dream team, and I don't know what I'd do without you.

Olivia Dade was gracious enough to read my first draft of this novella, and her expertise at writing in this form—as well as her kindness—was invaluable as I completed it. I am grateful more generally to my network of friends (writers and non-writers alike) who encourage each project I take on. A special thanks to Sarah MacLean, who talked through the art of the holiday novella with me, and to my first reader, Amy, who always live-texts along the way.

As always, endless gratitude to my loving family, and to my husband—the person with whom I'm always happy to be snowed in.

Kate

Keep reading for
a sneak peek at

LOVE LETTERING

The upcoming novel by
Kate Clayborn
Available wherever books are sold!

On Sunday I work in sans serif.

Boldface for all the headers, because that's what the client wants, apexes and vertexes flattened way out into big floors and tables for every letter, each one stretching and counting and demanding to be seen.

All caps, not because she's into shouting—at least I don't think, though one time I saw her husband give their toddler a drink of his coffee and the look she gave him probably made all his beard hairs fall out within twelve to twenty-four hours. No, I think it's because she doesn't like anything falling below the descender line. She wants it all on the level, no distraction, nothing that'll disrupt her focus or pull her eye away.

Black and gray ink, that's all she'll stand for, and she means it. One time I widened the tracking and added a metallic, a fine-pointed thread of gold to the stems, an almost art deco look I thought for sure she'd tolerate, but when she opened the journal—black, A4, dot grid, nothing fancy—she'd closed it after barely ten seconds and slid it back across the table with two fingers, the sleeve of her black cashmere sweater obviously part of the admonishment.

"Meg," she'd said, "I don't pay you to be *decorative*,"

as if being decorative was the same as being a toenail clipping hoarder or a murderer-for-hire.

She's a sans serif kind of woman.

Me? Well, it's not really the Mackworth brand, all these big, bold, no-nonsense letters. It's not my usual—what was it *The New York Times* had written last year? *Whimsical? Buoyant? Frolicsome?* Right, not my usual whimsical, buoyant, frolicsome style.

But I can do anything with letters, that's also what *The New York Times* said, and that's what people pay me for, so on Sunday I do this.

I sigh and stare down at the page in front of me, where I've used my oldest Staedtler pencil to grid and sketch out the letters

M-A-Y

for the upcoming month, big enough that the *A* crosses the center line. It's such a . . . such a *short* word, not a lot of possibility in it, not like my clients who've wanted a nice spring motif before their monthly spread, big swashes and swooping terminal curves for cheerful sayings ushering in the new month. Already I've done four *Bloom Where You're Planted*s, three *May Flowers!* and one special request for a *Lusty Month of May*, from the sex therapist who has an office on Prospect Park West and who once told me I should think about whether my vast collection of pens is a "symbol" for something.

"Other than for my work?" I'd asked, and she'd only raised a very judgmental, very expertly threaded eyebrow. The Sex Therapist Eyebrow of Knowing How Rarely You Date. Her planner, it's a soft pink leather with a gold button closure, and I hope she sees the irony.

Now I pick up my favorite pen, a fine-tipped

Micron—not symbolic, I hope, of any future dating prospects—and tap it idly against the weathered wood countertop that's functioning as my work surface today. It's quiet in the shop, only thirty minutes to close on a Sunday. The neighborhood regulars don't come around much on the weekends, knowing the place will be overrun by visitors from across the Bridge, or tourists who've read about the cozy Brooklyn paperie that Cecelia's managed to turn into something of a must-see attraction, at least for those who are looking to shop. But they're long gone by now, too, bags stuffed full of pretty notecards, slim boxes of custom paper, specialty pens, leather notebooks, maybe even a few of the pricey designer gifts Cecelia stocks at the front of the store.

Back when I worked here more regularly, I relished the quiet moments—the shop empty but for me and my not-symbolic pen and whatever paper I had in front of me, my only job to create. To play with those letters, to experiment with their shapes, to reveal their possibilities.

But today I'm not so welcoming of the quiet. Instead I'm wishing for some of those Sunday shoppers to come back, because I liked it—all the noise, all the people, being face-to-face with brand-new faces. At first I thought it was simply the novelty of having my phone put away for so long—a forced hiatus from those red notification circles that stack up in my social media apps, likes and comments on the videos I post, the ones I used to do for fun but now are mostly for sponsors. Me showing off brush-lettering pens I don't even use all that regularly, me swooping my hand through a perfect flourish, me thumbing through the thick, foil-edged pages of some luxury journal I'll probably end up giving away.

Eventually, though, I realized, it was more than being away from the phone. It was the break from that master task list I've got tacked above the desk in my small bedroom, the one that's whimsically lettered but weighted with expectation—my biggest, most important deadline ratcheting ever nearer and no closer to being met. It was the relief of being away from the chilly atmosphere in my once-homey, laugh-filled apartment, where these days Sibby's distant politeness cuts me like a knife, makes me restless with sadness and frustration.

So now the quiet in the shop seems heavy, isolating. A reminder that a rare moment of quiet is full of dread for me lately, my mind utterly blank of inspiration. Right now, it's just me and this word, **M-A-Y**, and it *should* be easy. It should be plain and simple and custom-made and low stakes, nothing like the job I've been avoiding for weeks and weeks. Nothing that requires my ideas, my creativity, my specialty.

Sans serif, bold, all caps, no frolicking.

But I *feel* something, staring down at this little word. Feel something familiar, something I've been trying to avoid these days.

I feel those letters doing their work on me. Telling me truths I don't want to hear.

MAY *be you're blocked*, the letters say to me, and I try to blink them away. For a few seconds I blur my vision, try to imagine being *decorative*, try to imagine what I'd do if I didn't have to keep my promises to the client. Something in those wide vertexes? Play with the negative space, or . . .

MAY *be you're lonely*, the letters interrupt, and my vision sharpens again.

MAY *be*, they seem to say, *you can't do this after all*.

I set down the Micron and take a step back.

And that's when he comes in.

The thing is, the letters don't always tell me truths about myself.

Sometimes they tell me truths about other people, and Reid Sutherland is—*was*—one of those people.

I remember him straightaway, even though it's been over a year since the first and only time I ever saw him, even though I must've only spent a grand total of forty-five minutes in his quiet, forbidding presence. That day, he'd come in late—his fiancée already here in the shop, their final appointment to approve the treatment I'd done for their wedding. Save the dates, invitations, place cards, the program—anything that needed letters, I was doing it, and the truth is, by then I'd been almost desperate to finish the job, to get a break. I'd been freelancing for a few years before I came to Brooklyn, but once I started contracting for Cecelia exclusively, handling all the engagement and wedding jobs that came through the shop, word about my work had spread with a speed that was equal parts thrilling and overwhelming. Jobs coming so quickly I'd had to turn more than a few down, which only seemed to increase interest. During the day my head would teem with my clients' demands and deadlines; at night my hands would ache with tension and fatigue. I'd sit on the couch, my right hand weighted with a heated bag of uncooked rice to ease its cramping, and I'd breathe out the stress from meetings that would sometimes see couples and future in-laws turn brittle with wedding-related tension, my job to smile and smooth ruffled feathers, sketching out soft, romantic things that would please everyone. I'd wonder whether it was time to get out of the wedding business altogether.

The fiancée—Avery, her name was, blond and willowy and almost always dressed in something blush or cream or ice blue or whatever color I'd be just as likely to ruin with ink or coffee or ketchup— had been nice to work with, focused and polite, a good sense of herself and what she wanted, but not resistant to Cecelia's suggestions about paper or my suggestions about the lettering. A few times, in our initial meetings, I'd asked about her fiancé, whether she'd want me to send scans to his e-mail, too, or whether she'd want to try to find a weekend meeting time if it'd make it easier for him to come. She'd always wave her slim-fingered left hand, the one with the tiny ice rink on it that looked almost identical to the rings of at least three other brides I'd been working with that spring, and she'd say, pleasantly, "Reid will like whatever I like."

But I'd insisted on it, him being there for the final meeting.

And I'd regretted it later. Meeting him. Meeting them together.

I regret it even more now.

We'd settled on a Sunday afternoon for that final meeting, and now it seems doubly strange to find him here again on another Sunday, my life so different now than it was then, even though I'm in the same store, standing behind the same counter, wearing some version of what's always, pretty much, been my style aesthetic—a knit dress, a little slouchy in fit, patterned, this particular one with tiny, friendly fox faces. Slightly wrinkled cardigan that, until an hour ago, was shoved into my bag. Navy tights and low-heeled, wine-red booties that Sibby would probably say make my feet look big but that also make me smile at least once a day, even without Sibby willing to tease me anymore.

Last year, *he'd* been wearing what other people call "business casual" and what I'd privately call "weekend-stick-up-your ass": tan chinos pressed so sharply they'd looked starched, white collared shirt under a slim cut, expensive-looking navy-blue V-neck sweater. A double-take face, that was for sure—so handsome half of you is wondering if you've seen him on your television and the other half of you is wondering why anyone would put a head like that on top of what looked like a debate team uniform.

But now he looks different. Same head, okay—a square, clean-shaven jaw; high cheekbones that seem to carve swooping, shadowed lines down to his chin; full-lipped mouth with corners turning slightly down; a nose bold enough to match the rest of his strong features; bright, clear blue eyes beneath a set of brows a shade lighter than his dark reddish-blond hair. Neck down, though, not so business casual anymore: olive green T-shirt underneath a hip-length, navy-blue jacket, faded around the zipper. Dark jeans, the edges of the front pockets where he has his hands tucked slightly frayed, and I don't think it's the kind of fraying you pay for. Gray sneakers, a bit battered-looking.

MAY*be*, I think, *his life is pretty different now, too.*

But then he says, "Good evening," which I guess means he's still got the stick up his ass. Who says *Good evening?* Your grandad, that's who. When you call him on his landline.

I feel like if I say a casual "Hi" or "Hey," I'll open up some crack in the space-time continuum, or at least make him want to straighten the tie he's not wearing.

I shouldn't be deceived by the clothes. Maybe he got mugged on the way over by a rogue debate team captain in need of a new outfit and that's why he looks the way he does.

I settle for a "Hello," but I keep it light and cheerful—*buoyant*, if you will—and I'm pretty sure he *nods*. As if he's saying, "This greeting is acceptable to me." I have a fleeting image of how it must have been at his wedding. Probably he did that nod when the officiant said "man and wife." Probably he shook Avery's head instead of kissing her. I really don't think she would've minded. Her lipstick always looked so nice.

"Welcome to—" I begin, at the same time he speaks again.

"You still work here," he says. It's flat, the same as everything I've ever heard him say, but there's a hint of question, of surprise in it.

So maybe he knows something of what I've done since I lettered every single scrap of paper for his wedding.

But surely he can't know—he absolutely *can't* know—why I'd decided his wedding would be my last.

I swallow. "I'm filling in," I say, and it's—less buoyant. Cautious. "The owner's on vacation."

He's still standing right inside the door, underneath the bright paper cranes Cecelia has hung from the ceiling near the entrance. Behind him, the window displays feature various sheaths of the new custom wrapping paper she'd told me about two weeks ago, the last time I'd stopped in for supplies. It's all so colorful, a springtime celebration of pinks and greens and pale yellows, a cheery haven from the mostly gray tones of the city street outside, and now it looks like a human skyscraper has walked in.

It reminds me of one of those truths about Reid Sutherland.

It reminds me of how he'd seemed a little lost that day. A little sad.

I swallow again and take a step forward, pick up my Micron from the crease of my client's notebook, prepare to close it and set it aside. **M-A-Y**, it calls, and this time something else occurs to me. It'd be close now to Reid and Avery's first anniversary. June 2nd, that was the wedding date, and sure he's planning way ahead, but probably he's that kind of guy in general. Probably he's got a reminder on his phone. And he'd be the type to follow the rules, too, all the conventions. Paper, that's the traditional first anniversary gift, and that's probably what brought him here. Very sweet, to come all the way to Brooklyn, to the place where they'd chosen their first paper together. Or I guess where she chose it, and he sort of . . . blinked at it in what she'd taken for approval.

I feel a blooming sense of relief. There's an *explanation* for this, for him being here. It's *not* because he knows.

No one but me could know.

I push the notebook out of the way and fold my hands on top of the counter, look up to offer help. Of course in the face of a human-shaped piece of granite I find myself struggling to muster the cheerful informality that's always made me such a hit in here, that had lifted my low spirits throughout today's shift. Ridiculously, I can only think of phrases that seem straight out of Jane Austen. *Are you in need of assistance, sir? What do you require this evening? Which of our parchment-like wares appeals most to you?*

"I suppose it's to be expected," he says, before I can

settle on a question. "You wouldn't need this job, what with all the success you've had."

He's not looking at me when he says it. He's turned his head slightly, looking to the wall on his left, where there's a display of greeting cards that Lachelle, one of Cecelia's regular calligraphers, has designed. They're bright, bold colors, too—Lachelle uses mostly jewel tones for her projects, adding tiny beads with a small pair of tweezers that she wields as though she's doing surgery. I love them, have three of them tacked on the wall above my nightstand, but Reid doesn't even seem to register them before his eyes shift back to me.

"I saw the *Times* article," he says, I guess by way of explanation. "And the piece on . . ." He swallows, gearing up for something. "*Buzzfeed.*"

LOL, I think, or maybe I see it: sans serif, bold, all caps, a bright yellow background. Reid Sutherland scrolling through *Buzzfeed*, the twenty gifs they'd embedded of me drawing various letters with pithy captions about how it was almost pornographically satisfying, watching me draw a perfect, brush-lettered cursive *E* so smoothly.

He probably got an eye twitch from it. Then he probably cleared his browser history.

"Thank you," I say, even though I don't think he was complimenting me.

"Avery is very proud. She feels as though she got on the ground floor, hiring you when she did. Before you became . . ."

He trails off, but both of us seem to fill in the blank. *The Planner of Park Slope*, that's what I'm called now. That's what got me out of the wedding business, that's what the *Times* wrote about late last year, that's what's had me on three conference calls in the last month alone, that's what's brought me the deadline I'm avoiding. Custom-designed datebooks and journals and desk calendars, the occasional chalk-drawn wall calendar inside the fully renovated brownstones of my most handcraft-obsessed clients, the ones who have toddlers with names like Agatha and Sebastian, the ones with white subway-tile kitchens and fresh flowers on farmhouse-style tables that never once saw the inside of a farmhouse, let alone the outside of a farm. I don't so much organize their lives as I do make that organization—work retreats and weekend holidays and playdates and music lessons—look special, beautiful, uncomplicated.

"Are you looking to have me design something for her?"

I haven't been taking on new clients lately, trying to put this new opportunity first, but it's clever, I guess, for the one-year paper anniversary. A custom journal, maybe, and it's not as if I don't secretly owe him an apology-favor. Of course, if this is what he wants, he's cutting it close, especially if he wants me to design the full year up front, which some clients prefer. Those here in Brooklyn I've mostly got on a monthly schedule, but Reid and Avery, I'm guessing they stay in Manhattan most of the time. Avery had a tony address on East 62nd when she was engaged; she's got the kind of money I don't even understand on a theoretical level, much less a practical one.

For the first time something in his face changes, a twitch of those turned-down corners. A . . . smile? It's possible I forgot what smiles are since he came in here, jeez. But even that brief flash of expression, of emotion—it changes him. Double-take face turns to triple-take face. Take-a-photo-and-show-it-to-your-friends-later face.

He's very tall. Exceptionally tall. I hate myself for thinking about the symbolism of my pens.

In the context of a *married* person, no less.

"No," he says, and the sort-of smile is gone.

"Well," I say, *extra* cheerful, "we have other gifts and—"

"I'm not looking for a shopgirl," he says, cutting me off.

A . . . *shopgirl*?

Now it's him that's made a crack in the space-time continuum, or maybe some kind of crack in my normally frolicsome façade. I wish I could unzip my forehead and release the Valkyries on his person. It'd be worse than the debate team captain mugging, I can tell you that.

I blink across the counter at him, trying to wait out my annoyance. But then, before I can plaster over the crack, I press up on my tiptoes, exaggeratedly looking over his shoulder (one of two excellent shoulders, not that I should care) to the street beyond, the dark green awning of a fancy shave shop flapping gently in the spring breeze.

"Did you come here in a time machine?" I ask sweetly. I lower back down to my heels, meet his eyes so I can catch the expression I'll see there.

Blank, flat. No anger or amusement. The *most* sans serif person.

"A time machine," he repeats.

"Yes, a time machine. Because no one has said 'shopgirl' since—" *Parchment wares*, is all I can think, annoyingly. So I finish with an exceedingly disappointing, "A long time ago."

I think my shoulders sag. I am truly terrible at confrontation, though this man, with his blank handsome face, seems unusually capable of making me at least want to try getting better.

He clears his throat. He has fair skin, an aesthetic match for the ruddy tone in the dark blond of his hair, and part of me hopes he flushes in shame or embarrassment, some physical reaction that would remind me of what I'd seen in him all those months ago. Something that would remind me he's not a man-sized thundercloud, come to monsoon on the rainy disposition I already felt taking hold before he walked in here.

But his complexion stays even.

I could've been wrong that day, thinking he was lost or sad. It could be that he's just a smug, stick-up-his-ass drone. Thinking of him this way—I wish it made me feel better about what I did, but it doesn't, not really. It was so . . .

It was so *presumptuous*. So unprofessional.

But I'm all out of patience now, no matter the error I made, especially since he doesn't even know about it. I may not be good with confrontation, but I am exceedingly, expertly good at avoiding it. I can paste on a smile and finish this shift for Cecelia and get him out of here, back to whatever doorman-guarded highrise he lives in with his fancy wife who never has ketchup stains on her clothing. A *shopgirl*, for God's sake.

"Anyway," I say, clenching my teeth in what I hope is an approximation of a smile. "May I help you with something?"

M-A-Y, I think, in the pause he leaves there. Flat, flat, flat.

"Maybe," he says, and for the first time he removes his hands from his pockets.

And I don't think I could say, really, what it is that makes me realize that *monsoon* was an understatement, that this is about to be a tidal wave. I don't think

I could say what I notice first: the fact that there's no wedding ring on his left hand? The corner of that thick paper he begins to pull from the inside of his jacket? The matte finish, the antique cream color I remember Avery stroking her thumb over, her smile close-lipped and pleased? The flash of color—*colors*—I used on the final version, the vines and leaves, the iridescence of the wings I'd sketched . . . ?

But I know. I know what he's come to ask.

MAY*be*, I think, the word an echo and a premonition.

He doesn't speak again until he's set the single sheet in front of me.

His wedding program.

I watch as his eyes trace briefly over the letters, and I know what he's seeing. I know what I left there; I know the way those letters worked on me.

But I didn't think anyone else ever would.

Then he looks up and meets my eyes again. Clear blue. A tidal wave when he speaks.

"Maybe you could tell me how you knew my marriage would fail."